Sisters of Ruin

Sisters of Ruin

Book I of of The Lucent Series

Darren Lewis

Copyright (C) 2016 Darren Lewis
Layout design and Copyright (C) 2016 Creativia
Published 2016 by Creativia
Cover art by Darren Lewis
This book is a work of fiction. Names, characters, places, and incidents are the product of the author's imagination or are used fictitiously. Any resemblance to actual events, locales, or persons, living or dead, is purely coincidental.
All rights reserved. No part of this book may be reproduced or transmitted in any form or by any means, electronic or mechanical, including photocopying, recording, or by any information storage and retrieval system, without the author's permission.

Dedication

To the two best brothers a man could have.

They've never failed to be there when needed.

Contents

The story so far	1
The Cold Universe	6
Ellie and the Battle (2008 C.E.)	8
Home again	17
Aftermath	20
Bound	23
Unprepared	24
Ten Years Later	**27**
The day we fell: 2018 C.E.	28
Silent Running	52
A New Order	55
Blue	58
Discoveries	70

Decisions	81
The day we feared	108
The Core — Gabby's memories	125
The Doctor — Gabby's memories	139
Testing — Gabby's memories	146
The village — Gabby's memories	154
Evolution — Present Day	179
Epilogue — The Prisoner	189
Afterword	192
About the Author	194

The story so far

As a young girl Ellie encountered and befriended a race of rabbits gifted with magic. Their one sacred duty; to keep this world safe and spinning through the uncertainty of our universe. Once a year (one turn of the seasons to the rabbits) they were bound to use this magic to keep the world turning. Mankind however had brought these most special rabbits to the brink of extinction through hunting and encroaching upon their lands and the world was in mortal peril. At the request of their leader, Rox, Ellie was transformed into a rabbit by Cast, the rabbit's magic keeper and Rox's father. Visiting the warren and using all of the remaining rabbit's borrowed magic Rox and Ellie journeyed into the past to find the source of their power, a legend only known to them as The White and Grey. On arriving at the birth of our world the two time travellers discovered that their presence in that moment caused two entities to visit this planet and begin its spin through the stars. Furthermore, the entities furnished this world with their own essence to create Rox's descendants. Little did Rox and Ellie know at the time but they also left something else of themselves behind to aid the future of the world. On leaving Rox made several jumps through time in order to assemble enough special rabbits from the past to bring to our time. They were successful and Ellie returned home safely.

Then fate, destiny or pure chance led to a meeting that would forever change Ellie's life and the future of the world itself. Standing next to her parent's house was a derelict building, an old farmhouse. In the cellar she discovered a young male dragon named Cole. Cole told Ellie the history of his race and the disastrous war fought between them and a small group of mankind. The outcome, the destruction and scattering of the dragons, condemning their existence to the dreams and fantasy of mankind's history. Cole and Ellie bonded, allowing

The story so far

the two access to the other's thoughts, emotions and memories. When the ritual was complete she became his rider. Together they set out to find Cole's father as his mother had died birthing him. What they actually found was nothing short of evil. With Cole's parents gone the remaining dragons placed their memories into an innocent named Malachite. The dragons entered a long sleep with Malachite to guard them. Over those many years with nothing but the terrible memories of betrayal, death and loss inflicted by man, Malachite became twisted, a darkness entering his soul that would not be touched by light no matter how bright. A thirst for revenge fuelled his existence and this is who they found.

Malachite released the hibernating dragons who then wished to drain Ellie of her memories to learn of the new world they now found themselves in. Fortunately, Ellie and Cole were saved by the quick actions of Rox and her kin close by. The dragons pursued the pair to Rox's home and set about the destruction of all around them. Ellie concluded they could not win against such fierce opponents. By the grace of fortune Cole's father arrived bearing an object of great power that Celestine, Cole's mother gave her life to create. With this device and the assistance of the world itself, Cole and Ellie, with a captive Malachite, travelled to the land of the dragons in the far reaches of the past. Using Malachite's memories to show what the future held for the dragons and humanity, Ellie convinced the dragons to transform themselves and leave this planet. The strange orb altered them into the beings that would become known as The White and The Grey and they vanished from sight.

Two surprises awaited the two lost souls, Ellie and Cole, in the past. First was Malachite. Bereft of his former personae. Eridan, Cole's father, had requested of Malachite to stay behind and protect the young girl and dragon, and secondly the great power from the orb had been used to grant them a long life.

An age passed by, thousands of years, Ellie kept her distance from humanity not wishing to interfere with what she considered history. But she was drawn back to her kind and it set Ellie's path to helping those who were persecuted for any number of spurious reasons, from witchcraft to skin colour. During this time, it was discovered the orb had become sentient. Its consciousness constructed from those it was closest to for so many years, Ellie, Cole and Malachite. The orb furnished the trio with what Ellie still considered history but what in reality was her future. Using this knowledge Ellie befriended many important figures, the most influential called the 'Father of Europe' King Charles, and more commonly named 'Charlemagne.' Charlemagne granted land to Ellie's cause, in effect planting the seed of what would become a global corporation named the Baiulus Institute, nearly a thousand years in the future.

Ellie's new path led her to Arianne and her young daughter, Isabelle. Both mother and daughter were magically gifted which brought about their being outcast from their home. Both would aid the three friends from the future as many others would but Arianne became a victim to the righteous mob that would push her daughter into murderous revenge. She slaughtered those responsible, injured Cole severely and stole the orb from Ellie.

Isabelle took everything Ellie and her two companions had stood for and turned it against them and the world, though she did this under the guise of oppressing the magically talented.

More years passed by and Cole suffered terribly. Ellie learnt that the newly named 'Baiulus Institute' could provide a liquid, essential to her dragon's survival. Ellie became an employee and worked her way to become their Chief of Operations. She used this position to 'capture' Cole and have him placed in suspended animation within this liquid. Ellie's own thoughts turned towards revenge but she also took it upon herself to protect the younger version of her, moving close by and keeping watch. Little did Ellie know that 'Isabelle' was in the village and set about her revenge on the younger version of Ellie. Punishing her for the past and the death of her mother. That day was the catalyst for Baiulus to move. Teams were sent to investigate the magical occurrences within the village and capture all inhabitants of Rox's warren. They tracked down Ellie but Malachite intervened in her capture and took her to the warren. From there, with only a few survivors including Rox and her son Flare, they came to the older version of Ellie for safety and both Ellie's were introduced to one another, the older version was promptly named 'Eleanor' to distinguish between the two.

Ellie had retrieved the orb during her encounter with Isabelle and Eleanor now knew it was time to free Cole and as many of the captured talented as possible. Eleanor went into the lion's den itself, the Institute's main facility in the city while Ellie and Malachite travelled to China to awaken the Terracotta Army to use as their soldiers. They were successful but Malachite paid for this success with his life.

In the meantime, the orb had convinced the Chief of Operations of Baiulus, Sloan, at the very least to assist Eleanor in healing Cole and allow Eleanor to

The story so far

leave. Little did either know that at the same time Ellie discovered the Isabelle she encountered in her home village was a clone, not in body, but in mind. It was revealed that Isabelle had brainwashed all those talented she'd dedicated herself to protecting and forced her mind onto theirs. Isabelle, the true Isabelle then revealed herself to Eleanor as she set Cole free. Isabelle initiated her final plan, to take over every government, military and judicial power in the world.

Ellie, now magically gifted thanks to her merging with the fake Isabelle, successfully moved the army to Rox's location and she was able to free all the rabbits, the only casualty being Rox's mother Storm. Isabelle now threatened to destroy the city and Eleanor ordered Cole to leave with the orb. Her threat was a ruse to separate Eleanor from Cole and the orb as she released all those brainwashed talents into the world.

Eleanor was taken to see Isabelle but unknown to her Ellie had taken the orb's power and with Cole restored to full health punched a hole through a magically constructed barrier of Isabelle's creation. Isabelle then brought forth a corruption of Cole's DNA. A malformed and hate filled white dragon. With Cole, Eleanor defeated it but in doing so left Ellie alone to confront Isabelle. Isabelle appeared to have defeated Ellie and absorbed all the orb's power from Ellie and make it her own. Eleanor was unaware that Ellie, with the orb, had orchestrated this and that at that very instance the orb was invading Isabelle's body and mind. Eleanor and Ellie then joined with Isabelle to create a bond and gave her a choice, let go of the hate and live or die in despair, alone. Isabelle chose life. But the damage was done. 'Baiulus' was online. Isabelle's talented had begun seizing control around the globe and nothing could be done to stop it.

The orb, or at least its consciousness, departed this world and plans were made to go into hiding. As Ellie and Eleanor were leaving the talented discovered them all and Eleanor was forced to surrender herself to Baiulus for everyone's safety.

Ellie, Cole and her family escaped but Rox was not so lucky. While leading her warren to safety they were attacked and Rox severely injured.

Baiulus was online and the world now belonged to the talented.

Begin with the experience and then investigate the cause.

LEONARDO DA VINCI

The Cold Universe

The anomaly was vast. Measuring at just over one million, eight hundred thousand light years across. Its existence in a seemingly infinite universe was still a spectacular phenomenon from Earth. Astronomers discovered the construct in the constellation of Eridanus in the southern hemisphere, approximately three million light years from Earth. What was known from maps pieced together of the cosmic background radiation in the universe was that this region was one of intense cold and lack of any kind of matter. Galaxy formation was sparse and in layman's terms this was an enormous cold spot in the universe.

Its presence was explained as an aftereffect of the Big Bang. The theories into what it was or what it meant to the existence of the universe were wide ranging. Explanations involved gravity, black holes or singularities, dark matter to dark energy. Any concept that this was an alien structure became popular on social media along with any number of highly detailed and sometimes disturbing conspiracy theories.

One of the most outlandish theories postulated that the cold spot was in essence a 'footprint', a place where the fabric of the universe came into contact with a "neighbouring" or parallel universe. Of all the theories posited on Earth this was the closest.

Regardless of the many theories put forth each one could never properly ascertain where this region sprang from. The type of energy required to cause the boundary of one universe to become susceptible to another could only be caused by one specific set of conditions. In this instance, the conditions relating to time travel. With this type of energy released the walls between universes, the walls between realities were gradually fading.

In the empty, dark region nothing of any note happened, at least nothing observable from such an immense distance from Earth. But changes were occurring that could not be explained by any form of science currently practised on planet Earth. The physics did not exist as yet for science to explain this phenomenon. The fabric between universes had been placed under enormous pressure and would soon distort space time enough to rupture. From the cold darkness a multitude of cries was emanating, but due to the vacuum of space it would never be heard except for the one mind it was intended for. The cries or voices travelled the vast distances required faster than any form of energy or matter had travelled since the birth of the universe in the Big Bang. To this voice the speed of light was not a restriction but merely something to outpace. It moved with a single-mindedness that suggested if not intelligence then at least an instinct that governed its passage through the cold black of space.

The journey came to a stop in interstellar space, a few thousand light years away from a boundary marking the beginning of galactic space. In that pause any creature sufficiently talented would now be capable of detecting a probe, a search for that one mind it needed. The search took seconds despite the enormous space involved, spanning one hundred thousand lights years in diameter and one hundred billion stars. The journey resumed into the target galaxy, passing a myriad of spectacles and sights no human eye had ever seen, but it did not pause to wonder or appreciate the majesty of nature as its singular nature would not allow it. Narrowing in on one small star the voice increased speed almost in excitement that its travels were now at an end. In the blink of an eye it gazed once more on what had once been, if not its home, then one almost identical, the planet Earth.

Ellie and the Battle (2008 C.E.)

Rainfall pummelled the ground without mercy. The summer that had started with such promise had quickly returned to the soul of a hard winter with plummeting temperatures and torrential rain.

The dark rip, for want of a better term, exploded into life, expanding and reaching out with almost evil intent. Dark itself, it enveloped the surrounding space, cutting off light and life from all sources. Ellie jerked and brushed the sodden fringe of hair away from her eyes as she walked with Cole towards the temple. The daydream was familiar to her. Since she could remember it would always intrude upon her consciousness, typically when she was trying to concentrate in school.

A quick glance back down the hill and she saw Eridan and Rox preparing to lift off and confront the remaining dragons. The fires in the distance were still raging despite the rain's onslaught such was the intensity of the dragon's fire.

ELLIE ARE YOU OKAY?

Cole asked into her mind, his tone soothing as he experienced Ellie's startled reaction to her daydream.

Just worried.

Ellie answered accompanied by an audible sigh. Cole leaned into Ellie's side and she placed an arm over his back. They reached the steps of the temple and ascended. Ellie lifted the orb to eye level and stared into the bright orange light. Eridan had somehow spoken with this device and communicated Ellie's plan. For her own part as she gazed into the swirling orange hue she fancied a split second contact with the raw power held within. The moment vanished as quickly as it had arrived and she dropped her arm to her side. Ellie hoped the black dragon knew what he was talking about.

At the centre of the temple, lying upon the embossed star design carved into the centre was the still form of Malachite. Ellie intended to take the insane dragon back with her and show the dragons of the past what lay in store for them and the world.

Are you ready?

Ellie asked her red dragon.

NOT AT ALL.

Cole quipped. BUT WE CAN DO THIS.

Ellie smiled with renewed confidence and gave Cole a quick squeeze before climbing onto his back.

Let's get this done then

. Ellie said before closing her eyes and concentrating on the orange orb in her hand. She imagined a time long ago, far from mankind. A beautiful island, lush and green. The beaches so white it would cause any being, man or beast to squint from the glare. Cliffs and mountains reared so high from the ground they seemed to pierce the sky itself. Ellie quivered slightly as Cole added his own mind to hers, reinforcing the imagery of the mesmerizing past.

The sound of falling rain softened and became waves upon a beach. Ellie smiled at the wash of water upon sand and she saw an orange glow through the closed lids of her eyes. The warm water of the sea tickled her toes and Ellie's skin tingled with energy as she strove for her body to *be* at the beach she saw. Ellie opened her eyes and looked down. The star carved into the temple floor itself began to glow with a bright white intensity to match the luminescence of the orb. Ellie clutched the orb to her chest and realised faintly that this would be the closest to prayer she had ever come.

Help us!

She pleaded, her thoughts directed below her, to this conduit of power Rox knew to be a connection to the living world itself. The bright white light intensified further causing Ellie and Cole to grunt with discomfort and close their eyes against the glare. Ellie heard a hum and sensed subtle vibrations from the stone floor through Cole's legs and spine. The hum increased in volume and Ellie now held her breath in anticipation as the energy seemed to reach a crescendo. The answer then came.

NO!

Ellie and the Battle (2008 C.E.)

Ellie gasped as the white light in one instant dissipated into the rain which fell quickly to the ground and became one again with the earth. The orange glow faded and Ellie brought the orb to her face.

"No!" She shook the orb viciously but the light returned to its normal level. Ellie's arm dropped as failure swamped her mind. Cole turned his head to cast one eye on his rider.

"How can the world abandon us?" He growled in anger. Ellie simply shook her head, her face a picture of despair. Her plan had failed, what was there to do now?

A loud screech from the sky brought Ellie and Cole's attention back and they saw a black dragon, not Eridan but his brother, Corvus, tumbling uncontrollably until he crashed in the vast pit caused by Plume a short time before. Ellie's eyes scanned the sky and she saw the three dragons had ceased their firing of the woods to intercept Eridan and Rox. Seizing on the moment and the imminent danger Ellie yelled to Cole.

"Let's get up there! Your father is outnumbered!"

Cole didn't hesitate, he bounded forward and cleared the temple before bunching his muscles and launching into the sky. The rain lashed against Ellie's face so she shielded her eyes and squinted into the sky again to find the black figure of Eridan. The three dragons were closing in on his position from above and Eridan was clearly unaware of their proximity.

WE'RE TOO FAR AWAY!

Cole shouted in frustration. Ellie felt her hand grow warm for an instant and glanced down. The orb, the repository of power created by Eridan and Celestine, was glowing once again. Ellie's eyes danced from the orb to Eridan.

Cole open a dragon thread!

Ellie instructed.

BUT THAT WON'T WORK.

Cole replied, reminding Ellie that a dragon can only travel fast between two points in a dragon thread *after* that journey had been made once before.

I know but we have to try!

Ellie felt a moment's hesitation from the red dragon before his mind concentrated on creating a dragon's most special form of travelling.

A small black hole appeared directly in front of Ellie and Cole. Blue streaks of electricity jumped and sparked from the edges of the rapidly expanding area of darkness. Though she had experienced the dragon thread already, Ellie held her breath and clenched her jaw tight as Cole crossed the threshold from this world into a dimension of infinite blackness.

* * *

Rox, using senses evolved since the dawn of her race, intuited rather than saw the imminent attack on Eridan.

"Dive!" She screamed at the black dragon. A roar from above distracted Eridan momentarily and both Rox and Eridan glanced upwards briefly into the claws of three dragons. Both rabbit and dragon knew it was too late to take any evasive action and braced for impact.

* * *

NOW WHAT?

Cole queried as he and Ellie sped through the black tunnel. Though Ellie could feel Cole beneath her and the orb in her hand such was the total darkness her eyes, in an attempt to detect any light, were round and trying almost by themselves to make sense of where they were.

Think about your father and where we saw him in the sky.

Ellie advised as she brought the orb to her chest and fixated her own thoughts on Rox sitting on Eridan's back. Image in place she directed her thoughts to the orb. If Eridan had communicated his intentions to this strange object maybe she could too.

Help me please.

Ellie pleaded for the second time in ten minutes but this time to a different power. *I need to get to Rox. Cole needs to get to his father.*

Ellie felt a brief pulse of warmth from her hand holding the orb and then it went cold once again. Ellie's shoulders slumped in defeat.

WHOA!

Cole yelled and the red dragon tilted sharply to the right and Ellie grabbed at his back to stay mounted.

What's happening?

Ellie asked fearfully as the dragon tilted even further.

I'M BEING PUSHED OUT OF HERE!

A white light appeared that quickly resolved into dark clouds and the rain of the outside world.

It worked!

Ellie yelled triumphantly and the orb began to throb with heat and Ellie could see the object glowing with power as she and Cole emerged into the sky. Cole's senses being more adapted to hunting immediately saw the three dragons descending on his father and he roared his anger at them. The dragon leading the attack, stunned by the sudden noise, glanced sideways and it was to be a mistake that would cost him. Instead of diving away, Eridan taking advantage of the distraction turned sharply to his left and whipped his enormous tail at the head of the dragon. Ellie heard the sound of the impact over the wind and rain, it reminded her of two rocks bashing together and the lead dragon dropped from the sky, knocked unconscious by Eridan's strike. Only then the black dragon folded in his wings and pointed his body towards the ground. Ellie glimpsed Rox hanging on for her life on Eridan's back as the two remaining dragons gave chase.

Let's go!

Ellie ordered but she needn't have bothered as Cole performed a sharp turn before executing the same manoeuvre as his father.

FATHER!

Cole called out. OPEN A THREAD, LEAD US ALL IN THERE!

BUT THEY'LL FOLLOW US WHEREVER WE GO!

Eridan protested.

NO. ELLIE FOUND A WAY TO OVERCOME THAT. WE CAN LEAVE THOSE DRAGONS IN THERE TO FIND THEIR OWN EXIT.

Eridan didn't reply but from their higher vantage point Ellie and Cole saw the beginnings of a dragon thread being created. The two dragons chasing Eridan roared in triumph at the seemingly pointless tactic and as Eridan's large form disappeared they added their own power to keep the entrance open. Both quickly disappeared and Cole was left alone in the sky above the woods. The moment didn't last long as Ellie gripped Cole's back tightly and once again they entered the darkness.

* * *

Eridan and Cole appeared in the night sky over Sydney, Australia in a wash of blue electricity. Cole had communicated to his father that he should picture Sydney harbour and then using the orb once again Ellie had directed it to help them break out of the dragon thread leaving the two pursuing dragons behind. Ellie had no idea if those dragons would be able to find their exit point or not and so had chosen this place instead of heading directly for home.

Remarkable.

Eridan observed to his son. Cole nodded and flared his wings to catch an updraft rising from the bay hundreds of feet below. Ellie stared at the lights on the bridge, her thoughts slow but tumultuous nonetheless.

No. Why? Why did you say no?

Ellie asked out into the night sky. Sounds of the traffic on the bridge dropped to silence. The wind passing Cole's wings was absent, Ellie could only hear the sound of her own heart beating. She closed her eyes and her vision merged with that of her dragon's. *Why?*

She asked again but her only answer was her heart pumping. Cole looked over at his father who was still carrying Rox on his back. Ellie tilted her head and ran her hand through her hair as something was bothering her.

The dragons couldn't follow us.

Cole and I never travelled from home to the temple or vice versa.

Ellie's entire body temperature dropped causing a violent shiver.

Eridan did.

Cole picked up on his rider's emotions and bellowed in alarm. He folded his wings and dropped out of the sky and with no warning to his father opened a dragon thread.

* * *

The sound of people screaming merged with the roar of flame. Malachite lashed out with his tail to swipe the already blazing house, smashing bricks and collapsing already damaged walls.

After waking on the hillside Malachite struggled at first to remember the sequence of events that'd brought him here but on moving his head the sharp, intense strike of pain in his jaw brought his memories back. A small brown rabbit had somehow cracked his jaw with a ridiculously powerful kick from such a creature, causing it to hang loose, broken on one side. He'd easily bashed that awful tiny animal aside and then set forth to find the girl and her traitorous dragon. Finding them had been easy but when confronting them near the destroyed temple his world inexplicably had disappeared. A cry from far above revealed the ongoing struggle between dragons including a dragon he had not seen for countless years, Eridan. Malachite snarled releasing a lance of cold fire in his jaw. His vision clouded with tears of pain but through those tears Malachite could see a streak of black belonging to Eridan. As dragons moved through their different space to travel quickly they left a trail in the world for other dragons to see. This trail could only have come from Eridan himself as Corvus, the only other black dragon in the vicinity had arrived with Malachite. Knowing then with some fury he was not in a state to confront Eridan, Malachite decided to lay in wait after travelling the black dragon's thread, reasoning with some hope, that the black dragon would return to his point of origin.

Leaving the fight behind Malachite rode Eridan's thread only to emerge almost instantly above a rain lashed house. Malachite's eyes were drawn to the roof as he watched raindrops fall and explode upon impact. The hypnotic effect drew the green dragon closer to the human dwelling and the steady, pounding beat of the water upon tile whispered dark secrets to his warped mind. Malachite grinned, ignoring the furious pain of his jaw and let loose a stream of fire.

Now the fire raged and when humans from inside the building had attempted escape another blast of Malachite's fire had sent them screaming back into their certain deaths. Malachite did not understand why this structure's destruction was so important, all he knew was that it was right. More humans had come but were sent either swiftly away by the sight of the dragon or had to be persuaded permanently by their destruction. Transports carrying humans with wailing noises and swirling lights approached disrupting Malachite's concentration upon the building but this time he rose high on the thermals created by the fire and he waited until they'd entered the building before descending and blasting orange flame from above.

Malachite landed in front of the burning wreck and he raised his face to the grey sky, allowing the rain to wash over him. For the first time in what seemed an eternity to him he felt a moment of peace. In knowing that he had landed the first blow in the war to come with the humans, the world felt right and just.

Bricks tumbled from the collapsing walls and Malachite lazily lowered his head and with satisfaction drifted his vision across the rubble and flame. A small pile of grey rubble shifted and attracted the dragon's attention. Malachite grunted and wandered over. A strange, surreal sight greeted him and Malachite leaned in for a closer look, not trusting his eyes. A hand, small and dust covered was standing like a monument to the dragon's wrath, amidst the remains of the house. Malachite scoffed with disdain and made to turn when the hand moved. Malachite jerked slightly, not in fear, but in surprise that anything could survive such an intense barrage of fire and the collapse of the building. Malachite used his sharp talons and flicked away pieces of rubble, uncovering the arm and then head of the person trapped. Malachite's eyes narrowed as he recognised the young of the humans. This one was extremely small and strange thoughts flitted about Malachite's head. To survive such an onslaught spoke of strength and a will to live that held Malachite's vengeance against the humans at bay. The human coughed and opened its eyes, finding Malachite's sickly yellow lantern eyes directed at it. It did not cry or call out and Malachite felt himself drawn into those innocent eyes. Malachite felt lightheaded and his mind called out to the young survivor still buried in the rubble. He felt the flow of his thoughts travelling outwards from his mind and into that of the child and in return he received alien thoughts, thoughts that were not his. A series of images flickered to life behind his eyes, some distorted, some clear of that of two older humans. When he thought of them a warmth flooded Malachite's body making him uncomfortable. Another sensation, that of loneliness in the dark, a crying out for human contact in the mind transforming into the cries in the real world bringing one of the humans to him and once again the warm feeling when they held him. A smaller human appeared with long hair. It spoke to him and though he did not recognise the words he understood the spirit of love behind them. Malachite reared back slightly, these thoughts and feelings totally new to the green dragon, conceived in darkness and implanted with the wicked deeds of man. A face resolved of the one with long hair and Malachite's thoughts seemed to shrivel with recognition. It was the girl, the girl with the dragon who'd found him and then escaped. The one he had sworn to kill first. Ellie. This young human was related to Ellie. Malachite stumbled backwards to break the contact and attempted to bring his fire to bear but his mind froze. The human sat up and simply stared at Malachite. The dragon searched his memories given to him by the surviving dragons and with pain, wonder and dismay he realised in his own form of innocence he had allowed himself to bond to the child just as Ellie had bonded with the red dragon, Cole. Malachite reared backwards and regardless of the pain in his face let loose a bellow of fear followed by a torrent of fire. He then collapsed to the ground, tears of anguish coursing down the rough hide of his face. A small touch opened his eyes and he saw the child had managed to free itself from the remains of the house and make its way to him. With a gentle touch it now stroked Malachite's injured jaw, an expression of understanding and grief on such a small face. Malachite rose to his full height and scooped up the child, he held it close to his chest and launched into the grey sky.

Home again

The house burned. The roof had caved in taking a side wall down with it, scattering debris and fire onto the driveway and the garage. Fire with a life of its own jumped and danced hypnotically not allowing Ellie to glance away, even for a moment. As the flames consumed the wreck of her home Ellie closed her eyes briefly and saw a wall of turbulent orange whipping wildly about her. Nothing was recognisable. Rooms were now mere containers of destruction. Furnishings if not ablaze had already been consumed by the fire. Ellie's vision shifted forward towards a small opening above and she recognised what was left of the stairs. They were now impassable, filled with the destroyed remnants of the roof itself. The image flickered into darkness as Cole blinked while continuing his search of Ellie's house. Safe from fire the red dragon had charged without thought or command towards the blazing house on arrival while Ellie had collapsed to her knees on the street. Fire not only raged in front of her but around the small village. Fire engines dispatched to deal with the inferno had met with disaster and sat smouldering in the road, overturned, their own fires dying quickly, their fuel tanks already consumed in what must have been a series of devastating blasts. Smaller fires set in seemingly random spots throughout Ellie's home village were gaining in intensity and Ellie was dimly aware of the multitude of screams around her.

Cole's eyes latched onto a strange mass in the kitchen and she felt her dragon's hesitation. She opened her eyes, squinting them against the orange fury in front of her, not wanting to see but needing to know.

Cole. Please, for me.

She pleaded. Cole didn't respond but their joining allowed Ellie to experience the dragon's emotions as he moved deeper into the wrecked house.

DISBELIEF! SHOCK! DISGUST!
No! NO!

Above the sound of the swirling flames Ellie heard Cole let loose a tremendous bellow of pain and anger. With her knees already on the floor, Ellie curled forwards, her head coming to rest on the grass with her hands covering her face, her fingers formed into talons, gripping her scalp harshly. She felt the pain of her nails ripping into her skin and it felt right, so she ripped harder.

ELLIE! COME QUICK! THE GARDEN!

Without conscious thought Cole's voice propelled her forward. She skirted the blazing house with her hands raised against the intense heat and followed the path to the back garden. She saw her dragon standing over a curled form in the centre of the lawn, his wings spread wide to protect it from the heat. Numbly, Ellie's feet seemed to move of their own volition as she screamed inside her mind to stop, stop, sit down and sleep. Ellie moved into the shadow of Cole's wings and she absently noted the decrease in temperature. She looked down at the poor creature on the ground, her mouth opened and a small whine escaped. She quickly placed a fist into her mouth and bit down hard, forcing the sob down. By the size she knew this was an adult but so much damage had been inflicted she couldn't tell who this person was. The skin was charred and cracked. She could see where boils had formed immediately from the heat and burst. No hair remained, nor could a stitch of clothing be identified. With silent tears coursing down her already wet cheeks, Ellie leaned closer to the tortured form. A terrible, rasped breath escaped from the faceless person and Ellie gasped and stumbled backwards, saved only from falling by Cole's strong leg to hold her up.

Cole?

She whimpered. *I don't even know who it is!*

Cole repositioned his wings so he could lower his head to his rider's level. He looked at the creature on the ground over Ellie's shoulder.

I... I THINK IT'S YOUR FATHER.

Despite what she could already see Ellie's eyes widened in shock. She crept forward and knelt at her father's head.

"Dad? Daddy?" Another breath rasped out and Ellie leaned closer. "I'm here, Daddy." A sigh was released and then terrible, tortured words were spoken.

"Ellie? Your mother and Jack, are they safe?" Ellie shook her head and looked desperately at Cole, knowing the awful answer as well as he. Swallowing her pain and wiping her face she forced a smile even though her father was now blind.

"Yes they're fine, Daddy. They're safe now." She lied. The figure on the grass gave a small nod accompanied by a long groan of pain. He tried to move an arm towards Ellie but the pain of the burnt skin stretching was too much and he cried out. "What can I do?" Ellie cried.

Dad shook his head.

"Nothing, sweetie. Oh, Ellie I'm so sorry." Dad croaked, his blind eyes searching her out. "Sorry, my darling." Ellie shook her head violently and made a move to wrap her arms around her father, but Cole held her back and she realised doing so would cause him terrible pain.

"For what?" Ellie said in a forced light tone. "What do you mean?" Despite the pain and sensing his end was near, Ellie's father moved his arm, holding out what was left of his hand to her. Ellie's tears flowed freely now as she gently cradled his burnt hand to her face.

"Don't be afraid." He rasped, his voice hardening ever so slightly. "Whatever else, never be afraid, sweetie." Ellie nodded and she felt his hand relax. His last breath escaped him and her father passed. Ellie continued nodding for a moment before taking his hand away from her cheek and laying it gently upon his chest. The shakes began in her hands and they moved swiftly around her body. She felt her mouth twitch and the heat from her own body seemed to surpass that of the still burning house even as a cold fire raged within her mind. Her thoughts were sluggish as she stared at the still figure of her father. Then in one quick movement she jumped forward and grasped her Dad's shoulders.

"Daddy! No! Please! Don't leave me! Wake up!" She shook his body as if by force of her own will she could restore the life taken. She howled and screamed at him over and over until she felt Cole's large paws on her own shoulders dragging her away. "No! Let me go! Cole!" Ellie turned into the red dragon's chest and clenching her fists and grinding her teeth Ellie let loose a silent scream into the heavens. The cords on her neck stood out and her eyes burned with fury.

I'm going to kill them all!

The promise made she collapsed to the ground, painful sobs wracked her entire body as she punched the grass. She was dimly aware of Cole's mind, pressing on hers, enveloping her, comforting her. Whatever he was doing she saw a black wall encircle them both and force her into sleep.

Aftermath

"Plume! Thank the White and Grey, you're alive!" Rox cried, throwing herself into the brown rabbit's chest. The last time Rox had seen Plume he'd been charging the green dragon Malachite all alone and Rox had feared for his life. Plume grunted in pain and shock but couldn't stop the grin that manifested itself on his normally acerbic face. Eridan had dropped the black rabbit off at a point far enough away from the fires where she could enter the warren undetected.

"I'm a little battered but I'm ready to take on those evil bastards again." Plume stated with venom. Rox pulled back slightly and Plume's eyes widened at the expression on his leader's face. "What? What's wrong, Rox?" Rox's mouth quivered, not wanting to speak the words. She took a moment to look about at the rabbits wandering terrified all around her. She grabbed Plume's paw and led him to an unoccupied hole. "What, Rox?" Plume repeated, his fears mounting.

"The dragons." Rox said, her voice weak. She cleared her throat and straightened her neck. "Cast saw what they did... they found their way to Ellie's home." Plume felt a streak of cold enter his body and he sat back on his haunches. "They killed them, Plume!" Rox sobbed. "Even her brot..." But Rox couldn't physically finish the sentence, her mouth refused to utter the word and Plume, though the thought was ridiculous, was glad of that. He slowly rose, moved to Rox and encircled her in his forelegs, his staff dropping, forgotten, to the dirt floor. Out of view of the rest of the warren Rox let her tears run freely and her emotions full rein. Her heart felt torn as her body convulsed with each cry of grief. Plume's face felt wooden and his mouth heavy. He could not think of one platitude or thought to give voice to. He remembered when Rox's mother, Storm, had been killed by a fox and though understandably devastating he knew instinctively that was the way of the world, parents will die before their offspring. To hear about such a young one dying by such a heinous act was almost beyond his comprehension.

"Rox?" Another voice came from the entrance to the hole. Plume looked up and with a great deal of relief saw it was Cast, Rox's father and keeper of magic for the rabbits. The old white rabbit looked utterly worn down from his heroic attempt to save Ellie and Cole earlier that day but Plume saw fire in the rabbit's eyes, eyes that had witnessed through magical means the destruction of Ellie's home and family. Rox took a moment to compose herself and turned to face her father, leaving Plume to retrieve his staff. The grief still burned her eyes and the fiery anger she felt rushed with abandon through her mind. Cast, though fully prepared to accede to his daughter's orders, knew the next words from Rox's mouth would alter the destiny of his race for good or bad. Staring at her father instilled a small amount of calm in the black rabbit and Rox took a quivering breath. Her responsibilities as leader, not only of this warren, but warrens like these throughout the world, came to the fore. Though she would aid her friend however Ellie asked, her duties must conserve as many rabbits as possible or every living thing would face the slow death of the world itself.

Cast entered and laid a paw on his daughter's shoulder just as Plume joined the small group.

"Send word to all warrens about what has occurred here today." She instructed her father. "Tell them their lives are under threat but under no circumstances are they to engage the dragons." Her eyes found Plume and she continued speaking while studying the warren's protector. "All our young and their parents will relocate to the nearest warren including those who wish to leave." Plume's eyes widened in expectation. "I'm committing those who volunteer to remain to help Ellie, in whatever she wishes to do next." Rox's voice had dropped to almost a whisper as all three rabbits contemplated their immediate future.

"I'll see to it." Cast responded, breaking the heavy silence. "Plume, will you organise the relocation of the families?"

Plume looked back and forth between Rox and her father before simply nodding and leaving the two of them alone.

"Am I doing at least one thing right, father?" Rox asked with a small snort of derision.

"You always ran your own way, Rox. But in doing so you found Ellie and all that comes with it."

"Well, we failed to save the world. If we're lucky enough to survive the attacks from the dragons, we still have to survive mankind."

"We can never know the consequences of our actions, Rox. We just do what we can."

Rox sighed and slipped her paws onto her father's shoulders.

"Thank you."

Bound

Malachite circled the destroyed house high above. He'd watched calmly as the red dragon carrying Ellie had emerged from a dragon thread. For now, the moment to unleash his fury upon the girl was quenched, the emotional confusion of the bonding tiring his thoughts and actions. So Malachite watched quite dispassionately as the girl and dragon raced about the destroyed house, neither pleased at taking so much from her, nor displeased at not wishing to descend and make good on his promise to her for a painful death.

Malachite turned and allowed the winds to carry him away on his outstretched wings. A slight wriggle from his chest brought his attention back to the child.

Cold. A tightness within the body. Short breaths.

Malachite instinctively lowered the child until it came into contact with his hide near to where fire was produced inside his body.

Warmth. Pain inside, growing.

Malachite tilted his head and his eyes widened as the child's thoughts impinged on his own body. From deep within he felt the turmoil of his stomach accompanied by a rush of hunger. He nodded and opened a thread to take him back to the temple. Perhaps he could track one of those interfering rabbits for the young human and feed it. Without a backwards glance or thought regarding his destruction over the last twenty minutes Malachite entered the blackness of a thread and vanished from the sky.

Unprepared

The steel grey sky above the temple, observed through human eyes, could easily have been interpreted as a grey shroud covering the world, never-ending, eternal. However, through eyes forged in the fire of magic the bleak sky revealed a wealth of information.

Corvus groaned flexing his right wing as he emerged from the deep pit. Mud caked his wings and when he was again on solid ground, he shook them viciously causing another groan to issue forth. His head pounded with the rhythm of his heart and the ache compelled the dragon to squint his large eyes. A groan became a growl as his memory replayed his traitorous brother, Eridan, swinging a bent metal bar at Corvus' head. The impact had resulted in a long painful descent back into the dark pit created by the troublesome rabbits who had saved the girl and her dragon.

Ignoring the pain Corvus looked upwards and studied the vast amount of dragon threads piercing the sombre sky. The threads used by the dragons for moving quickly from one place to another, left behind distinctive trails in the sky only visible to other dragons. Two were of immediate interest to Corvus, one of black and one of red. The threads circled and intertwined before vanishing in an electric blue mist followed by the colours of two of Corvus' group giving chase.

Despite his anger, Corvus found a knot of hesitation and worry in regard to his planned course of action. Initially his plan was to strip the girl of her memories to learn as much as possible about the new world he and his fellow dragons had woken to. Their slumber had lasted untold seasons and the black dragon was canny enough to acknowledge a lack of information may lead to their downfall. When the girl escaped however the path had led him here to this hillside and into the midst of a race of magical rabbits. Corvus snorted his disbelief at such a proposition but he had spoken to a member of their race twice now, and twice he had been made a fool of. Placing his confusion aside over the rabbits Corvus knew this day was lost and he and his kin must return into hiding while they considered a new course of action.

A flash of blue lightning from high above brought Corvus from his reverie and his spirits soared even as his heartrate accelerated as a dragon emerged into the lead sky. Perhaps his kin were bringing him the girl or his treacherous brother. His hopes were dashed as quickly as they were built as the dragon saw the green sheen of Malachite's hide.

* * *

Cold darkness gives way to light. However, not warm light.
Rush of wind beating its hard fist.
A roar of displeasure and the wind abates, stopped by…by…something.
Screaming, shouting, more anger but now tinged with fear.
Scared!
Do not be scared.
Protect!
I will protect you!
A flash of orange fire.
A warning. Away, we must go away.
We are unnatural. An abomination. Outcasts.
No. We are not. Malachite, we are not! We are together.
YES!
Kill to protect. Protect to kill.
Kill my leader for you?
For us, Malachite.
YES!

* * *

Malachite pushed Corvus' limp body into the dark pit. Defeating the black dragon was a relatively simple matter. Corvus was suffering the effect of falling into the pit by design of the rabbits and then receiving a tremendous blow to the head from a metal pole. As Malachite swooped to the ground he'd noticed the black dragon and leader of the dragons swaying upon his paws as he attempted to track Malachite across the sky. Gliding lower the green dragon had simply tilted his entire body and aimed his talons at Corvus' head. The weight behind the impact had driven Malachite's talons deep into Corvus' brain and the black dragon was dead before Malachite touched the ground proper.

Elation rose in Malachite's mind but its source came from his would-be rider.

Hide. Protect. Grow.

Came as a whisper, light, barely registering. Malachite's gaze was drawn upwards as the dragons returned unsuccessfully from chasing Eridan and his son. He looked down into the pit holding their deceased leader and then at the young human.

Malachite nodded.

Ten Years Later

The day we fell: 2018 C.E.

Mary leapt from the highest step of the coach and was instantly assaulted by an intense barrage before touching the ground. She yelped in something akin to pain at the cold onslaught. Wind and rain acted in unity, driving against her entire body, pushing her into the open door of the coach and causing her light raincoat to meld instantly with the contours of her body. Squinting and grimacing into the sharp deluge Mary heard laughing as some of her more well-dressed classmates grinned and chuckled smugly, comforted in the knowledge that even though their coats were more suited for an ascent of Everest, they were warm and if not completely dry, then close enough.

"Come on, Mary." Mary's arm was snatched and she was pulled away from the coach's door as others descended into winter's savage attack. Shrieks accompanied by yet more laughter told Mary she was not the only one dressed inappropriately for the day. The wind and rain lessened somewhat as Mary was pulled close into the minimal shelter offered by the coach's side. Wiping the water from her sour face Mary squinted and saw the smiling face of her friend Gabby.

"Bloody hell, Mary. This is fun isn't it?" Gabby smiled tighter and Mary sighed inwardly, not wishing to upset her friend. Gabby, as she promised she would, had successfully reigned in her excitement on the coach for today's journey under pain of a Chinese burn from Mary herself. Now however Gabby's exuberance had returned tenfold from, it seemed, being cooped up for far too long. Mary sniffed her agreement and displeasure and caught the sharp tang of salt in the air. Above the sound of the swirling wind and complaining students, Mary fancied she could hear the roll of the sea. Gabby caught her friend's look and she pointed towards a large building standing fifty metres away.

"The sea's that way, behind the main building. We're still quite a way inland as the site is massive."

Mary nodded absently and hunched her shoulders, not really caring what direction the sea was in or the size of what they were here to see. Her only concern was getting out of this ridiculous weather as soon as possible and into a warm room.

"Okay everyone pay attention!" A new voice intruded upon Mary's misery. "Please make your way to the main entrance. Remember we're still in a car park so no running. I said 'NO RUNNING!'" Mary snorted a laugh as nearly the entire class, as one entity, made a break from the coach to the safe harbour offered ahead. With a laugh, Mary grabbed Gabby's arm and propelled her forward. Gabby attempted to shake her friend's grip away.

"No, Mary! I can disobey our teacher perfectly well thank you." She protested. Mary grinned into the buffeting wind and kept pushing Gabby forward as they both giggled. Behind them, she could still hear the exasperated shouts of their science teacher attempting, with little success, to coral his students who had all become temporarily hard of hearing.

"It had better be warm in there!" Mary screamed into the rain.

* * *

Mary yawned and instantly jerked upright as an elbow connected sharply with her ribs.

"Hey!" She whispered fiercely to her attacker but Gabby was already facing the front of the room again and simply held a finger to her lips. Mary raised a finger of her own at her friend and tried without success to watch the 'Welcome!' with an exclamation mark, video, playing for them.

The promise of a warm, dry haven was short-lived. On entering the building, warm air instantly banished the ills of the winter weather. Even the harsh remonstrations over safety by Mr. Harris felt far away, as Mary bathed in the blasts of the heating system. The warmth was stolen away quickly however as all the class were herded into a dismal conference room. Its walls matched the grey of the outside world and without functioning heating either it seemed to be doing its best to match the conditions, with the added punishment of uncomfortable plastic chairs. After finding a seat, Mary quickly began shivering, her clothes still wet and hair hanging limply from her forehead. Misery descended upon the room as the door closed while they waited for their teacher to return and the windows rapidly misted blocking the dreary view. Gabby seemed to be the only student taking the room in, her classmates were holding whispered conversations as if talking at any volume would invite more problems. Though it did not seem possible at the time the video started, misery sank to new levels as nearly all realised the dull information doled out on screen by a fake tanned soap opera star would go on for a while. Mary shivered once more and rubbed her thighs.

"Remember, your safety is paramount. Elm-sea B operates a no tolerance rule on running, jumping and no..." Mary screwed her eyes and looked at the screen, "chewing gum!" The soap opera actor on the screen grinned inanely and Mary wondered how many teeth the man had in his mouth and if they were his. She heard a snicker of a laugh and raised her eyebrows at Gabby.

"Seriously?" She asked, nudging her friend with her shoulder. Gabby shrugged as the class groaned and cursed at the awful attempt at humour. Gabby leaned in close to Mary and without taking her eyes from the screen whispered into her friend's ear.

"His crap-eating grin just reminded me of that episode where he finds out his girlfriend is pregnant by another man but that's for the best as she might be his twin and the other man is wanted by the police for stealing cows and selling them on the black market." Despite her discomfort Mary snorted a laugh at Gabby's ridiculous breakdown of soap opera drama. Before Mary could add her own over the top storyline the video clicked to a stop which was met by a chorus of ironic cheers. The door to the conference room opened and Mr Harris and another man wearing a hi-vis jacket entered.

"Thank you for taking the time to watch our safety video." The man announced sardonically. "Now if you'll follow me the tour will begin."

Gabby squirmed on her chair and squeaked with excitement.

* * *

"The site was first developed back in 1964 as a caravan park but it was forced to close. The government's energy department purchased the land with a view to place a nuclear facility at the site." The guide stopped and pointed at the cement floor. "The first layer was put down by royalty itself in 1973." Gabby tutted, clearly frustrated by the type of information being imparted, Gabby wanted technical information and nothing else would satisfy her. Mary smiled at her friend's reaction and eased into a steady pace. As she thought about her friendship with this strange girl the words of their tour guide washed away and her movements became automatic as she was led about gigantic pieces of machinery. The two girls had only been friends for less than a year but the solidity of their relationship was clear for all to see. Mary, for her part, had only moved into the local area and school eighteen months ago. Her father had served in the army but injury on duty had forced an early retirement. She was quite used to being a 'barrack rat' as she was commonly known in schools and though it did not faze her it made cementing any long term friendships difficult. Even now the effect still resonated in her school life. Her parents promised this was the final upheaval as they relocated close to her grandparents, who she barely knew, and her place in a school a permanent fixture. Still the old fear remained and the difficulties in forming lasting friendships kept her at a distance from her classmates. Gabby however changed everything.

Ten months ago the teacher had introduced the new girl and Mary remembered grimacing in embarrassment for the poor thing as she had endured it herself not too long ago. With long, brown frizzy hair that matched the colour of her skin and clothes that seemed to hang as if unsupported by a human frame the teacher loudly announced the newest member of Class Heyerdahl. To make the situation infinitely worse the teacher sat Gabby next to a girl Mary thought of as the class bitch, Brooke. Even now Mary could see in her mind's eye the look of utter disgust on Brooke's face as Gabby slid ungracefully into her seat. Gabby it seemed either hadn't noticed or simply didn't care as she sat there with her shoulders hunched protectively and her hair forming a shield, obscuring her face.

The register was taken and five minutes after all hell broke loose.

Mary glanced up and saw the tour guide pointing to a container that would easily hold her and a few other class members and possibly their worldly goods. She smiled at the memory, and a bit guiltily for daydreaming instead of listening to their guide, but the droning chatter of machinery allowed her mind to lapse into its own world once again.

An eruption had occurred where Gabby was placed. The whole class reacted in shock accompanied with gasps of awe, replaced by the strange silence when major trouble is looming close by. The eruption was the desk scraping and screeching across the classroom floor as it was shoved forward. It was followed by chairs toppling backwards as their former occupants came swiftly to their feet. What Mary saw sent a trickle of fear straight into her stomach. Gabby was holding Brooke against the wall, seemingly with no effort for such a light frame, with one hand placed on Brooke's chest while the other was cocked back over Gabby's shoulder, trembling with effort and perhaps anticipation, aimed for Brooke's petrified face.

"Call me that again!" Mary had sworn at the time that Gabby had whispered but she was able to hear the girl clearly. "I dare you! Call me 'coloured' again!"

The teacher of course had rushed over, but rather than restraining Gabby had stopped very close to the girl and whispered into her ear. After ten seconds, or ten hours as far as Mary was concerned, the new girl had lowered her fist and released Brooke with a contemptuous snort. Then without pause or a backwards glance Gabby left the room. The teacher had turned a stern gaze on the class, muting the rumblings of excited conversation before returning the desk to its place, the chairs upright and Brooke to her seat.

"Line up outside the hall in five minutes for assembly. Mary please see to it." And with that the teacher left the room also, leaving Mary to nod dumbfounded at a closing door. The door clicking shut was naturally the sign for every member of the class to burst into voice, questioning Brooke about the incident, some laughing as at one time or another they'd felt the lash of Brooke's tongue, others quieter as they realised quicker than their fellow class mates that something troublesome had entered their lives and they would have to put up with it on a daily basis. That aside Mary couldn't believe that even Brooke could be ignorant enough to bandy about racial epithets and turned her gaze on the girl. Brooke's eyes were in constant movement around the classroom and she was pale enough for Mary to wonder if Brooke was going to vomit. A few of Brooke's 'friends' approached her and the small group tried to laugh off the whole situation. Mary sighed and banged her fist down on the table.

"Assembly everyone."

Mary cast a quick look at the unassuming girl at her side as they mounted metal stairs bolted to the side of some great piece of whirring machinery. As well as she knew Gabby now, Mary would never be afraid of her best friend, but on that day Mary had been frightened. Gabby sensed the look and turned an excited smile on Mary before her attention was drawn back to their guide.

The background and outcome of that day ten months ago quickly became common knowledge through gossip and rumour interspersed with the truth.

Mary listened to all the gossip in the playground and was amazed to find out that even her parents had a version of what happened that day. But whatever was true Mary made sure, as did nearly every member of the school, to avoid the 'troubled black kid.'

In class Gabby now sat by herself near the teacher's desk. She was there when Mary and her classmates entered and she would be the last to leave when the final bell rang. Mary couldn't exactly remember when the two of them spoke in earnest, only that their friendship was set on one particular day when Mary was standing by the teacher's desk reciting a speech made by Hamlet. The majority of the class looked bored but as Mary uttered the line "What a piece of work is man." She happened to see Gabby's face through the wall of hair used as a shield. "How noble in reason. How infinite in faculty." Mary had continued and though she knew the lines by heart she stumbled slightly as she saw the appreciation in the dark brown eyes of the girl before her. "Um…uh." The hair parted further revealing Gabby's face and her moving lips, whispering.

"In form and moving…" Gabby had prompted.

"In form and moving, how express and admirable." And Mary had continued after that without another stumble. Delight had registered upon Gabby's face at Mary's recital and as Mary continued to explain why Hamlet had become so disenchanted with the human race she saw the keen interest in the troubled girl's eyes.

It wasn't until a week later however when a chance encounter brought the girls together in the bathroom. Mary was washing her hands when Gabby entered the toilets and Mary cast her gaze towards the sink, concentrating furiously on the water and bubbles, her face reddening as she tried to finish up as quickly as possible. A murmur from her left shoulder caused Mary to look involuntarily for the sound and she saw Gabby standing behind her. Rather than her discomfort growing it was erased in an instant as the girl who'd nearly whacked a fellow classmate was offering a shy smile.

"Sorry?" Mary cocked her head while shaking wet hands into the sink. The smile twitched in embarrassed amusement.

"I love Shakespeare."

Mary nodded in agreement and then grinned.

"Me too, but the comedies are bloody awful." Gabby snickered a laugh and Mary caught a glimpse of the real girl behind the reputation. Mary turned fully and lifted a hand.

The day we fell: 2018 C.E.

"Mary."

Gabby paused but only for a moment before doing likewise and clasping Mary's offered hand. As soon as their hands met Mary cringed as she realised she hadn't dried her hands, but Gabby laughed it off and with her free hand swept the hair she used as a protective shield away from her face.

From that time forward the girls spent break and lunchtimes together, avoiding the playground and the snide and asinine comments of some over their blossoming friendship. Mary at first tried to in some way defend the words and actions of others as their school was located in the countryside and had yet to experience other creeds to the degree larger towns and cities had. Gabby had listened with great interest and sad eyes before shrugging and advising Mary she had heard worse but that Mary should never defend or apologise for what Gabby considered racist comments. Mary never apologised again.

The two friends sought solace within the quiet walls of the school library. Here Mary learned of Gabby's past while shrouded by the silence of the library, the atmosphere at times reminiscent of a confessional at church with Mary performing the part of priest. Abandoned by her drug addicted parents at the age of eight, Gabby had entered the care system and she deemed her fortune as astounding as her carers were kind, compassionate and trained to deal with a girl with Gabby's apparent emotional problems, not that they were going to vanish overnight. When Gabby spoke of where she lived at present her voice was marked by a soft tone, as if thankful in her own way that she'd escaped the hell of her parents. But when speaking of her parents Mary not only heard but saw the fire writhing within this damaged girl. That she hated her parents was clear, her anger towards them was almost a living beast in its own right. But Mary saw and sometimes heard beneath the anger was the loss, and the love. At times it would be the inexplicable love and need of a child for their parents regardless of how badly they had been mistreated. When this would fade from Gabby's eyes Mary saw the questions generated by that love but fuelled by anger. Why didn't you love me? Was I not good enough? How could you?

Mary simply listened. She offered no advice as she could think of none and refused to litter meaningless bullshit on such an open, sore wound. Arriving home from school that particular day, Mary embraced both her parents, shocking them both, before bursting into tears over another's pain.

From then on they studied together, gossiped together, spoke about all things music, television and film but above all that was a desire, a thirst they seemed to share, albeit in separate subjects. Mary was driven by the arts. She performed in the school plays, wrote prose and fiction and though completely untalented with oils and a canvas she had a wonderful eye through a camera lens. For Gabby her passion was mathematics and science, of any sort. While Mary read Dylan Thomas while sat upon the sofa in the library, shoes off and feet curled up under her, Gabby was sat at a desk close by, reading Stephen Hawking, Carl Sagan and Neil deGrasse Tyson. Both would also share their passion of Shakespeare and could often be found in the corner of the library whispering lines from Othello, The Merchant of Venice, King Lear and so on. Discussing characters, plot, the drama and one aspect that intrigued Mary, was Shakespeare a single playwright or many.

"So here we are at the main viewing platform. This offers us the best vantage point of the station and though not everything can be seen from here I'm sure you'll agree it's an impressive sight."

Mary blinked in surprise as Gabby rushed forward for a prime viewing spot, the excited girl turned and waved her friend over.

"Wow, Mary, look at this!" Mary smiled at her friend's keen excitement. When their science teacher had announced the visit to the nuclear power station the response was one straight out of the teenage manual of boredom for nearly all. Jokes were made and several of the boys wanted to invest in lead underwear but Gabby had been beside herself. To see such immense power and energy created, or at least the machinery and technology first-hand was a special treat for her. Mary was firmly settled in the 'boring' camp hence the threat to Chinese burn her friend if she let her excitement reach intolerable levels on the coach journey. Mary had to admit to a touch of appreciation for craftsmanship as she looked out over the machinery before her as it was big, extremely big, and noisy and that was as far as Mary cared about it. Their tour guide sensing at least one interested individual in Gabby moved close and pointed at the far wall, quite a distance away.

"We're permitted to take four of you at a time into the main control room over there." The man watched and tried not to smile too much at Gabby's widening eyes. "I assume you'd like to be in the first group?" Gabby nodded furiously and turned a stunning smile on her friend. Mary smiled in return and then sighed.

* * *

Mary cast a disapproving eye about the control centre as she, their school teacher, Gabby and somehow, Brooke into the large circular room. Judging by the comments made by their enthusiastic tour guide as they made their way across the station's main floor Mary expected to see something akin to the bridge of the Starship Enterprise, with fantastical displays projecting the inner workings of the station, stream lined furniture gleaming white and pristine. Unfortunately, she was met with a circle of bland, dull white facades on the rim of the room with a few diagrams and blinking lights. The office furniture was new, but a dull brown affair, made for its robustness rather than its aesthetic qualities. Two rows of desks housing computer screens were placed near the centre and temptingly showed more interesting graphics though Mary was sure one of the engineers or technicians was quickly attempting to close down a game of Solitaire. Their tour guide for the day had hustled them into the control room and handed them over to the station's Chief of Operations, Jeremy Anderson.

"All information feeds through to this room and to these gentlemen." A slight pause allowed each man sitting to turn and nod a greeting. "Information such as core temperature, pressure, energy production and so on. Suffice to say that we are the most efficient, in terms of logistics and conversion to electricity in the entire country."

Mary switched off from the technobabble and let her eyes wander away from the computer displays. Without consciously thinking her eyes settled on a display close by. It showed what she thought was the room she was in and the main station surrounding them, each area was lit by a green bulb which Mary took as a good sign. Below this display was another, the outer area the same size as the entire station but with much smaller compartments or rooms, each lit by a red bulb.

"Mary? What was that?" Mary turned with a bemused expression on her face to Mr Harris.

"Hmm?"

"You said something, or asked a question?" He prompted. Mary looked over to Gabby who was nodding with a slight smile and then over to Brooke who simply rolled her eyes in embarrassment for her. Mary flushed and cleared her throat.

"Sorry. I simply wondered what this area was lit by red? Red can't be all that good surely?" Mary finished quietly, biting a nail in nervousness. The technicians and Jeremy chuckled softly and he moved to where Mary was standing.

"This," he explained pointing a finger to the green bulbs, "is us. This area lit by the red is classified under the Official Secrets Act." Mary pursed her lips and nodded in understanding before frowning.

"But why would an area of a nuclear power station be classified?"

Mr Harris groaned and Jeremy smiled. Gabby raised her thumb to give Mary an ironic OK signal. Jeremy led Mary away, grinning all the while.

"Honestly it's nothing to worry about. I know after all these years nuclear power still gets a bad reputation which is why we sponsor these visits. But there's nothing here that need concern you." Mary shrugged and was about to apologise when a shrill alarm blared and every bright fluorescent light in the room flickered out to be replaced by dark red.

* * *

The terrible sound overrode nearly every other sense Mary possessed. Every technician in the room was shouting, some on telephones, others on walkie-talkies and also at each other, all in an effort to be heard over the pounding alarm.

Not a good design if it's too loud.

Mary thought, her mind sluggish, unwilling to come to terms with what an alarm at a nuclear power station could indicate.

One voice rose above all others in the dark red gloom.

"Shut that goddamn alarm off! Jesus Christ!"

A moment of silence, at least from everyone in the room, fell before a few taps on a keyboard brought total silence. Mary's ears whined and she screwed her eyes in pain. Gabby was busy holding her nose and pulling awful faces as she attempted to unblock her ears. Mary wanted to tell her that was pointless but she seemed distant to her surroundings. Everyone was speaking again but quieter and a lot calmer. Mr Harris was clutching Brooke's shoulders as the girl was only a few moments away from reaching hysteria. The chief, bathed in the red light of the control room resembled a shop mannequin. He had become stock still, the only indication of life was the sweat running down his face, already soaking his shirt collar in the short space of time since the alarm had begun. Random snatches of conversation seemed to drift towards Mary rather than any effort on her part to hear them.

"Core temperature is stable."

The day we fell: 2018 C.E.

"Turbines functioning perfectly."

"Water pressure is fine. I can't see what's wrong!"

"Then what the hell is wrong and who sounded the alarm!"

A high pitched whine made each person cry out and clutch their ears. Fortunately, it was over in a few seconds to be replaced by the crackles and pops of a speaker coming to life.

"Initiate quarantine, effective immediately. Code Manhattan, repeat Code Manhattan. This is not a drill, repeat this is not a drill."

The speaker died with one last crackle as the words played out in the imaginations of the rooms occupants. The lighting switched automatically from red back to the harsh fluorescent glare of five minutes ago. Gabby had wandered over to Mary and without thinking, they were holding hands for reassurance and comfort. What scared Mary more than anything though were the expressions on the station employees. All now bore a deathly pale countenance. It was their eyes where Mary could not bear to look. All of them, without exception, had the look of a person who'd gazed into Hell itself and seen it was where they were bound.

* * *

"Move! Come on!" Without pause for explanations the three girls and their teacher were each grabbed and propelled towards a metal door on the far side of the control centre. Any objections or questions were ignored as the door was quickly opened via one of the technician's swipe card. Banging on the far side of the control room drew Mary's attention and she heard muffled voices screaming incoherently. The door she and the others had entered into this area not ten minutes ago was the focus of the noise and Mary realised the voices were of her classmates and their tour guide. Her shoulder was grabbed once more and she was pushed through the open doorway. A long set of metal stairs followed and all four of the visitors fell silent as they were forced to negotiate the hasty trip down into the dark below. Mary tried to follow the short, sharp conversations being held around her.

"My class, my kids!"

"We're on lockdown now! There's no going back!"

"Christ. Oh Jesus, God, help us!"

"Keep going please!"

Mary heard a continuous call for help in between her own panicked breathing.

"Help me, oh god, help me, oh god!" On and on as she descended further into the blackness below. The phrase married with the clatter of feet on the metal treads created an almost hypnotic rhythm. Mary dimly realised the desperate voice was her own, out loud and in her head, this realisation nevertheless didn't halt her mantra.

"One more flight."

Mary flicked her eyes momentarily away from the steps and now saw a dim glow pooling at the bottom of the stairwell from a series of recessed lights. In the glow Mary saw another metal door which was now opening as the group reached their apparent destination. Space down here was limited but the operation's chief stopped everyone from proceeding further. Deep breaths were taken by all, many leaning on their knees before wiping the sweat from their faces. Mary looked for Gabby and saw her own fright and confusion reflected back at her. Brooke was sobbing gently into Mr Harris's shoulder and despite what she thought of the girl, Mary felt the need to comfort her.

"What the hell is going on?" Mr Harris demanded. "All my bloody students are up there!" The arm not wrapped around his student punched straight up into the air. Chief Anderson nodded as he drew a long breath. He looked back up the stairs to the door they'd entered from but it was now lost in the darkness above as their destination had been hidden below during their descent.

"I'm sorry, I truly am." The man ran his fingers through his hair and bit his upper lip before continuing. "Code Manhattan is a total disaster code. It's used in the event of natural disaster, invasion or nuclear attack."

Mary felt the sharp sting of tears pierce her eyes without the need to even contemplate this man's words, her body was reacting to the news seemingly of its own accord.

"I can explain more when we get to safety but please you have to realise that there is no going back. When the code was called the station's controls are set to automatic until an all clear. That means everything outside of the control room is sealed off." The man's voice became hard as he finished his sentence and Mary noticed he actually physically leaned forward as if to emphasise his point. Mr Harris squeezed Brooke's shoulder and cleared his throat.

"In other words they were locked out of the safe zone you have here, where we are now?"

The day we fell: 2018 C.E.

"We're not there yet, but essentially, yes." The man sighed and looked at his colleagues before addressing the surprise guests. "Before we enter I want you to understand right now that we will be sealed in. No getting out until it's safe, and that is a relative term until we know what's going on up there. My team and I have trained for these scenarios." The chief tried a half-hearted attempt at a smile. "But we couldn't just leave you up there could we?" Brooke groaned and Gabby shuffled over to Mary's side. The two girls placed their arms about each other's waist.

"But our family, our friends." Brooke sobbed. The man simply gave a shake of his head. He then closed his eyes and indicated towards the door. The technicians moved through the open door until, standing in the dim light, were the three girls, Mr Harris and the man who seemed to be in charge.

"I understand, miss. I really do. All of us, every person here, has family out there." He jutted his chin back towards the surface. Mr Harris nodded and guided Brooke to Mary and Gabby. Without words all four looked into the other's eyes and saw the truth of their situation. Mary took a deep, shuddering breath, trying to muster an ounce of will. She turned and nodded to the man who had led them down here.

Slowly the small group joined the remainder on the far side of the door and watched as it was closed shut, the clang of the metal reverberating in Mary's chest and it seemed stilling her fluttering heart.

* * *

Gabby could not resolve the images she was witnessing on screen with anything in real life. A few hours had passed since she and the others had fled to safety and as *guests* they had been dumped in a small lounge with a television, highly uncomfortable sofas and away in the corner two sets of bunk beds while the Chief and technicians went about their work in securing wherever they now were. With no real close ties to the outside world Gabby found herself the ablest to cope with the situation. If she was being completely honest she found it not only scary but quite exhilarating. But still, her best friend, Mary, was beside herself with worry, not to mention Brooke and Mr Harris. Mary had two brothers as well as her mum and dad to worry over so Gabby spent the time just sitting with her, neither really speaking but just comforting. Boredom as it often does however leaks into any situation regardless of the circumstances and the small group of four turned on the television, not expecting it to work and after a short while wished it wasn't. Gabby found the news stations straightaway and like her three companions had watched in a total state of confusion at some of the imagery they were seeing. Brooke would have none of it, accusing Gabby of turning to some stupid TV show rather than the news. The accusations grew louder and more hysterical until Mr Harris had been forced to intervene and calm the girl down. Gabby and Mary had continued watching and Gabby was sure if someone was recording them while sat there the video would show two girls with their jaws comically dropping to the floor.

The news feeds available were showing the same clips again and again, each with their own commentary, ranging from utter disbelief to numbed shock. The one main clip that each news broadcaster focused on was apparently from a tourist on vacation in the United States. The clip started out with a shuddery image of the ground accompanied by the user complaining about the shot. In the background were the normal noises for any city; traffic, footsteps of people passing by, chattering and shouting. While the video camera was still taking in the view of the ground a scream causes the operator to judder and turn in the direction of the noise. The screams multiply and the operator finds a group of pedestrians pointing to something over the camera user's shoulder. The image becomes blurry as the camera is spun quickly and at first the camera focuses on a set of large black iron railings. Then as the camera is pointed upwards the image resolves to that of the White House in Washington D.C. More screams add to the pandemonium and rockets are fired from the roof of the President's residence up into the grey sky. The camera user tracks the smoke trail the rockets leave behind until the intended target comes into view and the camera blurs once again as it attempts to focus on this new object. Here it becomes obvious that the camera operator is a man as the screams become his and then as the camera shakes in fright the image resolves to that of a huge yellow figure hovering in the sky. Beating its wings almost lazily the creature studies the rockets swiftly approaching, extending its long neck and letting loose a glass shattering scream of its own. The wings are thrust frantically and the animal gains height before disappearing from the sky.

A collective gasp is heard from those on the ground and the man behind the camera and silence returns for a short time. Conversations are picked up by the microphone and a few laughs as people think they've witnessed an elaborate hoax. The laughs are quickly replaced by shrieks, yells and screams as a mighty crunch is heard from the direction of the White House. On the roof of that most famous building is the yellow creature that a moment ago disappeared. Its weight has crushed part of the roof and the video clearly shows the men assigned to protect the President being dispatched in gruesome fashion. The man holding the camera begins to retch at the scene and he starts turning away as others around him are calling for help and fleeing the area. Just before the video loses focus on the White House roof a large stream of red and yellow fire can be seen streaking down from the roof, engulfing a large portion of the front of the house. Gun shots sound in the distance, sounding like nothing more than small firecrackers. Then with one final whimper for help from the man operating the camera the video and audio disappear.

Gabby watched the video again and again. The news stations were freezing the video and attempting to enhance the still picture of the yellow beast in the sky. Though the outline of the creature became blurry and detail was lost as the image was zoomed in the shape was apparent for all who were watching to see. Gabby herself knew what the creature was but it seemed none on the television dare speak the name, either through the thought of ridicule or simple disbelief. Gabby knew and when she looked at her friend sat next to her she saw in Mary's eyes the mixture of incredulity and foreboding she knew must show in hers at this fantastical creature, a dragon.

The video, before reaching any news outlets, had been uploaded to the internet via social media and from there quickly went viral. It was perhaps it's fantastical elements that created such a swift journey around the world as it was classed as an incredibly realistic CGI creation from persons' unknown or some sort of global advertising campaign designed to attract a large audience. Whatever the reasons it prepared the way for the mass of videos to follow.

After a few hours Gabby switched the television off and placed the remote control gently to her side. She kept her movements slow as Mary was sleeping curled into Gabby's shoulder. Gabby looked down and saw wayward hairs dropping across her friend's face so using a finger Gabby swept them clear. Mary's face, though still now, showed the ravages of emotions over the last hours watching news reports from around the world. That an overwhelming attack was underway was clear but Gabby sensed that in each report from government or military agencies the air of utter confusion was fogging any proper response. Gabby shook her head slightly. She knew the picture she was seeing being laid out by the media was a small one and if the media did anything these days it was to shock and encourage feelings of horror from their viewers, they still had ratings to think about regardless of the dire circumstances apparently facing the human race.

A short metallic squeak drew Gabby's attention to her left and the bunk beds in the corner of the room. Mr Harris their science teacher was rising, doing his best to do it quietly. In between watching the news reports the teacher had spent his time comforting Brooke who appeared to be in shock. The truth was they were all in shock but Brooke's fragility shocked Gabby as the girl was such a pain in the arse in school, not so much a bully as after their first encounter Brooke would never dare, but the occasional snide comment and enticing others to laugh at Gabby. Gabby's own shock at the situation had dissipated rapidly, having no real family in the outside world she was able to concentrate on the stories coming in, but it was her friend's distress that affected Gabby more than anything. Mary hadn't fallen apart as Brooke did but her tears were constant as she worried over her family. Gabby had tried to comfort Mary but in truth her friend's emotions brought Gabby's into play. Not only had she met Mary's family but they were warm and welcoming. Mary's Dad thought it hilarious to mention the incident with Brooke, much to Mary's and her mother's embarrassment. Gabby hadn't minded though, she sensed a subtle belonging after that as Mary said her Dad never would have said such a thing if he hadn't liked Gabby. Thinking of them brought tears to Gabby's eyes and the two girls had hugged tightly.

"Has there been anything new happening?" Mr Harris nodded towards the blank television screen, easing himself into an armchair close by.

"More eyewitness accounts and videos." Gabby replied without taking her eyes off Mary's face. "And most countries are declaring a state of emergency one after the other."

"Have any of those technicians, whatever they are, come back?"

Gabby now turned her head to respond and stared in dismay at the man sat near her. In his mid-forties, Mr Harris had been teaching for twenty years. His time in the classroom with teenagers had given the man the patience of a saint, not to mention the wit of a stand-up comic in dealing with the unruly elements of his classes. What he had looked like when he was younger Gabby hadn't a clue but in his class he became a science teacher and fitted the physical brief almost perfectly. Slightly hunched shoulders, brown hair, dappled with grey, a moustache that suited his face so well you knew he would look alien

The day we fell: 2018 C.E.

if he shaved it off. A pair of large round glasses added to the look, topped off with the customary brown jacket with elbow patches plus brown trousers and matching shoes. Gabby had thought each piece of clothing was an affectation, chosen and worn to complete the look to disarm students and teachers alike. But after a while Gabby realised this wasn't the case at all, Mr Harris simply dressed this way because that was who he was.

Now though the grey hair seemed to have taken a deep hold in a few hours. The large glasses appeared to have grown as the teacher's face looked sunken and haggard. It was the paleness of her teacher's face that caught Gabby's attention the most and sent a spasm of irrational fear through her thoughts as the man sat in the armchair beside her looked dead.

"How are you, Gabby?" Mr Harris whispered, placing his elbows on the arms of the chair and clasping his hands in front of his face.

"Tired." Gabby blinked and had to force her eyes open as sleep tried to quickly claim her.

"Hmm. I doubt you have much to worry about really do you?" Mr Harris didn't move but his eyes found Gabby's. She frowned at the question, shaking her head slightly. The teacher sighed and rolled his eyes. "You have no one do you? Your parents? Nope. Family? Absolutely not." Gabby felt her face flush with anger but her mind moved sluggishly as she tried to answer. "It's okay. I won't tell." Mr Harris brought a finger to his lips. "But you're one of them so you still have to die." Gabby whined in terrible fear. Her body locked in position, all she could see or think about was the man in front of her. Mr Harris smiled and he shuffled forwards, his knees meeting Gabby's own. He brought both hands to the sides of his mouth and reached in deeply with his fingers. He then pulled outwards, ripping the skin away exposing yellow teeth and a purple tongue. Gabby tried to scream but only whimpered. She tried to move but could only shake. Finished with the mouth the hands moved to the forehead where fingernails dug into the skin, slicing and then gathering the tattered flesh into loose balls, dropping them to the floor. Fingers then found the vulnerable eyeballs and ripped them clear in one motion revealing dark pits lit by yellow light. The jaws opened and cracked as the bone broke and grew forwards sprouting fangs as it seemed to reach for Gabby. Where the old skin was ripped away a new texture emerged, it was golden and looked to Gabby like lizard skin.

The transformed teacher rose from the chair and Gabby could not take her eyes away from the terrifying sight, she knew if she wasn't rescued soon she would lose her mind swiftly and her life a short time after. The creature bent slightly at the waist and Gabby heard a rumbling noise deep inside the chest of the thing before her. A dim red light appeared in the maw of the elongated jaws and with no conscious thought Gabby knew she now faced the end of her life and how it was to happen. The red light grew in intensity, swirling with yellow and orange as it danced deeply within the dark jaws. The creature leaned back and then thrust its chest and head forward violently at Gabby. A deluge of red fire emerged with the sound of a thousand trains racing by, directly at Gabby's face.

Gabby screamed.

* * *

Mary pressed down fiercely on Gabby's shoulders, holding her friend down on the bed as she thrashed and tried to shake Mary's hands loose.

"Gabby please!" Mary pleaded, panic taking a hold as she feared Gabby was losing her mind as she shrieked in terror.

"Gabby! Wake up!" Mr Harris's voice cut through Gabby's incoherent yells immediately, stilling the girl with such quickness that Mary feared her friend wasn't breathing. Mr Harris sat upon the bed opposite Mary and laid a hand on her aching arm, pulling it back from Gabby's shoulder. "Gabby, it's Mr Harris. You're safe now I promise. You were dreaming." The teacher's voice had softened considerably and Mary remembered that he had two children of his own, two boys, both young. Gabby didn't move but both heard the slight whimper as she drew in a quick breath. Mr Harris indicated to Mary to speak to her frightened friend.

"It's okay, Gabby. You fell asleep on the sofa with the news playing and Mr Harris placed you in bed. He's telling the truth you've been dreaming." Mary reached out and gently laid her hand on Gabby's cheek. Gabby flinched slightly at the contact but opened her terror infested eyes, moving them back and forth from Mary to Mr Harris, who both smiled comfortingly. Gabby closed her eyes and took a long breath and let it out through pursed, trembling lips. She raised her own hand and squeezed Mary's where it still laid upon her cheek. Opening her eyes again she took a shorter breath and blasted it out in frustration and embarrassment.

The day we fell: 2018 C.E.

"Okay. I'm okay, thanks. Just a dream, right." Mr Harris nodded and smiled in acknowledgment, Gabby's eyes once again danced from her friend to her teacher. "Though, could you both stop smiling at me while I'm lying down. It's quite unnerving."

* * *

The room in which the three students and teacher had been left in was bland to the point that Gabby was certain only a sick, twisted mind that worked for the government could conceive of such a terrible room. In her opinion it only qualified as fit for humans because it contained somewhere to sit, sleep and watch television. A bathroom was situated through a door at the back of the room but as Gabby sat down shakily she realised it was missing something of vital importance.

"How long have we been in here? I'm starving." Mary let out a bark of a laugh and rubbed her red eyes. Pulling her terrified friend out of a nightmare had led to a short burst of tears and Gabby realised that the four of them were barely keeping their emotions in check and a simple comment or action could break that thin emotional shell each of them were currently residing in.

"Only a few hours." Mr Harris replied taking a seat next to Brooke, draping a blanket around the girl's shoulders. "It seems longer I suppose because of the news we watched." Gabby grunted in response and stared at Brooke. It was clear to see how fragile she currently was. Her gaze seemed to focus on a spot directly in front of her and five miles away at the same time. Her face was deathly pale and Gabby shuddered as she remembered the white face of Mr Harris in her nightmare. She shifted her gaze to her teacher and cocked her eyebrow in question at him.

"I think she's in shock. I'm trying to keep her warm but you're right we do need food and water, especially Brooke."

Mary leaned forward from her seat next to Gabby.

"Do we turn the TV back on?" Her voice unnaturally timid, as if asking the question too loudly would offend some deity and make everything they witnessed true. Brooke's eyes fired into life and bore into Mary.

"Why would you want to do that?" She shrieked, her eyes flashed with such intensity at Mary that Gabby was sure Mary experienced a flash of pain. Mr Harris clamped an arm about Brooke's shoulders and he began whispering into her ear. Brooke shook her head violently, sending her curly blond hair back and forth across her tortured face. "No! No! I have to get home! Get off me!"

Mr Harris turned a desperate face to the two girls.

"See if you can find anyone out there, wherever we are, we need some help!" Both Mary and Gabby stood in unison, their own turbulent emotions forgotten as they made to leave the room. "A doctor would be good!" Mr Harris said in a strained tone as they left the room and closed the door.

* * *

"You know for an underground, secret lair, this place is quite well decorated." Gabby observed sarcastically, running a finger along the white, headache inducing, paint on the walls. As the floor and ceiling within the corridor they wandered along were also the same bright white Gabby couldn't quite dispel the notion she wasn't walking along a flat surface but somehow walking *down* a never ending white wall. The only interruptions in the white monotony were fluorescent strips in the ceiling, bright white again, and lines painted into the floor, six in total. Blue, orange, black, purple, green and, much to Gabby's chagrin, more white but at least surrounded by a black border. Mary had identified them as 'hallway markers.' A visit to a relative in hospital reminding her they were meant as a guide around the building. Gabby added in an exasperated tone that was fine as long as you knew what your destination was and which colour to follow. The coloured lines ran parallel to one another so far, but as the two girls had yet to reach a junction they couldn't fathom if they were going to or from any aid.

"Do you think Brooke will be okay?" Mary asked, linking her arm through her friend's for comfort as they wandered the hallway.

"No." Gabby shrugged. "But then, are you okay?" Gabby cast a sidelong glance at Mary and saw her friend purse her lips together until they matched the colour of the walls. "It's fine not to be you know." Gabby added in a conspiratorial whisper. "I mean take me for example. My folks, may they rot in hell, shit all over me and I still have 'issues' years later and now all this." Gabby waved her free arm about the hallway. "I'm buggered, is what I'm trying to say. Mental. Crazy. Ga ga." Mary sniffed a laugh and fumbled in her coat pocket for a tissue to wipe her eyes.

"I can't stop thinking of Mum and Dad. If they're alive…" Mary's voice broke slightly but she cleared her throat forcefully and with purpose. "And Ben and Alex of course. They must be so worried about me." Gabby nodded, sympathising in one respect and marvelling at the idea of caring parents in another. "But however weird this all is I'm sure it's being dealt with and we won't have to stay long." Mary finished her declaration with confidence. Gabby couldn't be certain if it was a false confidence or not and hoped her friend was right for all their sakes.

A few more minutes of quiet wandering brought the girls to a set of metal double doors. One side was opened inwards and as they moved closer they heard the sound of raised voices. Gabby squinted her eyes in the effort of listening as she walked. The voices at first were crackly, almost indistinct, coupled with clear speech and Gabby realised they could hear a radio conversation.

"Manhattan will stay online until the all clear." The girls heard the hiss and whine of static.

"Understood, sir. But from the Intel we're receiving here that could be a very long time." Mary and Gabby stopped walking as one of the men inside the room responded. Mary's arm tightened around her friend's.

"Major. We have no idea what's happening." The radio whined as if in protest causing all close by to grimace. "We are looking at a systematic attack on every nation capable of placing a military force in the field, sea and air." The voice paused again and the radio crackled during the silence, as if it was seemingly curious itself now as to what was occurring in the outside world. "Government buildings are also being targeted, there is no goddamn precedence for an invasion like this!" The radio fell silent without a crackle of static or whine in the air.

"Sir? Please respond!" The voice from inside the room responded to the sudden silence. After a minute of dead air, the girls heard the same man curse and he marched out of the room and almost into them. "What the bloody hell are…" He looked the girls up and down a look of utter confusion on his face. Gabby recognised him as the man who had given them the brief talk in the control room before the alarms had sounded, Chief, or apparently, Major, Anderson. The confusion was fleeting and the man's face became slightly softer. "Sorry, girls." He said with a sigh. "I'd forgotten we had guests." He looked back over his shoulder to the room he'd come from. "I assume you heard that conversation?" His face wrinkled and flushed with embarrassment and Gabby felt her own guilt at eavesdropping. Both she and Mary nodded.

"We've watched the news coming in as well." Gabby said quietly. The man closed his eyes briefly before giving them both quite a hard stare.

"Then you know what we face is real and why we're down here?"

Mary swallowed nervously so Gabby replied for them.

"Yes. But, why?" She asked with a shrug. "What's so important about this place?"

Mary cleared her throat.

"And when do we get to go home or speak to our parents?"

Gabby turned her head to her friend and nodded.

"And do you have a doctor down here? One of our frie…classmates isn't feeling well. And some food and something to drink?"

The man rolled his eyes and swore.

* * *

"The majority of the site is classified under the Official Secrets Act but I will tell you what I can." The man, the girls now knew as Major Jeremy Anderson, had listened to all the requests laid before him with a great deal of patience and promptly turned Mary and Gabby over to a junior officer, Lieutenant William McCaffrey, who was trying his best to bring his 'guests' up to speed as best as he could.

The three girls and their teacher had been moved further into the complex deep underneath the nuclear power station and shown into a common room where they were given food and drink. Brooke and Mr Harris left soon after to visit the onsite medic and returned shortly with some medication for Brooke. Brooke seemed a great deal calmer so Mary and Gabby didn't question what the girl had taken though they tried their best not to look too long in the girl's direction. Introductions were made and the Lieutenant attempted to explain what was going on.

"After 9/11 security reviews were mandatory at any potential terrorist target. One of the key facilities it was thought a group of trained radicals would attack would be a nuclear power station. Security here, as you know, requires a group to book a tour some months in advance and send information on all visitors that will be attending. Then on the day of your visit you produce your passport or other I.D and go through a metal detector and scanner. If anyone of the group have not brought their passport they get to sit out the tour in one of our secure rooms." The lieutenant paused as another man came over to the small group currently sitting about a long, metal table used for feeding tens at a time. The lieutenant was handed a note which he studied quickly and screwed into a tight ball. "Tell Dr Eames I shall see him shortly, but stay with him please." The order was acknowledged with a nod and the man left. "Excuse me." He apologised. "Dr Eames is one of our nuclear physicists onsite when this happened, I'll introduce you later." The officer's eyes drifted away and Gabby saw it happen when he'd said the word 'later.' At that point she guessed he was wondering if there was going to be a later. She reasoned it was an accurate guess as that thought had occurred to her. "Anyway," he continued, "in the event of an attack new protocols were to be put into place. The control room you saw would be sealed away until the crisis had passed. During that time any technicians or scientists would be effectively quarantined, to all intents and purposes, safely underground in this bunker. If terrorists were identified, then measures would be taken from down here to isolate them." McCaffrey cocked an eyebrow as he spoke the last words meaning that his idea of isolation was something quite permanent. "In our current situation the control room is locked down and we are secure in the bunker." He reached for a pitcher of water and proceeded to fill a glass.

"So my students are safe?" Mr Harris asked, casting a sideways glance at Brooke. McCaffrey nodded.

"Down here certainly, you are in the best possible place during a time like this." Gabby forced herself to the point of digging her nails into her legs so as to not roll her eyes at such a statement. "Your tour group would've been escorted away under military guard. All I currently know is that they were underway safely." Mr Harris flicked a nervous smile at the soldier. "Well, that's the basics anyway. We are still trying to ascertain what is going on out there but I'm sure your wait won't be too long." The lieutenant smiled and Gabby saw the strain in the man's eyes. As he rose from the bench Mary raised her hand in the air. McCaffrey raised his eyebrows in response.

"What you've just told us about his place is quite amazing." Mary spoke softly forcing the army officer to sit back down to hear her. "And it made me wonder that if you could tell us all about what's down here then what are you not telling us because of the Official Secrets Act." Gabby turned a shocked expression on her friend, in awe of her reasoning. The lieutenant smiled but it was a sickly smile.

"Let's not worry about that okay? You're safe. Major Anderson has assigned me as your liaison. We'll speak again later." He said rising quickly. A tremor caused the officer to lose his balance and he fell unceremoniously back into his seat cursing. Brooke shrieked in terror as the sound of a whip cracking came from the ceiling. Dust and tiny pieces of stone sprinkled the table and the lights flickered. Gabby grabbed Mary and shoved her under the table screaming at her teacher and Brooke to do the same. More upheavals shook the cement floor and a horrific grinding noise surrounded Gabby and Mary. Gabby squeezed Mary closer to her side and looked up to see lieutenant McCaffrey kneeling at the edge of the table just beyond Gabby's reach. He was shouting into a walkie-talkie demanding a situation report. The answer was unintelligible to Gabby so she shuffled forwards slightly and grabbed McCaffrey's arm. He jerked and swivelled on his knees to face her. His expression relayed any information she wanted. In the flickering light he'd aged twenty years in a matter of minutes. His skin was almost white and his eyes round and bloodshot from dust. Seeing the frightened civilians cowering under the table brought his own level of fear down and he nodded to Gabby and placed her hand in his.

"*We're under attack.*" He mouthed as shockwaves from the onslaught above reached them far below the surface. Gabby couldn't comprehend the forces at play for them to be felt in the bunker. Another titanic crack blasted away all conscious thought and Gabby screwed up her eyes and screamed her mind repeating one simple phrase.

I don't wanna die! I don't wanna die!

She sobbed in terror as larger pieces of cement hit the table above her head. Gabby had instinctively looked up at the first hit opening her eyes so she saw the moment the lights flickered one final time before plunging the entire room into black.

Silent Running

The International Space Station, so long a symbol of unity for the planet Earth circled her home planet in low orbit at four hundred kilometres above the blue world lifeless, her mission abandoned and crew departed long ago.

After the first wave of major attacks by the dragons upon mankind seemed to draw to a conclusion, military forces around the globe found themselves not only reeling in shock at the perpetrators of the destruction but to some degree became aware that nothing in the experience of mankind and the wars waged had prepared for a battle of this kind. To that end the crew were asked to utilise equipment originally built to monitor glaciers, agriculture, cities, coral reefs and the impact of mankind itself on the Earth, in conjunction with satellites in an attempt to track the dragons. The goal, to find where the dragons were launching their devastating sorties from. The crew, over the coming weeks, were unique witnesses to the dragon's ferocity, observing countless massive smoke plumes rising high into the atmosphere, as any city of appreciable size was put to the flame. Hours of footage was recorded and analysed back on Earth by militaries of many countries in a vain attempt to coordinate a defence and response.

With the dragon's apparently randomised attacks on crucial facilities around the world the decision to abandon the world's first multicultural space station was made swiftly, the safety of the astronaut's paramount. Six months after the dragons had destroyed several key installations of the American, Russian and Chinese military the equipment on-board the I.S.S. was set to receive its new mission parameters from the ground, for as long as that was possible and the crew departed for their home planet.

Cameras and satellites passively monitored the annihilation of airbase after airbase due to the dragon's immense power and fury. Planes, hangars and even housing for personnel were fired and reduced to so much rubble that nothing was left recognisable. The fastest interceptors from the nearest airbases were deployed and would arrive to find the carnage already well underway. Dogfights became reminiscent of World War II battles but mankind's technological advantages over those of small fighter planes of over eighty years ago meant nothing against the nimble and highly manoeuvrable dragons. Missiles that were used to lock onto targets miles away were completely ineffective against an opponent that could vanish in an instant only to reappear when the planes moved closer to the fight.

Planes of all nations were effectively grounded. Useless as fighter planes and equally redundant as transport for personnel and cargo. Escort duties quickly became voluntary though the human loss was considered too high a price to pay and air superiority was lost. Those remaining countries with enough of an intact navy still functioning, moved their ships within striking distance of their own capital cities and seats of government. The strategy, to defend these areas with missiles launched from distance. A strategy not too different from the fighter planes defending the land below them but the military had realised their losses were high and the situation desperate. At first the ships were considerably more effective than their air force counterparts but only in close quarters. Guns blazed on every deck around the world as the dragons launched their attacks on the mainland and at sea. The dragons suffered their first major losses, inflicting a rash hope in their human enemies. Any hope was short lived, the dragons adapted rapidly to the evolving human tactics. Single ships were located and targeted for destruction. When the fight commenced a single battleship was faced with well over one hundred dragons raining down fire from above. Battleships and aircraft carriers were unable to respond to such an overwhelming show of power. Ships by the hundreds and their respective crews were annihilated. The surviving craft were sent as close to shore as possible by their superiors who'd seen what fate awaited them, to offer safe haven to any in contact. The captains in command of the submarines were given one explicit order, *survive*.

Government control, commerce and infrastructures fell on a worldwide scale. Police and remaining armies struggled to stabilise the situation. The nature of the dragon attacks poured cold fear into the minds of every populace, as there was no discernible pattern for people to follow. Cities, towns, villages, farms, every place around the world where humans had established a foothold, no matter the size, suffered the same fate as the mighty battleships that were no more. The dragons did not relent. Riots became commonplace as food, water and energy came under threat.

Governments did not so much fall as vanish. Any forward plans by government leaders to sit out the destruction in relative safety to ensure the continuity of order were laid waste as the means of communication by technology were destroyed and the outside world was hidden from them. As communication networks died martial law was introduced, primarily by those army commanders on the ground as they strove to protect what was becoming a desperate situation for all.

The annihilation of the human race continued bloody year after bloody year. It fell to those still alive to band together with any surviving military to create conclaves, safe havens under the dubious and unreliable protection of surface to air missiles and any weapons to hand or could be fashioned. Great walls were erected as swiftly as possible to contain these last vestiges of mankind. Not all were successful as the dragons launched attack after attack until all but ash remained. Castles and their surrounding buildings became the most successful of these havens, medieval technology and craftsmanship proving by far more effective than their modern day counterparts. Humanity clung on in dark places underground. Making use of labyrinths constructed hundreds of years before.

Homo Sapiens was successfully replaced as the dominant animal on the planet as the dragons multiplied and flourished growing stronger with each passing year. The last bastions of humanity held on but only at the favour of the dragons.

Still the International Space Station collected its data and downloaded the information. But there was no one left to study it let alone receive it. The pictures of an Earth spinning dark far below marked clearly the near absolute perfect destruction the dragons had wrought on humanity. Cities no longer gleamed as a mark of civilisation as the space station traversed beyond the terminator and into night. Mankind had fallen into darkness.

A New Order

This architecture of my kind... why keep it? Surely they do not deserve such reminders of these great buildings of their lost past.

AS WITH EVERYTHING THAT REMAINS INTACT IT SERVES A PURPOSE. A CONTINUATION OF SORTS, THE ILLUSION OF CONTROL, THAT DESPITE THE FACT THEY NOW SERVE NEW MASTERS, YESTERDAY WAS THE SAME AS TODAY AND TOMORROW PROMISES THE SAME. WITH A FAUX GOVERNMENT INCLUSIVE OF HUMANS WE HAVE THAT CONTROL.

Such a lot of effort to expend on them. Why bother?

BECAUSE WE NEED THEM, THAT'S A SIMPLE TRUTH. WE MUST SIMPLY DISREGARD OUR PERSONAL FEELINGS IN THE MATTER AND THINK OF OUR BROTHERS AND SISTERS AND THE FUTURE OF OUR RACE. WITH THE HUMANS THAT MAKES OUR TASK SIMPLER. THEY WILL TEND TO US, HARVEST AND SLAUGHTER FOR US AND EVENTUALLY THEY WILL ALL FALL ON THEIR KNEES TO US.

To you. Not me.

NO. US. YOU WILL SERVE AS THE HEAD OF OUR ORDER WITH ME. WE SHALL REPRESENT THE BEST OF BOTH KINDS WHILE STRIPPING EVERY HUMAN WE SEE FIT OF THEIR SOUL IN THE PROCESS OF OUR JOURNEY.

I shall require followers as you have kin. Brothers and sisters if not in blood then in purpose to join me.

A New Order

AN ARMY? A RELIGIOUS ORDER?

Perhaps. The selection must be severe. Infants would be most suitable and then only the best will be chosen for the honour I intend to bestow upon them.

YOU WISH TO CREATE RIDERS?

Yes. And also find a use for humans suitable for our purposes of change.

VERY WELL.

* * *

The raids upon human settlements began in earnest six months after humanities final surrender of the short lived 'Dragonwar.' Human regional governors were put in place and electricity was slowly restored and facilities reopened though at an extremely reduced capacity. Society resembled the Soviet Union before the collapse of the Berlin Wall. Food lines dominated every city and town. Inhabitants of villages unable to support themselves flooded the nearest towns creating overwhelming pressure on the meagre supplies available. With transport limited to the newly formed police serving under the regional Governors many took to the roads not only as a means of travel but as a source of accommodation. Coaches, buses and lorries were used by thousands seeking shelter. Food, water and supplies were moved around countries, where possible, by train. The dragons reasoned they could track and monitor this mode of transport more effectively. In countries where train services were poor or non-existent the people suffered, thousands were to perish long after 'peace' was established. Supplies were eventually moved by cart and horse or physical strength. Telephone exchanges were destroyed eradicating the digital age at the start of the 21st century. Schools, colleges and universities became housing and within the cities the great buildings and skyscrapers that once held vast economic power were the new ages tenement buildings.

Despite the awful conditions humanity now found itself in, as a race it never questioned why at the time hospitals were the main focus of their new masters. That the dragons ordered humans fit and as healthy as possible was a cause for some to extol the virtues of the planet's new dominant species, in sending humanity back to a simpler time without the use of technology and science.

What these people failed to appreciate was why the hospitals were valued so. Under the guise of treating people of any age and any disease the dragons were able to begin their harvest without much attention at first. But as time went on word was spreading from town to city and ever onwards. Shock and outrage from people was met with terminal intensity, the dragons would not suffer any hint of resistance and displayed this quality with no regard for the people who would speak out. In time it was accepted that the dragons would harvest or procure their lot once a year in return for hospital care for the sick, injured and dying that people experienced before the war. For many this new life became the norm but for one group. It would cause them to live in continual fear. Parents. Couples who lived in dread that their newborn child would be taken away from them by the dragons.

Blue

"Come on, Blue! If we're late they'll stick us on cleaning duties again!" The teenager referred to as Blue leaned his head back against the cold window pane and closed his eyes.

Twelve years. He thought raising his eyebrows at his time at the academy. *And now, oh I can't think about it!* The young man's stomach rolled and gurgled and he was forced to take a cleansing breath followed by a careful swallow. The nausea fled as swiftly as it had arrived and Blue leaned forward, grimacing at his delicate stomach.

"Hey? You okay?" The same voice chastising him for being late returned and Blue offered a wan smile to his roommate of the last six years, Copper. Blue reached out a hand which Copper grabbed and hauled his nervous friend from his chair next to the window. A cold, December wind whipped through the open window causing Copper to shiver. "Had enough fresh air?" He asked, a sly smile on his face. Blue huffed.

"You just wait three months and see how you like turning sixteen." Copper grinned inanely and slapped Blue hard on the shoulder making him wince.

"Two months and twenty-two days thank you." Copper was shorter than Blue's six foot by at least six inches, but what he lacked in height over his roommate he more than made up for in mass and build. He also wisely ignored other student's choice of wearing their hair long as his red hair had a tendency to frizz when Copper let it grow longer than five millimetres. Blue turned and studied his outfit for the day in the long mirror attached to the door. He brushed his long black hair from his eyes and studied the leather riding jacket he'd owned for the last three years. The seams were straining and the panels in the shoulders and back needed replacing as Blue was beginning to add bulk to his lean muscle. He fingered the frayed edges of the sleeve cuffs and sighed. Each student was responsible for the upkeep and upgrade of their riding jacket as they aged and grew but Blue detested this one duty even above cleaning out their mount's stables. The leather was soft and supple through years of Blue applying oil to the skin and the dark brown of the leather was almost black from the stain the oil left behind. His outfit was finished with a pair of dark blue trousers that resembled, much to many rider's dismay, jodhpurs, but with additional protection of padding on the inner thighs and calves. His feet were clad in black leather half boots bought a week ago for today's occasion and he still had a tendency to hobble where blisters were healing.

Copper laid a hand on Blue's shoulder and leaned into him, pushing him away from the mirror.

"Please." Copper said with a roll of his eyes. "If you're going to crack the mirror with that bloody ugly face of yours then at least let me in first." Blue cocked an eyebrow and ran a forefinger along his most defining feature, at least in his mind. From the edge of his left eye in a curved, almost calculated arc, ran a deep, white scar down Blue's face to his neck and then it became hidden in his jacket, but the scar continued to his collarbone. Copper tutted as he saw what his friend was doing.

"I told you, if you keep doing that something will fall off."

"Oh, ha bloody ha, Copper. Don't be a dick." Blue shoved Copper's shoulder as the shorter teenager laughed. Copper stumbled to the door and swung on the doorframe.

"Come on, Blue" Copper added more seriously. "Let's get you ascended." Blue straightened his jacket and with one more look in the mirror marched out of the room.

* * *

The Academy did not need any addition to its title or qualification to its purpose. The buildings that housed the instructors and students were not known in the formal sense as a centre of education and learning. In its previous life before the war it was used by the privileged few as a grand home while people roamed the streets homeless and children went hungry. A fact the teachers at the Academy used as an example of the immorality of the human race. The choice of such a grand building offered space for its occupants inside and mounts in the outbuildings. Acres and acres of woodlands and fields combined to gift the most important aspect, privacy. It was also an area that managed to escape any destruction during the war and that became, whether by accident or design, an integral part of a student's education.

As the two young men walked briskly down a wide, grand hallway, Blue wondered, for what seemed to him like the millionth time, who from mankind deserved a building such as this for a home. No original furnishings remained but Blue had always noted the finely constructed handrails on the many sets of stairs and though he was unaware of the proper names for the many carved or moulded items about the house he admired them for the craft involved in their production. When students were old enough, usually eight, or nine years old, a brief history of their home was given and consisted of tales of heroics by dragons and their riders in defending this house from the might of the human armies. It captivated them all of course. The story of a last stand resulting in victory against an overwhelming enemy made for satisfying listening and students afterwards became prouder of their heritage and their inclusion at such a privileged site. Blue as much as any was fascinated by the tale and badgered instructors constantly until they threatened him with the switch if he didn't quieten down and concentrate on the here and now. As Blue recalled the story he recited the short poem or saga written by an instructor a few years before Blue's time at the Academy. It was required reading and Blue sang out the words in his mind in time to his marching feet.

> *Death is a blade that's cold when it strikes*
> *Our lives will mean nothing! Unless we all fight.*
> *Our armies, our warriors, are gallant and true.*
> *Leaders of men, are corrupt and are few.*
> *But enough to cause chaos and war to descend,*
> *They send us their soldiers and we must defend.*
> *This castle, this rock. This bastion of hope.*
> *If not, we'll feel the tug of the hangman's rope.*

Blue's lips moved on the last two words and he swallowed against a tightness in his throat. He tried to imagine as he had so many times what it must've been like to have humanity's evil engines of war descending on this place he considered his home. The riders and their dragons would've been terrified naturally but as the song and history spoke of, they found so much strength within each other they were able to rise up and defeat the armies ranged against them. No documents existed detailing the events that led up to the war or what happened that fateful day but Blue had spent many a night as he drifted off to sleep placing himself in the battle that day. Imagining what he would have done and how he would've been victorious while leading his army of dragons.

"Come back, Blue." Copper nudged his friend's elbow as they approached the main entrance. Blue swallowed and found his throat sore and dry with anticipation. His fingers nervously fumbled with his jacket and he managed to assure himself one last time that all was in order. Satisfied he ran his fingers once again through his black hair. Copper smiled, not at Blue's nervousness but with genuine pride at his friend's day of ascendancy. Blue inhaled sharply and exhaled with force through his nose with a nod of determination.

"Let's go."

Blue and Copper reached the massive main doors to the Academy. Much to Copper's dismay they stood open allowing the cold chill to penetrate the grand reception area.

"Bollocks." He cursed earning a smirk from Blue. "You can laugh, my friend but just you wait until…" Whatever point Copper tried to make was cut short as a golden dragon's head and long neck peered around the edge of the open door. "Um, uh, oh no." Copper stammered, his shoulder's slumping.

"I suggest you take your place immediately, Copper, before I become concerned over your suitability to be here." The dragon's chastisement caused Copper to pale and tremble slightly.

"My apologies, Andromeda." Copper bobbed his head to the dragon. "I didn't realise the time. I was helping Blue with his formal attire. I wanted him to be at his best." The female dragon Copper had named as Andromeda growled deep within its throat silencing the young man immediately and Blue wondered at his friend's inability to keep his mouth shut. The dragon flicked a talon towards the open door and Copper wasted no time in exiting the building.

The dragon turned its gaze to Blue and he gave a short bow of respect. Andromeda, bonded to Tarvos, and a legendary figure amongst students and mature riders alike, studied Blue to the point of discomfort. He held his position and hoped his anxiety had not manifested itself in his expression.

"Choose your friends and comrades wisely, young Blue." The golden dragon commented. "Many a warrior or leader's downfall came at the machinations of those closest to them." Blue nodded automatically and swallowed nervously as he felt a thin sheen of sweat on his face. "Although despite his nature, Copper should be counted amongst those you call 'friend.'" The dragon sighed and moved backwards slowly, her eyes never leaving Blue.

"Come, Blue. Attend your ascendency and may fate grant you the world you deserve." Blue puffed his chest out slightly at the encouraging words and followed Andromeda out of the Academy and into the cold air of winter.

* * *

"Blue Cal-Tea." A solemn voice called out. "You come before us today as it marks your sixteenth year and the twelfth of your education here. Step forward." A faint murmur ran through the assembled children of ages ranging from four to twelve, each whispered their excitement at what they would witness this day. Amongst the older children near the rear of the gathering a single person rose from the grass to stand above his contemporaries.

Not friends. Never that. He thought. *Brothers and sisters.* Whatever their age, gender, personality he would gladly perish to save any of them. Blue once again straightened his leather riding jacket, making sure the toggles were correctly fastened. He weaved his way around the sitting children to the centre of the assembly where an aisle was left free allowing someone to walk to the front and his future. Blue's breath plumed into the cold, biting air. The ceremony of Ascendency was performed on the green fields to the front of the great house. Blue's exact birthdate was unknown so the day he had arrived at the Academy marked his rebirth as a student. As proud as Blue felt this day he secretly hoped for a large snowfall and having the ceremony take place in the Great Hall.

Calda never would have forgiven me.

Blue thought and as he strode forward he attempted to locate the dragon discreetly, flicking his eyes beyond the seated students to where the dragons waited patiently, surrounding them all. Blue felt a twinge of disappointment that Calda wasn't closer which disappeared rapidly as he experienced the soft touch of the dragon in his mind, warming and comforting Blue considerably.

Blue ignored the whispers around him from some of the younger students and looked up at the stage erected before the assembled students, instructors and dragons. Three people occupied the stage, two sitting and one standing and each terrifying in their own way as instructors and Blue winced as memories of finding himself at the wrong end of a switch from each of them popped into his head. The two instructors sat were responsible for the student's education in the matter of fighting, from a one to one fight up to battle tactics involving hundreds if not thousands of soldiers. They had no names or formal title other than "Sir" or "Ma'am" and it was a quick, harsh punishment to any child who forgot to use either mode of address. The two on the stage Blue looked at now had not always been his teachers, a few had been assigned to the children's training over the years and these two were relatively new to all, which meant they were a lot harder, tougher and quicker to anger than instructors used to the children. The man standing who had called Blue's name was not a newcomer. Sir Tarvos was and had been the main instructor since Blue could remember. Sir Tarvos was named after successfully bonding with a dragon. It was considered bad form for the older riders who survived the war to keep anything of their past including their names after joining with a dragon. Names were chosen as closely as possible to resemble some characteristic, physical or otherwise about the new rider. Tarvos was a deity, a bull God, and it was plain to see why this particular name was chosen. Sir Tarvos was gigantic, not only in a muscular sense but he also towered over every student and instructor to have ever attended these halls. He kept his blond hair long and tied back in a tail but kept the sides shaved to within a millimetre of his scalp. His eyebrows, a shade darker than his hair formed a vicious 'V' above his nose imparting a look of furious attention to whatever he was doing. It was the eyes that captured and stilled many a heart, but not in acknowledgment of their beauty, but in the darkness held within. With a shade of brown bordering on black, to be caught in that gaze was many a student's worst nightmare. Only once in Blue's memory had those eyes inspired anything but cold fear. In his earlier years, when the possibility of getting caught breaking the rules was a worthy risk, Blue and a few of his fellow students would dare one another to sneak about the foreboding, empty corridors, late at night, dodging instructors performing their nightly rounds. It was attempting such a dare that Blue was forced to duck into a corridor leading to Sir Tarvos's study to avoid running into an instructor and the beating that would surely follow. Edging along the cold, stone wall Blue saw a dim light shining from the open door of the study. Daring himself now, for what a tale it would be for his classmates, he moved closer, as slowly as his wired senses and body would allow. A soft voice drifted to him through the open door, a voice that he did not recognise. His curiosity now piqued, Blue marked himself a few feet from the doorframe and with one ponderously slow and large step he came to rest next to the open door.

"I know what I am doing is for their benefit. But that is difficult when holding a leather strap in one hand and a crying child in another."

The soft voice paused and Blue craned his head as far forward as he dared, straining his entire body in an effort to hear.

"No I won't. I will remember that always. I just wish it wasn't so."

Blue closed his eyes, hoping by shutting down one of his senses he could make another stronger.

Rarely are we given a choice, my friend and even if we both were given a different path to follow we wouldn't take it. Both you and I have seen too much and know what is at stake.

Blue's forehead furrowed as he heard the other side of the conversation for the first time. Strangely the voice was clear and he was puzzled as to why he couldn't hear it previously.

"No. No we wouldn't. Have you received any news about our friend's whereabouts?"

No. Nothing.

The 'voice' offered sharply and Tarvos sighed in response.

"I see. We can but hope. I'm sorry for contacting you like this...thank you...goodnight."

Anytime. Goodnight, my friend. Sleep well.

The creak of a leather chair echoed into the hallway and Blue could picture the chair being used. A great, hulking leather beast of furniture, it was Sir Tarvos's favourite to use as a match to his physical presence when dressing down a student. It was also just beyond the line of sight of the door. Sweating and risking possibly a great deal more than a leather strap or switch to his backside just to satisfy his curiosity, Blue gripped the edge of the doorframe and leaned into the room and found himself looking straight at Sir Tarvos. His hand clenched the wooden frame of the door so hard he feared the wood itself would crack and Blue thought he might lose control over his bladder. His heart seemed to falter causing a fresh sheen of sweat to erupt on his face. But Sir Tarvos didn't move, he was sat in his leather chair with his great arms resting on his legs, leaning forward. Blue could see him as the instructor had moved the chair to where a student would normally be standing. Sir Tarvos's gaze was somewhere far from his study and far from the walls that made this place. In that look Blue could see emotions he'd never equated with this man, worry, trepidation. As

Sir Tarvos remained in place, staring into nothingness Blue heard the wooden thud of a door closing nearby and realised his luck must be at breaking point. He ducked back out of the doorway and into the dark corridors, making an uneventful trip back to his dorm room. Once there he celebrated the fact he didn't run afoul of the instructors with his bunk mates and settled down for the remainder of the night. He didn't know why but he had no intention of telling anyone what he'd seen and it was only when sleep was close that he remembered he didn't see anyone else in Sir Tarvos's study for the instructor to hold a conversation with. Puzzled, Blue had assumed he'd fallen asleep as he remembered a voice, though slightly different in tone, once more that night.

Goodnight, Blue.

It was now, a few years later that the memory returned to Blue while walking down the aisle towards the man he'd seen that night looking quite lost. Regardless of whatever expression he wore back then, Sir Tarvos was every inch the dominating presence he usually projected, his face as expressive as granite and his eyes as hard as that particular stone. In front of the stage was a lectern, placed so students could stand before their peers. When a student was ordered to take this position it marked that student's most important day in the Academy, so far at least. Blue finished his walk and stepped onto the small step leading to the lectern. As was customary the student would remove their riding jacket and place it on the grass behind them. No matter what happened next this would be the final time they would wear the riding jacket of a student. Blue did as hundreds before him had and turned to face what those approaching their sixteenth birthday called 'Doomsday.'

"Blue Cal-Tea." Sir Tarvos invoked Blue's formal name, referencing Blue's sponsors through the academy, the rider Galatea and her dragon, Calda. "Today is the day of ascension. Today you may ascend into the light or descend into the darkness." Blue nodded and swallowed nervously at Sir Tarvos's words and he hoped his anxiety did not show. "For twelve years you have acquitted yourself with honour towards the goal every student here aspires to." Blue experienced a shiver ripple the length of his spine and the large breath he took that filled out his chest was one of intense pride that his studies and achievements hadn't been in vain. "But though some can enter this establishment with their hearts pure and intentions good it does not qualify them for the privilege they seek." Sir Tarvos paused a moment and any whispered conversations occurring among the students stopped immediately to be replaced with an awful silence. Blue frowned and flicked his eyes over each instructor on the stage. "Despite your intentions and fortitude we find you, Blue Cal-Tea lacking and we must offer you into darkness." Blue's mouth moved, repeating Tarvos's final word but no sound came forth. His face was heavy as if disbelief had robbed him of any expression. His confusion was absolute. Though anxiety and nervousness could dream up any black future in the dead of night, Blue was sure, no, certain that today he would ascend! His instructors had not spoken to him on any fault he needed to correct, his classmates, envious that he would be first to ascend, had the decency to compliment him and assure him that his sixteenth birthday would be one of celebration.

"Lady Galatea. Please escort your charge Blue Cal-Tea away. His name will be struck from our history and the name Blue will never be assigned again at this hallowed place. This matter is closed."

But I'm one of the best riders.

Blue screamed in his mind. *Calda told me so himself and he wouldn't have lied!*

Blue took an involuntary step backwards and his arms were grabbed none too softly. He was turned and led back down the aisle. Faces of those sitting about him didn't register and he searched for Copper to no avail. Every face was as clear as the sky. Every face was a blur. Blue made no protest, could make no protest, as the person called to handle him, guided his path all the way back to the Academy where two large wooden doors marking the main entrance were standing open to receive him.

* * *

Lady Galatea was infamous within the stone corridors of the halls. As a person she was fiercely loyal to Sir Tarvos and equally dedicated to the students under her tutelage and sponsorship on condition she was shown complete dedication by her class and absolute respect for the mounts the students trained upon. At just under six feet in height she did not often find herself craning her neck up to speak to someone. As befitting such a prestigious rider her clothing was black leather, each piece handmade and crafted just for her use. For practical purposes in the air, Galatea wore her hair short which emphasised the pixie quality of her face. Many a student, both male and female, had developed a crush on the instructor. She was demanding, fierce, passionate and above all else a rider of high calibre. Every student, regardless of age, had watched

Galatea and her grey dragon, Calda, take to the skies to demonstrate the spectacular flying manoeuvres achievable between a bonded human and dragon. But it was not only the prowess of the pair shown in the air that accounted for their fame. What all trainee riders saw was the adoration and respect that so clearly existed between the two. Rather than an emotion such as love to be the topic of many a joke amongst children and teenagers they witnessed a pure form of affection, the likes they themselves had never experienced. In addition, the fact that the affection was bestowed by such an incredible creature as a dragon was something they all dreamed of.

Blue was one of the select few entrusted to ride upon Calda's back. That honour alone accounted for many at the Academy thinking Blue would ascend with ease, along with Blue himself. The young man was still shocked at the decision levelled at him and he replayed the event over and over thinking Sir Tarvos must be mistaken and that any moment the doors to the large gardens would swing open and apologies would be bestowed upon him. The doors remained resolutely shut, and Blue irrationally hated them for not opening. The two continued moving along a dark corridor lit only by oil lanterns every thirty feet towards the rear of the large building to a set of winding stone stairs. Galatea gently positioned Blue ahead and nudged him to proceed her. As he took the first step downwards, the jolt of hitting the cold stone seemed to jolt the grey dragon's words loose into Blue's addled mind.

"You were born to this, my friend. To ride dragon back with ease is a formidable task. Galatea's sponsorship of you may one day change the Academy itself." Calda had spoken to Blue as they'd soared into the pristine sky above the low murky cloud level chilling the land below. Blue had shivered uncontrollably, not with cold but with the intense pleasure of approval.

"My thanks, Calda. Ascension is close and despite my frayed nerves I think I'll do well."

"You should." The dragon had agreed, turning his head to fix an eye on Blue. *"But remember that nothing is certain and ascension itself is to not only open oneself to another but the reality of the world we live in."* Blue had nodded perfunctorily, not really paying attention to the final piece of advice, but it seemed that nothing was going to stop his success on his sixteenth birthday.

Blue screwed up his face in confusion once again and shook his head. Calda's words from that day faded and he experienced the walk to the lectern once again, taking in Sir Tarvos's eyes and their grim appearance. Blue stopped his descent causing Galatea to curse and place her hands on his shoulders to steady herself.

Those eyes.

Blue thought. *Maybe Sir Tarvos did see me that night in his doorway. I saw a weakness, a different man that night. Perhaps he'd planned this all along!*

Blue brushed the hands from his shoulders and turned to face Galatea.

"This is wrong, Lady Galatea! You know it! Calda knows it! I shouldn't be here; you know that Ma'am. He wants me gone. I…I don't know why." Just as had happened that night, Blue found he could not share what he'd seen in Sir Tarvos's eyes and what he'd heard. Galatea sighed impatiently.

"Remember your station, Blue Cal-Tea." The lady rider chastised the young man. "I feel for you, Blue. But the decision has been made. I'm not privy to everything that goes on here but Sir Tarvos must have his reasons."

Blue's lips moved soundlessly and for the first time he felt the enormity of the last ten minutes as if a gigantic weight were suddenly pressing him down into the ground. His knees trembled and Galatea's strong hands caught Blue under the shoulders to stop him from falling.

"But what now?" Blue whispered and he looked up into Galatea's eyes. There he saw his instructor was not lying. He saw regret, but something else that scared him more than creeping about the halls late at night, Blue saw pity. His own eyes widened in response as the rumours and especially the horror stories that were told late at night to all new students, in a cruel initiation, of what would happen to them if they failed to ascend. Blue had not thought of them for years and now the memories cruelly returned. He recalled sitting in his bunk at five years old and listening to an older student retelling the story that would induce nightmares in many of them.

"You don't think a dragon-rider, even a failed one, is allowed out of here, like that?" The older student snaps his fingers and it's the sound of bones breaking. "First they take your memory. The Lord of all dragons strips it away and it's like acid upon paper!" The boy hisses and waggles his fingers in the air. "Once the fire in your mind is raging the instructors burn you with a brand on your chest, so everyone knows of your failure. You'll be an outcast amongst humans and riders. Reviled by both and chased away from anywhere you dare lay your head!"

"Kill me." Blue pleaded, tears of anguish and loss falling unashamedly down his cheeks.

"I have no choice, Blue. Remember that above all else I beg you." As Blue was already in such a confused state it took a few seconds for him to realise that an instructor such as Lady Galatea would never speak such words. He quickly blotted the tears from his eyes, but before he could question her further, Blue saw Galatea's eyes look briefly over his shoulder. He began to turn on instinct but the sharp, icy jab on his neck merely led him into the dark.

Discoveries

"As far as we can ascertain we actually have two problems. The breach or rift is one and we know where that is and can actually see it. The second problem is a bit trickier." Murmurs began in the small audience and Blue drifted lazily above their heads to get a better view of the speaker.

"It was called the Great Attractor. The best we can say in position is that it sits on the other side of the Milky Way, millions of light years away. The glare of stars and the centre of our own galaxy prevents us from observing it directly." Blue could see the speaker and he snorted a laugh. It was Copper! Blue drifted to the ground and sat down on a bench, he nodded respectfully to the two dragons sitting either side of him. He didn't recognise them and he didn't really wonder at how they could fit inside this room.

"What we can see is a slew of galaxies being drawn in, pulled towards this expanse." Copper explained hitting a stick against a blackboard. Blue squinted at the blackboard as at first he saw nothing at all, but the longer he stared the deeper the blackboard seemed.

"That's right, Blue. Keep looking." Copper told him, as a forked tongue wriggled from his lips. Blue concentrated further and in the next moment felt himself surrounded by the black and accelerating out of control into the void before him. Blue screamed but there was no sound.

"Calm down." A voice advised. "I will see you soon." The voice didn't return but Blue was left with a feeling of confidence. He smiled and continued his race down the dark tunnel.

* * *

Blue rose from the murky depths of sleep in pleasant fashion. He was warm, comfortable and more than anything could not wait until he chose his dragon after ascendency. That blurry daydream brought him fully awake in an instant. He pushed up from the bed and hit his head on a wooden beam.

"Bollocks." He hissed through clenched teeth rubbing the back of his head rapidly. Shaking his head in annoyance Blue rolled carefully over and came face to face with a chicken. It stared down at him with the disdain that the majority of fowl carried on their faces when confronted with humans. Blue rolled his eyes left to right as he tried to remember the night before. "How much did I drink last night? And where the hell am I?" He asked the chicken but it simply pecked at something more interesting on the rafter than Blue before trotting off. As Blue frowned and followed the chicken's progress along the beam he was able to study where he had ended up. Blue lay on a shallow cot, just big enough for his shoulders to squeeze on. His legs and waist were covered in a grey wool blanket. To his left was a wooden wall and judging by the darkness above, Blue assumed he was near the roof. A look to his right confirmed this and Blue saw he was on a narrow platform, twenty or thirty feet above the floor. Hay bales were stacked as neatly as hay bales could be stacked and at the far end of the building Blue could see the foot of two large doors.

"What on earth am I doing in a barn?" Blue could still not retrieve any memory of the night before and assumed all this was Copper's idea of a practical joke.

Blue rolled back onto his front and inched his way off the cot, the gap between the cot and a nasty fall was less than two feet and Blue did not want to ruin joining with a dragon by breaking any bones, though he was quite adamant that Copper might not be quite as lucky when Blue got his hands on him. Blue caught sight of the top of a ladder close by and he breathed a sigh of relief. He crawled over and gingerly eased his legs onto the rungs. The wooden ladder creaked and groaned at Blue's weight and he screwed his face up in anticipation of a crash landing amidst sharp stakes of wood. The ladder held firm enough so Blue descended as quickly as he dared. On the ground Blue checked himself out. His fine riding clothes were gone and replaced with a simple pair of black jeans and t-shirt, white trainers and a light grey raincoat. Blue scoffed in disgust, never thinking that Copper would stoop so low as to hide his clothes as they were the most valuable items Blue possessed. Appraisals of attire complete Blue studied the barn but gleaned nothing more than it was daytime and sunny from the streaks of light coming through the wooden planks making up the wall.

The chicken by now had somehow made its way to ground level and was standing near a smaller, man sized door in the larger barn door clucking to be let out. Blue cocked his head and then rolled his eyes.

"Fine. That's just fine, now I'm playing bloody servant to a bloody chicken." Blue sighed and walked the short distance to the door and opened it. Golden sunshine streamed into the barn causing Blue to squint, and he was temporarily blinded as he stepped through the door. The chicken clucked once more at Blue before racing off to whatever it needed to do next.

"You're welcome." Blue whispered in a sour tone.

As Blue's eyes adjusted to the glare the shape of a large house across a field of corn became visible and he could hear the deep grumble of an engine being started in that direction. Blue figured he would have to extricate himself from this embarrassing position devised by Copper and return to the Academy under his own steam. With that in mind Blue started walking towards the chugging engine.

* * *

Blue paused as he neared the large farmhouse. The entire front of the house was catching the hot sun's rays making the off white wood shine almost painfully and turning the windows into square holes of pure white fire. He took a deep breath and closed his eyes and despite the predicament he now found himself in Blue was quite relaxed. The aromas of the farm mixed with the sound of the gentle breeze over the cornfields almost made him wish for more time in this place. Something troubled him though, all he had learned of the majority of the human race led him to believe that places like this didn't exist. That as lower creatures than that of dragons and riders they were forced to eke out a small existence for themselves, scavenging and relying on their betters for sustenance.

"Hey! You!"

Blue opened his eyes and turned to the source of the voice and saw a young girl, perhaps nine or ten, with long brown curly hair, wearing a simple summer dress, staring at him while swinging back and forth on a rope swing hanging from a massive tree.

"You're new here aren't you?" She asked scuffing her feet on the ground, bringing the swing to a stop. "That's okay." She added before Blue could answer. "My daddy can always use a helping hand around here." The girl approached Blue completely unafraid and took his hand in her own. He looked into the girl's dark eyes and thought how pretty they were and how they matched her dark, wavy brown hair perfectly. "Thank you." She seemed to reply to his unspoken thought and led him towards the farmhouse. Blue shrugged half-heartedly. Obviously the girl was offering her thanks in advance for aiding her father in whatever he needed.

They both stepped onto a wooden veranda that encircled the house. Blue felt slightly uneasy at finding himself on someone else's property without the permission of an adult but hoped they would understand and be able to point him in the right direction to walk at least.

"I think daddy's inside." The girl pulled on Blue's hand and he followed.

"What's your name?" Blue asked as the girl pulled back the screen door and entered the house. She pulled Blue over the threshold and smiled, almost condescendingly Blue thought, and continued to lead him through the house to a large kitchen at the rear. A long and broad wooden table occupied the centre of the room with a bench either side that could easily seat a dozen people if not more if the occasion demanded it. The light of the clear day was more subdued and Blue immediately felt the drop in temperature. He looked about the kitchen noting the large cooking range and the wealth of copper pots and pans hanging above the table itself. A pot was bubbling away on the range, the lid jostling and clanking slightly from the escaping heat. Blue drew a deep breath and began coughing, quickly followed by violent retching. Blue fell to his knees, the odour was overpowering and with every retch he felt sure he would never stop to draw another breath. Through watery eyes he saw the girl approach and rub his back. Tears streamed down Blue's face and as a retch ended and he half sobbed the kitchen appeared to darken, the wood of the cabinets and table changed colour to a dark grey with touches of green and black covering their surfaces. Another retch took him and he doubled over. In the instant before he closed his eyes, he saw black mould beneath him, on every inch of the kitchen floor. Blue's head shook with the pressure from within and once again he swore he would never take a breath again but as he did his stomach relaxed enough for him to gasp.

"It's okay. You're fine. Too much beer I'm guessing, I've seen my grandaddy with a hangover, it was so scary. I'll never drink." The girl's words were so sincere that Blue let out a half sob, half laugh. He wiped his eyes on the sleeve of his new raincoat and looked around. The farmhouse kitchen was as he'd originally seen it, with no trace of decay. He sniffed tentatively but could only smell whatever was cooking on the range, and whatever it was it didn't smell like how he imagined death smelt. The girl grabbed Blue's upper arm and he pushed himself upright.

"Come on, take a seat, Blue." Blue nodded and sunk gratefully onto a bench, turning so he could rest his head in his hands.

"Sorry about that." Blue mumbled, totally at a loss to explain what had just happened to him, though he renewed his vow to kick Copper very hard in a sensitive area when he saw him. The girl laughed and Blue smiled at the girl's amusement regardless of how he felt. Blue heard the clink of glass, the squeaking of a tap and rushing water.

"Here you go, Blue." She placed the glass of water under his supported head. "Try that." Blue nodded his thanks gingerly and took a sip of water. The taste of water caused Blue to start to his feet, spitting the water from his mouth as he threw the glass away spilling it on the table. He cringed and felt his gorge rise yet again but Blue held his breath and released it slowly, concentrating, calming himself. The taste lingered and to him he imagined it was probably akin to drinking straight from an animal's water bowl left out for weeks. He looked down at the table and saw the remaining water in the glass was a pale brown with black flecks circling the glass.

"What the hell is going on?" Blue didn't think even Copper would go so far as to drug him and cause hallucinations.

"Don't you like my house?" The girl asked, her voice betraying her upset at Blue's behaviour. Blue sat down heavily on the bench.

"I don't know what's the matter with me." He explained placing his hands on the table to reassure him for the moment it was real.

"Don't you like my house?" The girl asked again but with a more insistent tone. Blue gave the girl a lopsided smile, though that was the last thing he felt like doing. He turned his newly bloodshot eyes to the window and stared into the cloudless sky.

"It's beautiful." He whispered and then he frowned. "But I didn't think that places like this existed, at least not for humans." The girl stayed silent provoking

Blue into speaking. "We... we were told that humans either served their masters and lived comfortably as servants and the like or denied them and lived in squalor." Blue swept his hand around the kitchen, indicating the farm in general. "I can't fathom this place." The girl pursed her lips thoughtfully and nodded.

"You're right, Blue. That is the way of things, even here." Any discomfort Blue still carried fled with these words.

"So you do serve the same masters as I? Can you help me return to the Academy? I'm due for my joining." Blue rose, expecting the girl to acknowledge his request. Instead she took his hand once again and led him to the back door.

"My father is late." She laughed sadly. "He was always late. My mother would say he did it purposefully but the truth was he was a dreamer, his head always in other places." Blue frowned at the change in tense the girl was using. She shrugged and pushed her way through the back door of the kitchen to a porch and the golden fields beyond. Once again Blue was struck by the astounding beauty of the farm he had woken in.

"Do you like it?" The girl whispered and Blue saw the tears swelling in the girl's eyes.

"Yes of course!" He answered immediately, not wishing to upset this strange but welcoming young girl. Blue studied the fields quickly to try to add to his rather bland comment. "May I ask why you have three separate fields instead of one?" Blue had noticed this feature in the cornfields at the front of the farmhouse. It wasn't the best question he had to admit but his head and throat were still sore from being ill. The girl didn't answer and instead led Blue off the porch to stand in front of the middle field. A small wooden cross was staked into the ground and Blue saw two more crosses placed in front of the cornfields to his left and right.

"Do you wish to be a dragonrider, Blue?" The girl asked releasing his hand and kneeling in front of the wooden cross. Before Blue answered a dark billowing cloud moved in front of the sun, casting the house and fields in a sombre grey. Blue shivered at another rapid drop in temperature.

"Of course. I've trained for it my entire life."

"Would you kill to be a dragonrider, Blue? Would you die for the chance to be one, Blue?" Blue shivered again and rubbed his arms. The conversation was taking quite a grim turn and Blue was uncomfortable answering such questions to one so young, so he changed tack.

"Do you know when your father will be back? Maybe he can help me get back to the Academy?"

The girl, still turned away from Blue shook her head.

"He's not coming back. He's over there." She pointed to the field on their right-hand side. "My mother is over there," she raised her hand indicating the field to their left, "and I was meant to be here." The girl's head sunk down until her chin was resting on her chest. A breeze rippled across the fields, sending the corn swaying and Blue was overcome by the thought that what he saw wasn't real. He stepped back and his shoe cracked against something on the ground. Looking down Blue saw a small white bone, no longer than his forefinger, curved and snapped in two. He grimaced and stepped sideways eliciting yet another loud crack. The bone this time was more substantial in thickness and length. Blue looked up with a disgusted expression straight into the girl's watery eyes. He couldn't say why but an important fact suddenly came to him and sent a wave of fear down his spine.

"I didn't tell you my name? How do you know my name?"

"I will tell you." The girl answered as a few tears escaped and ran down her cheeks. "But in return I wish to show you something?"

Blue hesitated slightly and the girl stepped forward to reassure him.

"No harm will come to you, I swear."

Blue sighed, in part as he believed this was just some incredibly complicated ruse Copper had a hand in or the celebrations of his ascendency ran out of control and he was paying the price in this nightmare of his mind.

"Okay. Show me."

The girl sobbed and reached for Blue's hand.

* * *

There are hundreds of us here. All huddled together in small terrified groups. The only sounds that have any meaning are the cries of infants, children, men and women but they are the sounds that are ignored. To our captors they are nothing more than a wound left by a mosquito. But like that mosquito it may be infected, so they will eradicate the source, disinfect their world, eliminate any threat.

I don't remember the journey here, I'm too young, too scared to pay attention to such detail. All I know is that my parents are petrified and that is something that scares me more than anything I've encountered or witnessed before... until this day.

They move among us, they separate and segregate. Men here, women here, children over there. Some are chosen and are taken away, kicking and protesting, but all to no avail. Those who try to fight back are beaten to unconsciousness or worse.

I'm not with my parents anymore. They told me to be brave before we were sent from each other. I cannot stop crying; I want them so much. The gentleness of my mother's hand on my cheek, the strength of my father's arm about my shoulder, it has been taken from me and now I am weak, I cannot stand alone... but here I stand.

My group has smaller children than I, they cry terribly and look lost. I remember my mother's hand and father's arm and comfort these little ones. Their crying abates a while and my heart beats stronger.

Night approaches and we are cold and hungry. We are promised food and drink soon. As the night wears on and I watch my breath plume in front of me I huddle in closer to my small group to steal some much needed warmth. Sleep does not come so I look about and try to see my parents, but fail. My fingers and toes have become numb and I cry in pain at the emptiness in my stomach.

The new day brings a red band across the horizon and we are ordered to our feet. Some of the older men and women do not rise, the cold has claimed them. They are the lucky ones. Digging equipment and tools are given to every person and we are ordered to dig a pit. One for each group. I don't know why but some of the adults do and run away. They do not get far.

We dig and shift soil. The work makes me warm but my energy is fading quickly from lack of food. Each pit is dug in short order as there are so many of us. When we are finished we are permitted to rest a while.

The day's work has taken a toll once more and these bodies are casually tossed into the pit. No words of comfort are said over them, no remembrances, no prayers are offered but those in our minds.

As evening comes and we weaken the order to stand is given and we are led to the pits. I know now what they are and I do not care. I only care that the final indignity or cruelty of being separated from our loved ones at this moment takes precedence for these monsters.

Heavy thumps ring out. I jump with each and begin to shake. The smaller ones' start wailing and I try to comfort them as I would like to be comforted but my words have no meaning. Screaming heralds the arrival of night and does not cease.

Pitiful cries to a failed God are repeated over and over until they are silenced. They now come among my group and I close my eyes. I hear the wicked sound again and again. I clutch the small bodies to me when they go limp. The terror I feel seems to petrify my body and mind and I wait for a final instance of pain and then nothing.

A heavy crack of bone is accompanied by white light and a high pitched whine. Then nothing...

My mouth is half full of something grainy and I spit it feebly away. My head aches with the rhythm of my pounding heart and I groan in pity for myself. I open my eyes and immediately blink and rub away the dry mud covering my face. I feel a soft breeze caress my hair and I open my eyes once again to stare at a blue sky. There is no sound. No birds sing in the trees and no insects chirp in the grass. I sit and see my body half covered in dirt. The landscape around me is sculpted by three rises and has the look of fresh turned soil. I ease the rest of my body slowly upwards and cry out as a limp hand falls from my foot... and I remember. The heavy thump on my head and the white light of pain. I explore the back of my head and feel the matted blood.

I don't know how I've survived or how I've dug myself out of my own grave. Tears spill down my face washing away the grime. Apart from me there is no evidence of the horrors that have occurred here and I weep for each person buried below me.

As my tears dry and I think of my parents and the little ones I tried to comfort. I push my hands into the soil and force myself upwards on shaking legs. I'm weak, but only physically. I'm weak, and I don't know if I will get stronger.

Maybe I cannot stand alone... but here I stand.

* * *

Blue fell to his knees in front of the wooden cross the girl had guided him to. He tried to scream as tears fell to the soil beneath him. The grief overwhelmed him and Blue wanted nothing more than to wail, to cry and sob relentlessly for the lives taken so coldly that night. But he couldn't. The scream he wished to release was silent as if he unconsciously knew that no display of grief could ever be enough for what had happened. Instead he pounded the ground with his fists until exhausted and rested his head on his arms.

A hand squeezed his shoulder and he heard a sigh.

"I'm sorry to do that to you, Blue. But everything you felt was true." The girl's voice had changed albeit subtlety but Blue could not bring himself to look at her yet.

"Why did you show me? What did I do to deserve that?" Blue whispered, his voice wavering still.

"Nothing." The girl replied bluntly. "Just like everyone here that night. They did nothing to deserve or justify what happened to them." Blue heard the girl sit down next to him and felt her breath on his ear. "It was important for you to see what your past, what your education was built upon. You were chosen from birth, Blue to be a rider. Your talent was apparent even then. Now think of all those others at birth who weren't suitable." The girl paused and placed a hand on Blue's back. "do you think they were simply adopted out to human families? What do you think happened to them?" Blue tried to reconcile what he was hearing with his life at the Academy. In all his years he had never heard a story such as this. His education had taught him that mankind was the aggressor and tried to eliminate the dragons from the world and it fell to a few humans to become riders and save both species. Blue shook his head violently and thrust himself upright, his lips quivering in anger to repute what he was being shown, he would not be a pawn in some ridiculous ploy. But the words died on his lips. The golden fields of corn were gone and the clear blue sky replaced by a dirty brown haze rising from the horizon to far above. All that remained were three wooden crosses, placed as they were when Blue had first seen them. Behind the crosses were three stretches of land measuring at least ten metres on each side. The three areas of land were dead, nothing grew at all anywhere and Blue could not help but stare at the mass of bones that lay close by.

"The farm was an illusion but it existed here at some point. I wanted to show you how much had been lost even in this small part of the world."

Blue turned to look at the girl and was not really surprised to find a young woman standing next to him.

"What you showed me happened years ago?"

The young woman nodded.

"But how? Who are you? Where am I?" As the questions poured from Blue his memory returned in such a fashion he stopped speaking and his eyes widened. The young woman gave Blue a sympathetic smile. Blue sat back down heavily and he groaned. "I failed my ascendency. I was to be cast out."

The young woman chuckled, not with malice though Blue still levelled an angry gaze at her.

"No, Blue. I told you. You were to be a rider. It was decided your skills were needed elsewhere and now you're here." Blue once again tried to speak and untangle the situation he'd found himself in, but he felt utterly lost and decided on a simpler question.

"Who are you?"

The young woman fixed her green eyes on Blue.

"I'm Cerys. Pleased to meet you, Blue."

Decisions

A single oil lamp lent its soft yellow glow to the kitchen of the abandoned farmhouse Cerys brought Blue to. He acknowledged in passing that the waves of illness that had affected him so, happened in this ruined room he thought a hallucination at the time. He sniffed cautiously but didn't detect any of the odour that had made him sick.

"That was part of the illusion." Cerys explained noticing his reaction while retrieving a small rucksack from an empty cupboard. "You were experiencing the horror of this place as a physical sensation. It made you ill." Blue grunted noncommittally and seated himself at the table. Cerys gave Blue a long stare before emptying her bag in front of him. "Here. Food and water. Not much I'm afraid but you'll get used to it." Blue cast a cynical eye on the fare placed before him. He gave a paper wrapped square a poke and waited to see if it would poke back. When nothing happened he unwrapped the small package revealing a sandwich of dark bread and something that smelt questionable. "The bread is made for travelling long distances so it has to last. The meat..." Cerys had the grace to look away, whether from amusement or embarrassment, Blue was unsure. "Well, it's edible at least." Cerys pointed at him without turning. "Eat!" Blue picked up the sandwich, noting the singular hefty weight of the bread, and took a small bite. It wasn't good in any way and although his muscles still ached from earlier his stomach cried out for sustenance and he made quick work of the meagre bounty. Cerys sat across from Blue nodding in satisfaction. As he swallowed his last mouthful she pushed a plastic bottle towards him. "Just water." Blue didn't hesitate this time and chased the hard meal down with the slightly warm water. "Good." Cerys commented. "We have a journey to

Decisions

make and you'll need to keep your strength up." Blue paused with the bottle halfway to his mouth.

"What? I...I want to go home. I want to go back." Blue protested, hating the weak tone of his voice. Cerys didn't reply but simply stared into Blue's eyes. He couldn't hold her gaze and looked down at the table.

"I understand, Blue." She said after an uncomfortable minute. "You've experienced something terrible about the world as it is now and for you to know it was perpetrated by the ones you aspire to be; I cannot imagine how difficult that must be for you." Blue continued to stare at the table. The lamp gave just enough light for him to see that someone, probably many years ago, had scratched their initials into the wood. He tilted his head as he followed the curved lines.

You're ignoring her on purpose you coward.

Blue flushed as he said those words to himself. He looked up and saw Cerys smiling at him.

"You're not a coward, Blue. Overloaded, overwrought and tired I expect." Cerys now let out a small laugh at Blue's expression. "Yes sometimes I can see inside people's minds. It's a gift at its best and a curse at its worst."

Blue shook his head, groaned and put his head in his hands.

"I was meant to be choosing my dragon today." Blue mumbled into his hands. "I still want to do that in spite of what you've shown me." He admitted.

"Hardly surprising, Blue. You've spent your life working towards it. A lot has happened to you today. It will take you time to process it all."

Blue opened his fingers and looked at Cerys through the gaps.

"So are you part of the resistance? The Grey Rose we were told about?" He asked, wondering how this young, slight woman could be any such threat to those in charge. Cerys lifted her hand and tilted it from side to side.

"Sometimes, when I'm needed like now. But I can promise you one thing, Blue. If you will travel with me you will learn a hell of a lot and," Cerys leaned forward and took Blue's hands from his face. "You may yet join with a dragon."

* * *

How did it go?

A lot better than expected. He'd forgotten about failing 'ascendency' so was quite open to me.

Will you have any problems?

I think it will take him some time to get used to the idea that those he served were and are trying to wipe us out.

If you have any doubts, Cerys then you must…

I know what I must do. Please don't lecture me on that point. I decided to return on your word about this one. Remember I was done converting potential riders from the Academy.

Sorry. We're still wary after the last incident.

I know. I'm sorry too. But his mind is different, more like mine.

Then you can confirm he's gifted and his connection with Calda and hearing your conversation with Tarvos wasn't some kind of fluke?

Yes, but I doubt he knows it. I think it would explain why he felt my memories so intensely, so personally.

Okay. Well, we shall see you soon, Cerys.

Soon? It's a bloody long way on foot and we don't all have a dragon.

* * *

Blue rolled and shuffled in agitation on the hard floor with a groan, wishing he had returned to the barn to sleep on the cot. Then he scoffed at such a thought and wished for his own bed at the Academy. That thought brought him fully awake and Blue's mood darkened. He turned his head slightly and saw Cerys asleep under the kitchen table. She had no mattress, pillow or even blanket and was sleeping soundly it seemed, much to Blue's dismay. He sighed and pushed himself up, then with light steps made his way outside. Blue walked a short distance bringing him to the three mass graves. Blue had always prided himself on his memory, it was a gift that helped him to be a good rider and jump between two places blind. Now it was nothing more than an accursed trait. He could still hear the shovels biting into the earth as hundreds of people worked on their own graves. He could smell the fear, as daft a concept as that was to him. Most of all he could see and hear the cries of the children as seen through Cerys's eyes.

"No!" Blue whispered through clenched teeth. "It can't be true. She's lying!" Blue had never felt at odds with himself in his entire life. Anger rose swiftly coupled with the belief he was being used. Without a look back he marched off away from the farmhouse, away from the graves and Cerys. He needed answers.

* * *

Cerys watched from a broken kitchen window as Blue stormed away into the night. She felt nothing but pity for him. She'd experienced a great deal of grief and loss herself and had no wish to cause it in others, especially those like Blue who were programmed almost from birth to be good little soldiers. Amazingly she sensed Blue's mind was quite open to seeing another truth about their life and their world. Cerys sighed and sat down with her back against the wall. She closed her eyes and tried to doze off. Blue was easy enough for her to follow and he needed to see the state of things for himself.

* * *

Blue ran his tongue around his teeth nervously, grimacing at the night's fuzz covering them. He'd walked through the night until just before dawn when a small settlement came into view as Blue reached the top of a low rise in the landscape. Blue had never seen anything like it. Cars and vans were arranged as a makeshift circular wall on the outskirts of the strange village. Metal corrugated sheets were then affixed in a number of fashions to the roofs of the vehicles, creating a single, if wavy, continuous roof. The metal did not extend to the centre of the village and from here Blue saw pale blue smoke rising into the chilly, early morning air. The smoke gave rise to a set of chills running through Blue and he became very aware at how cold he was standing at the top of the rise. He hesitated for a moment, while rubbing his arms and stamping his feet to inject some warmth into them, as he wasn't sure what type of people he would find here. His inner voice came back to haunt him.

Coward.

Blue snorted a laugh at his own reluctance and set off down the small hill.

As he neared Blue saw a small gap between two large vans, creating a gate just wide enough to admit one person at a time. Rather than a gate however Blue was faced with four large metal, horizontal rods, blocking his entrance. Each rod had a handle so it could be pulled out of holes punched through the back doors of one of the vans. Blue frowned as he couldn't really see the point in such a construction that was meant to keep people out.

"Surely I just open it." Blue said to himself, reaching for a handle. A snap of metal sounded to his right and he looked instinctively to its source to find a black tube pointing at his face.

"You can, laddie." A man's tinny voice from an opening in the van said. "But I'll blow your face off if you move that hand of yours another inch." Blue froze and tried to think of an appropriate response while staring at the end of what he now knew to be a rifle. A snicker of laughter came from inside the van. "With your eyes crossed like that you look like the mother in law!" Blue attempted a fake smile in an attempt to win some favour but failed miserably.

"What's going on, Al?" A man's voice from the other side of the gate piped up.

"We have a wee visitor in the wee hours it seems."

Blue cleared his throat and swallowed with difficulty as his mouth was nearly bone dry.

"I'm sorry. I'll go. I wasn't looking for any trouble." Blue eventually explained, his voice tense.

"Well you're a rare breed then, laddie." The man identified as Al commented while, to Blue's relief, he withdrew the rifle slightly. A clank of the metal rods drew Blue's attention forwards and he saw a man leaning casually against the gate, studying him.

"Not looking for trouble? As Al said that's rare. But then you're hardly dressed for scavenging or raiding are you?" Blue looked down at his simple wardrobe and shrugged.

"In all honesty I don't know what I'm dressed for." The man on the other side of the gate didn't smile but an amusement of sorts shone in his eyes.

"Hmm. Well I like a good mystery, young man. What's your name?"

"Blue."

The laugh from the van returned and Blue's face flushed.

"Well, *Blue*, come on in. I'm Rick."

Decisions

* * *

Blue watched with interest as the camp bustled into life as the sun peaked over the horizon. Once through the gate and under the escort of Rick, Blue saw the inside of the circle of vans was separated into segments by wooden or metal panels, blankets or scraps of fabric sewn together. Blue surmised, as he watched people emerge, that each area was home to a family for the night but come the morning they gathered, as they did so now, around the central column. From his view outside Blue had only seen the smoke rising from the hole in the middle of the 'caravan' but now he was sat next to a few large black ranges, providing heat and stoves for cooking. As Blue watched curiously these people in turn watched him until he was forced to turn his head away in embarrassment only to start his observations again a few seconds later. A quick head count gave Blue a total of thirty people, at least those up and about and including Al at the gate but what surprised Blue given that number of people which included children was how quietly they went about their early morning business. Apart from the clanking of metal pots on the ranges and whispered conversations, about him Blue had no doubt, there was no noise that Blue considered 'normal.' He recalled breakfasts, lunches and suppers at the Academy, certainly there were more students than here but still the amount of noise at meal times just generated by talking was a constant loud drone.

Rick walked over carrying two metal cans, each with steam rising from them. He sat down next to Blue with a soft groan and handed him one of the metal cans.

"It's not great coffee but," Rick paused, "actually I can't finish that sentence, it's shit," Blue nodded before very carefully setting down the can in front of him. Rick took a tentative sip of his own drink and shook his head. "Jesus H Christ that's bad." Rick followed suit and placed his can of coffee down. "So, Blue, why are you here? I guess you've surmised from Al's greeting we don't get many visitors and let in even less."

Blue watched a woman carrying a baby sit down before the heat of a range where she pulled aside her shirt and began breastfeeding. Blue flushed and looked away.

"Only an imbecile is embarrassed by nature, Blue." Rick told him, frowning at Blue's reaction. Blue bit his bottom lip and gave Rick a glance and then the woman who was still breastfeeding. She noticed his attention and gave him a small smile. Blue nodded and turned back to Rick.

"I'm sorry. I didn't mean any disrespect, I've never seen a baby or... well, that." He finished at a loss for words.

"You've never seen a baby?" Rick asked, his eyes wide with incredulity. Blue shook his head which Rick copied. Both men fell silent for a time. Blue once again let his gaze roam about the caravan, noting the shabby clothes and gaunt appearances of many and though there seemed to be quite a number of children Blue could see no one he thought was over sixty years of age.

"Why is it so quiet?" Blue asked suddenly. Rick once again fixed Blue with a look of stern disbelief.

"Christ, Blue, you're either from another planet or taking the piss? Now which is it?" Blue spread his hands to display his innocence, eliciting a cynical huff from Rick. "Okay, I'll play." Rick said reaching for his coffee. "Reason one; we may be quite an obvious little community here with our circle of vehicles and smoke from our cookers but to keep silent or quiet at least keeps the attention down from scavvies." Rick saw Blue's frown. "Scavengers." Rick took a drink of coffee his eyes never leaving Blue's own. "They're not too much trouble but you occasionally get a band of Raiders passing through. Now some would say, make a lot of noise and scare them away but I prefer sitting silent until they're close and then raising merry hell over the speakers!" Rick barked a short laugh, pointing to various points around the camp. Blue saw black wires trailing up posts to large conical speakers. "It works more often than not. If not, then we are ready to defend our little community here." In already meeting Al, Blue was aware just how seriously wrong his morning could have been if not for Rick's intervention but Blue was also impressed by the passion this man clearly showed when speaking about his home. "Reason two." Blue noticed Rick's voice dropping as if speaking the next explanation out loud would involve severe repercussions. "The bloody dragons." Rick took a moment to spit with disgust onto the ground. "They see our lights and smoke, they know we're here, but we keep quiet, keep still, act like good little humans so those bastards leave us alone." Blue covered his surprise at Rick's heresy by reaching for his coffee. "Last time they came here it was to round up some of the younger ones." Rick's voice wavered and Blue leaned in to better hear. "We had five little ones, from one to two years of age. They were taken. Taken from their families, while their mothers, fathers, brothers and sisters screamed for them to stop.

They didn't of course." The hand Rick was using to hold his coffee was shaking and Blue, without thought, reached out his hand and steadied the older man's. Rick's mouth twitched in an attempt at a thanks. "One family, the Fords, there were two brothers and a two-year-old sister. Well the riders wanted the girl of course but her father was having none of it. He grabbed a club and threatened anyone who went near that girl." Rick's eyes were glazed over as he relived the past for Blue. "They got her of course, but not without the riders getting a few lumps and bruises. The rest of us did nothing. They decided on a punishment for the father. Ten lashes. You know what that is?" Rick's voice turned hard and he looked at Blue. Blue nodded. "Except those bastards have their weird sense of honour and loyalty. They actually respected the father for making a stand! Can you believe that? And then chastised the rest of us for being cowardly. Anyway, as a final lesson the lashes were to be dealt by the leader of our little clan. I guess you know who that was?" Blue could see the guilt in Rick's eyes and simply nodded. "Clever buggers I'll give them that." Rick gazed off again, upwards towards the roof and the escaping smoke. "He didn't survive, the father. Ten lashes might not sound much but we have no doctor, no medicine. His wounds became infected and then one night, gone. His wife followed him a short time after. Who said you can't die from a broken heart eh?"

Blue closed his eyes and felt the ground shake and tilt, back and forth. He gripped his knees though he knew the sensation was not geological but mental. The firm ground upon which his life was built was literally cracking underneath the strain of the past twenty-four hours. But Blue's mind fought back, rebelled against what he'd learned.

"Why did they take the children?" Blue asked, not daring to open his eyes lest they betray the truth of his origins.

"No idea. We hear rumours from passing traders but I always wonder where the hell do they get their information? Worst gossips in the known world they are." Blue groaned quietly as a single piece of Rick's story span about his swirling mind.

Children. They were taken. Taken from their families.

Blue's own memories at the Academy started at four years of age and there was nothing about his parents or possible siblings before that.

Is that what I am? Is that what I was? A stolen child?

"Blue are you alright? What are you saying? You've gone white as mother's milk!" Rick grabbed Blue's arm and gave it a small shake causing Blue to open his eyes and grab Rick's shoulder.

"I... I was one. They must've taken me. Oh no, please." Blue's mental strength seemed to be leaching his physical as it fought a battle within.

You're a rider! Now act like one!

No! I am not!

You're better than anyone here. You were born for this, destined for your own dragon until humans interfered!

Blue released Rick and went to his knees.

But it's a lie, all of it.

This is just one sample of humanity but it shows you what kind of creatures they are. Living off the scraps we throw them, fighting amongst themselves, unwilling to stand for one another! He even told you that!

He was afraid. He didn't want others to suffer.

That's no excuse.

No. But it is a reason.

Blue heard raised voices behind and turned to see Rick speaking with members of the camp. They were gesticulating at Blue and shouting; many were holding wooden clubs.

You see. They know what you are. They are afraid of you.

Blue heard a strong voice shout above the others and though he couldn't understand the words he knew that accent. Al strode to the front of the group of people, his face red from shouting, his rifle slung over his shoulder.

They will kill you now.

Rick came back to Blue's side and knelt with him in the dirt.

"Jesus, Blue. You just had an entire conversation with yourself out loud! And it didn't sound all that good for us!" Rick let out a frustrated sigh. Blue watched as Al unslung his rifle. "Who the hell are you?" Blue shivered as Al walked closer. His vision was gradually darkening and Blue was certain these were his last few minutes. As his mind circled downwards he thought of Cerys and then nothing else.

* * *

"You're telling me that not only do I have an ex dragon rider in my camp, but you're a member of the Grey now?" Rick asked pointing first to the sleeping form of Blue and then Cerys. Cerys rubbed her already red and tired eyes and slumped heavily into the chair offered her. She was frustrated and angry with Blue, she had hoped that giving him a little leeway and finding out a few things on his own would help him to see the world as it was and not the fantasy he had been spoon-fed the majority of his life. If she'd even harboured a hint of a suspicion that he would meltdown fully *and* in front of a group of people she never would have let him out of her sight.

No.

She thought grimly. *I never would've allowed him to jeopardise my mission.*

That thought made her angrier but this time at herself.

Cerys batted the air in front of her with both hands trying to instil calm into the camp's leader. As soon as she had heard Blue's mental cries of torment Cerys had left the farmhouse and followed Blue's trail. During the morning she intermittently heard Blue's dreams and nightmares. As she walked they would come to her resembling sound waves crossing the landscape but only visible to her because of her gift. By the time she encountered the camp it was midday and Blue's dreams no longer visited. Cerys thought the worst had occurred.

"Yes but he's not a risk to you." Cerys explained. "And neither am I."

Whether by luck or fate Cerys knew the inhabitants of this particular camp and Al, knowing Cerys well, had let her in immediately.

"How the hell do I know that, Cerys? Your word? Fat lot of good that will do us when ten or a hundred dragons pay us a visit!" Rick screwed up his hands into fists in sheer frustration. "I've got my people to think about. They wanted to kick him out of here straight away, a few wanted him dead." Cerys shivered at Rick's casual mention of murder. "I told them if they did come looking for him at least he'd be alive!" Rick sat back in his chair and stared at Blue sleeping. "Why have you done this, Cerys? The Grey make as many enemies amongst our kind than allies."

"Oh come on, Rick!" Cerys whispered harshly. "That's bullshit and you know it. They are working to rid us of 'our masters.'"

"Yes well the majority of folks I've spoken to tend to see them as the types who would kill you to cure you of a disease." Cerys scoffed in disgust and fell silent, her anger simmering. Blue mumbled in his sleep and Rick leaned forward to check on him.

"Why him, Cerys? He's clearly not able to deal with what he knows." Cerys pursed her lips. She was fine with Rick knowing her affiliation with The Grey and she would offer information on Blue if it aided them both but she was not about to divulge all that she knew. She was also not above lying to get her own way out of a difficult and dangerous situation.

"They believe that he is special. That he was to be raised by dragons and then by humans and only then could we beat our foes."

Rick gazed at Cerys with narrow eyes wondering if he was being toyed with. After ten seconds of scrutiny Cerys threw her hands in the air.

"Oh fine. The Grey want him okay. I was his contact and was supposed to get him... somewhere." Rick nodded though he showed quite clearly in his expression that he knew Cerys was still not revealing everything. Cerys leaned closer to Rick. "If I don't tell you any more, then you can't tell them." Rick bit his upper lip as he considered Cerys' advice.

"Alright, young lady. You have two days, no more, then you're gone."

Cerys' shoulders slumped as the tension left them, she hadn't realised how on edge she had become.

"Thank you. Now if I can only convince him to trust me."

* * *

Tears of utter joy spilled down Blue's face as Calda, Galatea's beautiful dragon, emerged from grey cloud into the icy blue of a clear sky. The wind swept them from Blue's cheeks leaving tiny frozen trails behind. Coupled with a half laugh, half sob, Blue rubbed his cheeks against his gloved hands to warm them. He then released the reins attached to the dragon. Not that they were there to guide the dragon, dragons were a long way from horses, they existed purely as a safety feature for the rider.

Calda glanced over her shoulder at the impulsive young rider, noting the dropped reins. The dragon chuckled and looking forward once again dipped her wings. The affect was immediate, the dragon tilted downwards at an alarming angle causing Blue to cry out in shock and grasp ineffectively at the loose, flapping leather straps. Calda righted her angle to horizontal just as quickly and Blue's mouth hit the hard spine of the dragon.

"Never lose your concentration, Blue. You could be in the most normal of environments, even a place of safety and your life maybe in danger."

Blue tasted blood in his mouth and felt the warm run of blood from his nose.

"I think I've broken my nose." He complained.

"I'm glad you said 'I' and not 'you.'" Calda noted with approval. Blue fumbled in his riding jacket for a cloth he normally used to clean his goggles and pushed it against his nose, wincing as he did so.

"Okay." He mumbled through the cloth. "What would I do in a situation like that?"

"First you must ascertain if there is an actual threat as the reverse may also be true. The situation may seem full of danger, full of a threat to your life, but in reality allowing events to play out would be the best course of action." Calda tilted her wings bringing them in a wide arc, on a course to the Academy. Blue screwed his eyes up.

"How on earth do I tell the difference?"

"What I said 'concentration.' Take heed of every moment and the people around you. It is said that you shouldn't judge people too quickly or harshly but in truth we all do, even dragons. It's how we survive. It just depends on how good we are at making those judgements."

"Doesn't it depend on what type of person, or dragon." Blue added, caressing Calda's back. "One is?" He finished.

"Yes." The dragon admitted. "But we're not just animals surviving on instinct. We must use instinct but temper it with intelligence."

Blue closed his eyes and thought on the dragon's words. He felt the soft thump of them landing and frowned. They shouldn't be touching down just yet.

"Open your eyes, Blue." The dragon commanded. Blue opened his eyes and found himself standing in front of Sir Tarvos on the day of Blue's ascendency.

"I know this is a lot to process, Blue, but please use that brain of yours and think." Blue scoffed at his former master's words. He turned and saw the rest of the students of the Academy standing and watching, each with expressions as lifeless as statues. "These here do not possess your talents and I'm not just speaking of your riding skills." Blue and Sir Tarvos were now walking through the halls of what had been Blue's home for the last twelve or so years. "You heard me speaking to a distant figure many years ago but that conversation was in here." Tarvos tapped his finger against his head. "From then we knew you were one to watch, to educate to the best of my abilities before passing you onto those who would continue to teach you for the betterment of our world."

Blue stopped and waved his hands in frustration.

"But what's wrong with the world?" As soon as the question was spoken Blue pictured the night the graves were filled with the bodies of men, women and children. Tarvos reached out to steady the young man as Blue's legs trembled in horror.

"Any world that allows such an atrocity to happen and disappear as smoke on the wind needs healing, Blue. That was a fact I was convinced of long ago just as I'm trying to convince you now." Blue wiped the tears from his face and was surprised his hands weren't covered in blood. He touched his nose expecting a flash of pain but he pressed it with no reaction. Tarvos allowed himself a small smile at Blue's confusion. "Yes, Blue, this is a dream."

"Then you're not real. Calda wasn't real either?" Blue sighed morosely, feeling more distraught that his home had been ripped away from him. The windows to his right shattered with a titanic crash of glass. Blue ducked instinctively and shielded his face but he still saw the magnificent form of Calda enter the long hallway.

"Of course I'm real, daft boy! You just happen to be dreaming." The dragon growled and sat back on her haunches. "Dreams are the only avenue left to me to communicate with you, Blue." Calda relaxed and Blue stared into her golden eyes.

"Trust me." Calda whispered.

* * *

Blue walked alongside Calda through the sodden grass and onto the mud infested road. Storms had apparently washed a great deal of mud and debris from high in the valley, depositing a great deal on the tarmac, concealing the majority of the black road. The sky was now clear and the wind light. The season should've made for a frightfully hot day. Blue stared into the sky and watched his warm breath rise and mist away. The cold penetrated his riding clothes and Blue acknowledged vaguely he should be shivering, perhaps wailing in pain as the frigid air burrowed deeper into him, surrounding his bones and making them ache. The pain was missing, it wasn't dulled through medication or his mental state, it was simply not there. Blue shrugged, if he wasn't to feel the pain that was fine by him. The road continued and so the young man and dragon continued walking in silence. A few moments passed and Blue realised the silence wasn't a lack of talking on his or Calda's part. Soft though it was, the breeze caused no noise as it washed through the nearby trees and bushes. Birds that Blue could see wheeling and soaring low to the ground and high above his head did so without the chorus of song. Intrigued but not alarmed, how could he be when in the presence of Calda? Blue addressed his own movement. As he walked he was leaving large footprints in the mud. Again there was no associated sound. No squelch of compressing wet earth and no sharp thump as his foot heel struck the exposed tarmac.

DON'T WORRY ON IT, BLUE.

Calda reassured the young rider. *I CAN SENSE YOUR DISQUIET. THESE EVENTS YOU ARE EXPERIENCING MAY SEEM LIKE FANTASIES AND YOU THINK YOU'RE BEING MISLED, DECEIVED. ALL WE CAN ASK IS FOR YOU TO CONSIDER ALL YOU KNOW; ALL YOU'VE LEARNED OF THE WORLD IS A LIE.*

Blue tilted his head and reflected on the dragon's strange words. Whenever Calda spoke to him during instruction Blue had never 'felt' the dragon's emotional state during mind-speak. Now Blue was able to detect distress from the dragon coupled with the odd sensation of tumbling or vertigo, as if the dragon's emotions were out of control within and attempting to be released.

WE WERE DIFFERENT BACK THEN, GALATEA AND I. WE REVELLED AND FLOURISHED IN OUR ZEAL.

The dragon spoke through her own emotional distress as they carried on down the road. *TO BE A PART OF THE RIGHTEOUS CHOSEN IS TO BE ONE WITH POWER ITSELF. ONCE YOU ARE CAPTURED BY IT, ABSORBED BY IT YOU WILL DO ANYTHING THAT POWER DEEMS THE RIGHTFUL PATH. NOW IT'S TRUE ENOUGH THAT SOMETIMES ANYONE, DRAGON OR HUMAN WILL HAVE TO ACT IN A WAY RESULTING IN TERRIBLE CONSEQUENCES TO ACCOMPLISH A RIGHT RESULT. THOSE WHO DO WE HOPE ARE BLESSED WITH A CONSCIENCE AS THEY SHOULD FEEL THE PAIN EVERY DAY FOR THE REST OF THEIR LIVES, BUT THEY SHOULD ALSO EXPERIENCE THE GOOD THEY DID AND PERHAPS THE UNIVERSE WILL FORGIVE THEM THEIR SINS. FOR US IT WAS NEVER THAT WAY. WE DID AS WE THOUGHT RIGHT, WITH NEVER A THOUGHT TO WHETHER IT WAS CONSIDERED 'WRONG' AS THAT PURELY DEPENDS ON YOUR VIEWPOINT. WE HAD NO SUCH VIEWPOINT AS FOR US ONLY ONE EXISTED. THE*

DIFFERENCE IN US? WE NEVER QUESTIONED OUR DECISIONS OR ACTIONS. WE NEVER GAVE THOSE WE DID HURT A MOMENT'S THOUGHT. THE DOCTRINE WAS WITHIN US AND WE FOLLOWED IT AND AT TIMES WADED IN BLOOD TO FULFIL OUR 'RIGHTFUL' DESTINY.

The dragon stopped abruptly and Blue took a moment to process Calda's thoughts. He frowned as philosophy was not high on the learning agenda for a would be dragon rider.

LOOK ABOUT YOU, BLUE.

Blue did as he was asked and wasn't surprised that their surroundings had changed, merely curious as to how Calda had accomplished such a feat. Five caravans were standing twenty feet away, arranged to form a horseshoe or cul-de-sac with two caravans sitting parallel to another two and one creating the base of the shoe. Men, women and children were rushing about, their expressions, ones of mortal dread. Parents shooed their children into the caravans as swiftly as possible and slammed the doors, leaving a young couple and their child standing alone. To Blue this was performed in silence, the only sound being Calda's voice in his head.

WHEN YOU WERE TWO YEARS OLD A TITHE WAS DEMANDED OF YOUR SMALL TOWNSHIP. IT WAS THE SAME AS IT HAS EVER BEEN SINCE THE END OF THE WAR. ALL CHILDREN, MALE AND FEMALE BORN WITHIN THE LAST YEAR TO BE PRESENTED TO US FOR SELECTION. YOUR MOTHER AND FATHER HAD ALREADY SUCCESSFULLY HIDDEN YOU AWAY FOR TWO YEARS AND FOR REASONS BEYOND ME ONE OF THEIR NEIGHBOURS INFORMED ON THEM, SEEKING TO ELEVATE THEIR OWN STATION WITH US. WE HAD THE LOCAL LEADERS BRING THE THREE OF YOU BEFORE US FOR JUDGEMENT. YOU KNOW OUR WAYS. DISOBEDIENCE IS NOT TO BE TOLERATED. THERE ARE NO GREY AREAS, ONLY ABSOLUTES.

For the first time in this strange existence, Blue's hands began to shake. He looked down briefly in bemusement to discover the trembling was rapidly rising through his arms and into his shoulders.

FORGIVE ME, BLUE. I'M HOLDING YOUR EMOTIONS IN CHECK BUT THEY ARE MANIFESTING EVEN HERE 'PHYSICALLY.' LET ME FINISH MY STORY AND YOU WILL UNDERSTAND. THE THREE OF YOU WERE SENTENCED TO DEATH. YOUR PARENTS BY THE FLAME AND YOU WERE TO BE LEFT OUTSIDE, UNCLOTHED AND UNCARED FOR AS AN EXAMPLE TO OTHERS, OFFER YOUR CHILDREN TO

US AND RISK US TAKING THEM OR HAVE THEM DIE ALONE FROM EXPOSURE, HUNGER OR WILD ANIMALS.

YOUR PARENTS WERE BRAVE TILL THE END AND FOUGHT. I SAW IN THEIR EYES THEY WOULD RATHER BE THE ARCHITECTS OF THEIR OWN AND YOUR DEATHS. IT WAS OVER QUICKLY; WHAT RESISTANCE COULD TWO UNARMED HUMANS OFFER US? THE WOMAN, YOUR MOTHER, WAS MORTALLY WOUNDED AND SHE FLUNG HERSELF ACROSS YOUR BODY. I MOVED CLOSER, CURIOUS MORE THAN ANYTHING AT THE TIME AT THE UTTER RIDICULOUS NATURE OF HUMANS. THAT WAS WHEN YOUR MOTHER MADE HER FINAL STAND. SHE SWEPT AROUND WITH A LARGE KNIFE SHE HAD HIDDEN WITHIN YOUR BLANKETS AND SLASHED MY FORELEG. I REACTED ON INSTINCT AND THRUST MY CLAWS FORWARD. THEY... THEY WENT THROUGH YOUR MOTHER AND INTO YOU. THE SCAR YOU BEAR WAS RECEIVED AS I KILLED YOUR MOTHER.

Blue stared at the ground at his feet. The blood soaked woman had collapsed backwards, her spine arching almost protectively over her child. He watched as Calda bellowed in agony and strode forward lifting his mother and tossing her aside with ease. The two-year-old boy lay upon the muddy ground his eyes wide with fear and cheeks wet from his tears. Calda leaned in close to put an end to the infant, her own blood running swiftly from the knife wound and dripping to the mud next to the child's hand.

THERE!

Calda announced triumphantly and through the roiling emotions of the dragon Blue recognised the elation sweeping all the pain Calda was experiencing aside.

THIS MOMENT, BLUE IS WHY YOU ARE SO SPECIAL AND STOPPED ME FROM ENDING YOU.

The images of the younger Calda and Blue froze. I DIDN'T THINK IT POSSIBLE. DIDN'T BELIEVE IT EITHER, NOT FULLY, NOT UNTIL YOU WERE OLD ENOUGH TO MIND-SPEAK. YOU MUST'VE WONDERED WHY YOU WERE MY BEST STUDENT, MY BEST RIDER? WE BONDED, BLUE! RIGHT THERE ON THE MUD CAKED GROUND!

Blue took a few steps forward and fell to his knees. The shaking was affecting his entire body and for the first time in this odd place his thoughts coalesced into something coherent.

"You're lying!" Blue cried out into the silent world. "You and Galatea are bonded. You are lying to cover past sins!"

No.

Calda spoke gently into Blue's mind, caressing it with a soft mental touch. *That is your gift, Blue. You are able to bond with any dragon. It changed mine and Galatea's path as we saw the simple innocence and goodness of an older child rather than the pure instinct of a baby. An innocence we'd purposely ignored to do our kind's bidding. It forced us to confront what we were and what we'd done.*

Blue drove his fists into the side of his head and dropped forwards, grinding his forehead into the ground and let out a howl of frustration. A sob escaped him despite Calda's control.

"What am I supposed to do?" Blue's breath hitched. The sight of his dying mother and father replayed again and again in his mind's eye. It wasn't grief that was causing him to cry, not yet, it was the conflicting tales he'd learned over the past twenty-four hours. He shook his head violently to dislodge his thoughts as he believed if they remained in his head much longer his mind would be lost.

"Thomas?" A woman's gentle voice reached Blue over the swirling mess in his head. It calmed his breathing and dried his tears for reasons he couldn't understand. A hand laid upon his shoulder and pushed him up to his knees. His watery vision found a young woman crouched in front of him, a gentle smile matching the gentle tone she'd spoken to him in. "Or, Blue, now I should say." She continued with an amused curl of her lips. Blue's eyes twitched to the bloodied body of the dead woman a few metres away. "This isn't easy but please hold on tight. We're here for you." Blue frowned and a shadow passed behind the woman. Blue looked upwards into the face of a bearded man, in his twenties, at Blue's guess. The man's brown eyes were filled with love and worry. He placed his hands on the woman's shoulders and squeezed.

"If you need us, Blue. Now you know where we are. Where we've always been." The man leaned forward and tapped Blue's head. Both adults smiled though the woman could not suppress the tears from falling.

Blue!

Calda called out distracting the young man. He turned to gaze wearily at the dragon before returning his attention to the couple in front of him. When he turned they'd disappeared.

I'VE SHOWN YOU WHAT I CAN, BLUE. HOW YOU PROCEED IS ENTIRELY IN YOUR HANDS. TELL CERYS THE ROAD YOU WISH TO TAKE. AND IF WE DO MEET AGAIN I HOPE YOU CAN FORGIVE ME.

The dragon turned and walked away from the bloody scene leaving Blue alone in the silent world.

* * *

Blue awoke to the sight of green cloth suspended five feet above his head and the sound of snoring from his right hand side.

"Another cot." He whispered to himself. Considering his last memory before passing out was one of terror and his dreams were ready to cause a mess of emotions, Blue felt surprisingly clear headed. He levered himself onto his elbows and saw Cerys half lying, half sitting in a rather uncomfortable looking chair close by. Seeing her with her eyes closed the young woman seemed at least five years younger than when Blue had met her. Not that her face bore the weariness of a strangled existence or hard upbringing, it was her eyes. They held such depth of pain when awake it aged her. Cerys snored again and Blue turned away smirking, certain it wouldn't be a good look for anyone when sleeping.

"Ha ha, Blue." Cerys mumbled as soon as the snore was complete. "I can hear your damn laugh in my head."

"Sorry." He apologised swinging his stiff legs over the edge of the cot so his knees touched Cerys'. Cerys sat up slowly, her eyes never leaving Blue's.

"Interesting dream I take it?" She asked, her eyes flickering back and forth, searching his. He nodded.

"I assume you had something to do with that?" This time Cerys nodded.

"I figured a little help wouldn't go amiss. Tarvos, Calda and Galatea were always keen to help their former students." She answered with a sad smile.

"How on earth do you know them?" Cerys held up a finger.

"One thing at a time, Blue. First, breakfast and second we need to get out of here, I promised Rick we'd be gone in two days and we've been here four!" Blue's eyes widened.

"I've slept for four days!"

"Oh yes."

"And you've watched me for four days?"

"Yes."

"Who? Well, who took care of me?" Blue glanced down at his clothes for the first time and realised he wasn't wearing the clothes he'd passed out in. Cerys smiled slyly and beckoned Blue forward.

"It was Al."

* * *

"Thank you." Blue clasped hands with Rick. The older man smiled and handed Blue a small medallion on a silver chain.

"Something about you, Blue. Not sure what but I figure as you're tied up with her," Rick said pointing at an offended Cerys, "you might need this more than I." Blue took the medallion and held it up to catch the early morning light.

"It's a St Christopher medal." Rick explained, seeing Blue's puzzled expression. "Belonged to my father, the catch is broken but he'll still protect you on the road." Rick saw Blue hesitate and held up a hand. "No arguing. Just do the thing justice and stay out of trouble." Blue stayed silent and placed the necklace into his jacket pocket. Cerys stepped forward and nodded at Rick.

"Thanks again, Rick. And please do as I ask?" Cerys' tone became long suffering. Rick grinned mischievously.

"Maybe. No promises. You know I never make those." And with that he turned and walked back to the gate of the camp.

"What was that all about?" Blue asked as he and Cerys started walking.

"Rick's been travelling for years. He knows the roads, the people and dangers, and perhaps more importantly when and where to hide and when to fight. A man like that is extremely useful."

Blue and Cerys walked on in silence for a time before Blue had to share his thoughts with this odd young woman.

"Cerys. I'm still not sure about all this. For all I know you're casting some kind of spell and conjuring images of my instructors to confuse me, I mean how would I know the difference?" Blue came to a stop and turned to look back at the camp. "That's real and the farmhouse is real." Blue shrugged. "But I don't know if what you're showing me is real." Cerys sighed in frustration but nodded her understanding.

"I can't make you believe, Blue. I promised I would show you what I could of the world as we travelled. Then perhaps you'll come to understand why you're needed." Blue frowned at Cerys.

"What? That I'm special?" The memories, real or fake, of Calda mortally wounding Blue's mother and then bonding with him as a child played in his mind. "Why does my ability to bond make me special to you? Is it because I represent more of a danger to the Grey? Are you trying to 'win' me to your side?" Blue's face was flushed with anger. Not only did he feel betrayed by the people and dragon he was closest to, now he couldn't shake the sense of manipulation, as if his path was being chosen for him. Cerys's eyes became distant for a short time and even through his frustration, Blue almost sensed words spoken in Cerys's mind as actual spoken words. A few minutes passed and Blue's temper, rather than increase at such an irritating delay, slowly dissipated and a small flicker of guilt arose in speaking to Cerys in such a way.

"Don't worry about it, Blue." Cerys comforted him, sensing his distress, as her eyes came back into focus.

"Why am I important, Cerys?" His tone verged on pleading. Cerys laid her hands on Blue's shoulders and she stared up into his eyes.

"Firstly, you're something of a rarity in dragon-riders, you have yet to lose your humanity. Secondly, yes, I will tell you. It will be just as difficult to hear as anything you've learned from me and perhaps Calda." Blue was about to nod eagerly hoping more information would inform him as to whether he was being used with callous or true intentions. Cerys's expression made him freeze however. He saw emotions playing on her face he'd never witnessed. Empathy and instinct allowed Blue to experience a leaden weight in his chest that was somehow hollow also. He gasped slightly and Cerys grabbed Blue's hands.

"You're not the first, Blue. You're not the first dragon-rider we've tried to save."

* * *

Blue stood in one of the farmhouse's large reception rooms after refusing vociferously he didn't want to spend another night in the dank kitchen with three mass graves just outside.

Alleged graves. He corrected himself and experienced a flash of guilt at the horrid thought that Cerys might be lying.

Blue and Cerys's journey had led them back to the desolate farmhouse. As uncomfortable as the place caused Blue to feel he'd decided he wanted to hear Cerys out before their travels went any further, if they were to travel together at all.

Twilight painted the farmhouse in a sombre shade as they'd approached and Cerys was grumbling to herself.

"I hate twilight. Can't see by it and certainly can't read by it."

"Can't you read in the night either?" Blue asked, glad for the strange distraction.

"No. I sleep at night, I'm not a bloody vampire, Blue." Cerys had chastised him before walking off ahead leaving Blue alone in the fading light wondering if staying at the farmhouse again was too much for her.

"Are you ready?" Cerys asked bringing Blue out if his reverie. He grunted in acknowledgement and walked to the bay window and sat waiting for Cerys to do the same. She paced the floor in agitation, flexing her hands into fists over and over again. Blue didn't have to be psychically gifted to recognise the amount of consternation emanating from Cerys. Cerys stopped abruptly with a loud, suffering sigh. She crossed to the large bay window Blue was sat upon, that once looked out upon acres of farmland, and perched on the wide sill.

"No special tricks, no magic, no dream states to divulge information okay?" She said quietly as she stared out the window.

"Okay."

"You've been smart enough to realise that someone gifted can show you what they want within a vision or dream, not just the reality you seek, and besides," Cerys paused to chuckle morosely. "I get a bit sick of them myself." Blue smiled at her honesty.

"So?" He prompted. Cerys turned her shoulders slumped in resignation, sparking a sliver of doubt in his search for answers.

"Just ask me, Blue. Anything you want, then you can decide if I'm telling you the truth."

"Alright." Blue took in a deep breath and the many possible queries circled and circled as he let it out. "What is so special about me? My talent?" Full night didn't allow Blue to see Cerys's expression and he lent forward to gauge her reaction by starlight.

"Calda wasn't the first dragon to realise a person can bond with another paired dragon and rider." Cerys began. "The Grey have worked with dragons and riders dedicated to peace before you and Calda bonded when you were a child."

"But why would a dragon decide to help the Grey? If a person can bond multiple times so what?" Cerys nodded at Blue's question but enough light caught her face for Blue to see Cerys's eyes filling with tears.

"The first dragon who realised such a feat was possible did as you would think. He took the child back to the Academy and informed them of his suspicions. They were confirmed. The child was… disposed of." Blue saw the moment the tears fell from Cerys's eyes in the deep blue light. She sniffed and laughed mockingly. "It was the first time the phenomenon was discovered but not the last. This particular dragon had to witness these gifted children being killed for no other reason but to protect the leadership. By the time the dragon and his rider made contact with us the human race had lost too many innocents to this new order." Cerys's voice had become monotone as she finished the sentence, distancing herself from the horror she spoke of. Cerys stood quickly and went to her pack. With shaking hands, she retrieved a small box. She opened it and tipped whatever was inside into her mouth. As she did this Blue considered her words. It was difficult for him to fathom, just as the imagery of the three graves and Calda's memory had been. He wanted to walk away already, simply place his hands over his ears and turn his back on Cerys and the farmhouse. He was sure with the information he'd discovered about Galatea and Tarvos working with the Grey he'd be welcomed back to the Academy.

Cerys returned to the bay window flashing the small box at Blue.

"Nicotine gum." She explained. "Can't find any cigarettes anymore." Blue frowned, ignoring her as his legs were tense, readying him to get up and leave. But one piece of information stopped him.

The dragon and his rider made contact.

Blue's thoughts went back to his Ascendency and the unbelievable fate Tarvos had meted out. Further back and Blue saw the head of the Academy looking lost and desolate in his chambers, late at night, speaking to an invisible comrade.

"It was Tarvos wasn't it?" Blue asked, his voice barely a whisper in the deafening silence of the farmhouse.

"Yes." Cerys whispered back but in a much firmer tone. "Tarvos came to see how warped and paranoid his leader had become. To extinguish what he saw as a potential threat in an infant." Blue slumped back against the window causing the wood to creak and crack ominously from his weight. "What Tarvos came to realise in time was that his leader was actually right."

"What? Tarvos thought? No!" Blue was incensed that his former instructor could think such a thing.

"No, Blue. He didn't think it was right, he merely realised his leader was right to be fearful. You see when you bonded with Calda you gifted him, well, your innocence. When a dragon bonded with a baby there are no thoughts or memories to share, only an instinctive need for comfort and sustenance that the dragon would provide. As an older child you fundamentally changed Calda's viewpoint on the human race. Never before had she experienced such purity. You have to remember that Galatea was brought up like you, to be a rider, similarly biased. When Calda changed, Galatea changed as Tarvos had. Can you imagine the threat that opened up? A 'peaceful' revolution was a possibility, led by a human bonded with potentially hundreds of dragons."

Blue ran a hand through his hair and then over his chin, noting distantly he needed a shave.

"So these children could ultimately change any dragon. Make them see their enemies for actual living beings?" Blue recalled many lessons on the scourge of humanity. How they had squandered this world and its resources for its own pitiable desires and wants. Humans like Blue were the chosen few. To be accepted by a dragon was to be acknowledged by the planet itself as its saviour. "You say I'm not the first." Blue stated. Cerys shifted her position and shuffled next to Blue. Both could now see the other's expression and in the blue-black light of the room, Blue saw the consternation written plainly on Cerys's.

"Tarvos and Galatea formed a pact to rescue these talented children. For every child found another dragon and rider were brought into the fold. For every child found not only did they run the risk of being discovered or informed on but the death of the child itself. A decision was made to hide the gifted children within the Academy and then for them to be released to the Grey on the day of their Ascension." Cerys swallowed around the chewing gum and grimaced. "Twenty-year-old gum." She removed the wad of gum and pressed it firmly to the wall behind her. As her finger squelched into the sticky mass she continued her story. "You're in a perfect position obviously to know the mental stress inflicted on a sixteen-year-old discovering who they are to their own kind and what the world is truly like. To be hunted by those you grew up with and reviled by the rest of humanity." Cerys prodded the gum with increasing strength.

"You're not the first, Blue." Cerys repeated her earlier statement. "You're not the first." She turned and drew up close to Blue, close enough for him to see her eyes properly. "I won't bore you with how I became involved with the Grey, suffice to say when this 'opportunity' arose I leapt on it. I wanted to be the one to encourage these twisted minds to see what their kind had inflicted upon the world. That there was no mercy, no justice except for the harsh law of dragon-kind. I and I alone would be the light in the dark for them." Cerys slapped the palm of her hand against her chest. Blue involuntarily leaned back at the vehemence in Cerys's eyes. "I failed them." Cerys whispered her face becoming motionless as the tears fell once more. "All but one of my charges committed suicide. Sixteen-year-old boys and girls who expected to be bonding with a dragon were caught up in the desolation of humanities remains. To be told *they were the one. They* were so important, but the price was to be hated by your fellow riders." Cerys shrugged and she scoffed at herself. "It was like running the most terrible experiment you can imagine. What shall I tell them? Is it safe to disclose information on the Grey? Shall I begin with the war? Maybe the stories of mass graves in every country around the globe? Your dragon friends are genocidal bastards so will you help us thank you so much!" Cerys drew a calming breath and ran her fingers through her hair hard enough for Blue to hear her nails scraping on her scalp. "I left, after I found the last one with their veins open, I left the Grey, not before expressing my full opinion on waiting until a rider was sixteen to tell them the truth." She interlocked her fingers behind her neck and blew out a deep breath, her eyes distant, wandering through scenes of horror that Blue could scarcely conceive.

"What became of the one who didn't..." Blue couldn't finish the question.

"He seemed fine. I was so thrilled, so happy that finally I'd broken through all those years of brainwashing." Cerys barked a laugh, sniffed and moved away from the window and into the darkness of the room. "We rendezvoused with the Grey and the change was so quick, like a lightning strike. You know? It's so powerful, so terrifying and awesome that it captivates you for an instant. He killed two of the Grey, two of my friends before he was... restrained."

Blue sat unmoving on the window sill. He felt an incredible sadness at the loss of his fellow brothers and sisters. A loss apparently perpetrated by those he trusted and the woman standing in the dark not ten feet away.

"Then they told me about you." Cerys whispered from the dark. "They said you were different. That your mind was open, gifted in a way we'd never encountered in a dragon rider."

"What does that mean?" Blue closed his eyes, came to his feet and then forced his lips together as his sadness was replaced by a growing anger.

"The way you saw my memories of the graves. The night you discovered Tarvos speaking to me far away from the Academy. Allowing your dreams to be a conduit for Calda to communicate with you. Everything pointed to you being different. So I agreed to come back."

"To what?" Blue scoffed. "To 'experiment' on me? Find out which method would keep me from going crazy and the sharp knife out of my wrists?"

Cerys was in front of Blue so quickly it startled him into silence. She grabbed the lapels of his jacket and twisted them around her fists.

"Yes! To keep you alive!" She yelled into his face. "To do the crappy job of telling you your life is complete bullshit, a complete bloody lie!" She shoved Blue backwards. The backs of his thighs caught the window sill and he lost his balance, crashing into the fragile woodwork. Glass shrieked as it shattered and Blue felt Cerys's grip once again as she hauled him away from the broken glass. "I could've turned away. I wanted to. Oh I really wanted to." Cerys smoothed Blue's jacket and readjusted the front so it was hanging straight. "But I didn't want the burden to fall to another. I wanted this chance no matter how selfish. A chance to reach your gifted mind, Blue as I believe you will see the world as it is and not how you're told it is."

"But all everyone has been doing is telling me how it is." Blue protested. "For all I know you set me up to meet Rick."

"Fair enough." Cerys acknowledged calmly. "That's why I'm asking you to come with me. Give me a chance and see for yourself. Find your own truth, Blue."

* * *

Stars speckled and glittered in the night sky. A vast range of cloud was visible on the eastern horizon and would soon prevent the beauty of the night a witness.

Blue stood motionless at the rear of the farmhouse staring intently into the heavens seeking an answer. As turbulent as his mind currently was he'd decided to not act as rashly as the others before him had done. He sighed, he knew that was unfair. To be thrown into this world and learn of things that cast your entire life and future into doubt was as terrifying as it was overwhelming. The lack of control over his own fate or destiny was as abhorrent to him as to anyone but Blue suspected something that made him cringe in embarrassment no matter how true he thought it was. To be standing here now after being 'banished' from the Academy, to meeting Cerys, Rick and speaking to Calda, the wealth of information imparted, he realised was quite useless to him at this moment. If Cerys was being truthful and Blue believed she was regarding the deaths of former riders like him then it was that single piece of knowledge that kept him standing here rather than walking away or seeking his own exit from life. He felt the depths of despair his comrades surely experienced. The darkness in front of him was held at bay by the hands of those who'd been consumed by it and he thanked them. For without the knowledge of their fates he would follow the same path rather than the bleak future awaiting him.

Blue still wanted to reject Cerys's words and memories. Reject them completely. He couldn't and wasn't sure why.

It's your gift, Blue.

Blue recognised the voice in an instant. He'd first heard it as a boy when spying on Sir Tarvos just as he fell asleep.

I remember you. Your voice came to me as I began to sleep.

Blue thought into the ever expanding dark cloud above. Blue sensed a wry amusement from his visitor.

Indeed, and I've watched you ever since. When possible anyway. Speaking like this doesn't come naturally to me.

You're not gifted then?

Blue found his curiosity overriding any black thoughts.

In a fashion.

Again there was that warmth of amusement. *A couple of my friends help me out but I wouldn't be able to do it at all without my friend.*

Blue cocked his head in interest and he felt an overpowering sense of affection, of *belonging* flooding this method of communication.

May I speak to your friend? Or meet them?

You may meet him. He wishes to meet you very much.

Blue instinctively reached out and allowed his mind to become enveloped in this being's stream of thoughts. He followed them to their source. He opened his, their eyes, and saw a massive red body towering before him or them, a few feet away. Swirling colours regarded him from two eyes and Blue gasped at the revelation of what he was seeing.

That is part of your gift, Blue and what the others before you could not see. Trust me, Blue. Allow Cerys to bring you to me. See the world.

Blue smiled with genuine delight.

Yes.

He replied to the other's mind.

"Yes." He replied out loud to the increasing wind around him. Blue opened his eyes and bowed his head in respect to the graves. He then turned, and as the first few drops of rain fell upon the soil, Blue walked with resolution back to the farmhouse and Cerys.

The day we feared

Mountains tremble in awe at the weapons unleashed upon the earth.

Bodies of dead creatures piled high enough to rival the tallest of peaks shudders and then collapses, crushing and breaking apart skin, bone and sinew, transforming each to dust under the terrible force of gravity. Dust storms rise from the debris and twist and search the land around them, ever seeking, ever seeking.

A lone figure is witness to all this. The last of her kind, she tries to weep at the emptiness but her face is dry, her eyes as cold as the desolate, barren land as she knows the fault is hers. The wind whips the mighty dust clouds around her and she screams in silence for there is no one to hear.

The sky turns black as the sun is gorged upon and as the world grows cold the wind and dust storms die. The figure is left in darkness upon her knees, weeping her cold tears. The death of every creature has invaded her and torn her down with their memories of life and the very moments of their death.

A burning white fire rips across the black sky, the final illumination this dead world will ever witness. The woman stands and is shocked to find she is able to look straight into its fierce glare. A white tendril reaches out for her and she feels warm and comforted the closer it comes. A sense of finality overcomes her and she reaches with her own hand for the questing white fire. The ground beneath her cracks apart and a hand grabs her ankle. She screams and the white fire pulls away. The crack widens but rather than be pulled in the hand pulls harder and a figure climbs from the cracked earth. It stands and growls at the comforting light and it recedes but does not disappear. The naked figure is covered in dry mud from their hair to their feet. It moves forward until the lone woman can see blue eyes boring into her soul. The creature from the ground opens its mouth and a forked tongue is revealed.

"Begone!" The creature hisses at the white fire. The blue eyes widen and focus on the woman. "It is time." The world turns black again as the white fire is extinguished.

* * *

"Gabby! Gabby wake up!"

Gabby lifted her head quickly from her folded arms and winced at the stiffness in her neck. She looked up with blurry eyes and saw the mud stained figure from her dream at her side. Gabby rocked backwards, almost falling from the chair she'd fallen asleep in but for a pair of hands stopping her. Gabby grabbed the edge of the desk as the hands righted her position and she took a calming breath. Gabby looked again and this time saw Mary, wringing her hands. As Gabby's mind moved further from the strange dream she now heard a persistent alarm sounding outside her room.

"What's going on, Mary? I haven't heard that alarm in fifteen years?" A fleeting rush of desperation swept over Mary's face and Gabby cursed her half-awake brain, there was only one reason the alarm would be sounding. "They're here?" Though both Gabby and Mary knew it wasn't a question.

* * *

"I can't believe it's taken so long for them to find us." Mary stated wrapping a heavy scarf around her neck to ward off the icy chill from the sea. Gabby nodded and smiled at her friend who she knew was attempting to be flippant in such a dire situation.

"The reports we do get say The Grey have been causing this lot quite a bit of grief, more with each passing year." Mary had overcome her nerves from earlier and refused to be left below, wishing to see for herself what was occurring above ground. Now the two young women and their most trusted advisor were standing at the highest point of the power station's surviving building, surveying the scene.

"If they come at us all at once how long do you guess we can hold them?" Gabby asked, her eyes searching and analysing the bleak landscape around her.

"All at once, perhaps twenty minutes. That assumes they attack with half their numbers in the first volley, the other half in the second and so on."

"And even if they don't do that straightaway and they take some time figuring it out then allowing for worst case scenario the station will fall eventually." Gabby concluded turning to look at the man standing next to her. Former lieutenant McCaffrey was perhaps Gabby's most trusted friend, at least after her oldest friend Mary. The army officer was one of the few surviving members of the original military staff based at the nuclear power station.

The attack upon the power station at the beginning of the war resulted in a great deal of cosmetic damage to the bunker and several severed power lines. As emergency generators activated the new residents of the bunker came to realise the immense forces ranged against them. Whether the dragons were aware of the importance of this particular nuclear power station or they simply were knocking out energy supplies the bunker's inhabitants realised quickly how fortunate they were to be sequestered below the surface. Only one casualty resulted from the attack in the form of Mr Harris. A concrete beam had cracked and pinned the teacher's leg, shattering it instantly. Staff and the medical team successfully rescued Gabby's injured teacher but were unable to save his leg. In a short period of time his mental health deteriorated. To the girl's horror they watched as their former teacher grew weak. He refused to speak and refused any sustenance to nourish his body. The doctors even went so far as to introduce a drip feed and a food tube directly into the man's stomach. The physical damage that was so easily treated could not compare to the mental damage the teacher had suffered and the weaker he was the more prone to illness he became. The medical staff tried their utmost to counsel the suffering teacher even to the extreme action of promising his family were safe and on their way to him. The mental damage was too strong a wound. Six weeks after the attack on the power station Mr Harris succumbed to pneumonia. The first real casualty the girls were to witness of the war.

During this period, communications were re-established with the outside world. Dire news started coming through that the war was taking a heavy toll on military and civilians, and the soldiers quartered in the bunker started to become understandably restless. Their fellow soldiers and in most cases, friends, were high above, on the ground, fighting a losing battle. Every soldier knew it was extremely unlikely their actions on the field of battle would alter the outcome of the war but the call to defend their friends, their fellow brothers and sisters, and country was undeniably strong.

The armed force within the bunker were given just one order. Maintain their posts and defend the site at all costs. The station was a valuable asset that required a military presence. But as news of loss after loss came in dissent grew. It was the final message that caused every soldier and a number of the civilian staff to disobey orders and leave. The enemy were beginning their assault on the nation's capital. Even though a surrender had been issued by the human leadership it had been ignored by the aggressor, so every soldier; army, navy or air force were being recalled to defend the heart of their country.

Gabby would still experience chills when she thought of that moment fifteen years or so ago. Watching those brave men and women pack up and leave. Seeing in their eyes that they were ready to face death. The fear was great but she never once saw one of them falter that day. At the time she thought them foolish. Ridiculous simple minded people who had no other thought but to shoot and kill others in some overblown game of 'war.' That they marched off thinking that this was their glorious moment, that they alone would be the hero and save the human race in its direst hour of need. It had taken Gabby a few years of maturing, reading, thinking and talking to the soldiers ordered to remain that changed her views. Not on war, never that. But on those who fought and died. That all they wanted to do was serve and do it alongside someone they could trust to have their back as they would watch another's. Among Gabby's many hopes and wishes, meeting even one of those soldiers again would fulfil her fervent desire to apologise for her scorn the day they left the safety of the station.

"Do you think they'll offer terms?" McCaffrey asked, leaning out over the high roof of the station's main building to ensure every person housed at the station was out of sight. Gabby grabbed McCaffrey's arm and pulled him back, shivering as she did so.

"Don't do that." She complained. "You know heights give me the willies." McCaffrey snorted and ran a hand through his greying hair. Gabby studied the man she'd known for over half her life. When they met on the first day of the attacks she thought he encompassed everything typical of an upper class army officer. His accent was so proper it made Gabby's jaw ache as she clenched her teeth listening to it. But through those first days, that ultimately led to weeks, months and years McCaffrey had taken the responsibility of taking care of his charges as seriously as if they were his own children. Throughout the emotional turmoil brought on from news about the war, being unable to contact

The day we feared

their families and finally not being able to leave the facility at all, McCaffrey was on hand to deal with the three teenage girls, helping them through their grief, anger and frustrations. He ensured their education continued under the tutelage of one of the professors onsite, Professor Eames, known to the girls as Elliot, locked away underground with them. It came as no surprise to anyone that Gabby was the most proficient student and that in her intelligence, Professor Eames proudly acknowledged his student would surpass him, though he tagged 'eventually' onto that thought.

Gabby sighed at the sight of her ageing friend, now in his late forties, and she worried that any course of action she chose would mean one of her dearest friends would not reach fifty. She turned from McCaffrey and focused on the sight arrayed in a huge semicircle around the nuclear power station. On her last count she had found one hundred and twenty of them, most in the air and the remainder poised like beautiful but deadly statues around the station's perimeter fence. Now she estimated another fifty had joined the ranks of the small army amassing in front of her but one especially drew her attention. Gabby reached out a hand and McCaffrey responded automatically and placed the scope in her hand. She raised it and focused on the one all others on the ground were paying deference to.

"I guess we'll find out soon, my friend. And when we do it will be that one making the decision." Gabby lowered the scope and had to suppress the fear threatening to make her dash madly for the safety of the underground bunker. It was frightening enough to stand off against over one hundred and fifty dragons but the one that truly gave her pause was of the human she had seen sitting astride the terrifying green dragon. His face was young, handsome even, but contained such a wealth of sorrow and anger that his true age was eclipsed by the shadow of his memories. Even now with the scope lowered and detail now a blur Gabby could feel that face turned towards her exuding hatred and malice from his eyes. The dragon's visage was a match for its rider's but only in emotion. The huge jaw of the beast was tilted, lopsided, allowing several sharp yellow fangs to be on display on one side of its face. Gabby couldn't think of any circumstances that another human or creature could perpetrate such a wound to a dragon.

"Lord Andas has come for us."

* * *

In the early years after the war, or at least what those in the bunker thought signalled the end of the war proper, the complete breakdown in communications, there was no exploration above ground. Protocols were in place and were followed to protect the integrity of the site and the secrets it held. Regardless of who the enemy was, whether it be an invasion from a human army, or in this case, no matter how ridiculous it sounded at the time, by dragons, the station was not to fall into enemy hands under any circumstances. Therefore, no personnel were allowed out of the bunker lest they draw attention to the station's ongoing occupation. But with the main bulk of the military presence gone the resolve to stay underground for what seemed year after pointless year to the majority of its residents wavered and eventually died. Any lingering arguments concerning the official secret act or duty to one's country were ground down by the ongoing relentlessness and boredom of a life below ground. All those below without exception ached to see the sky once again.

In addition, as the years passed and no cessation to their duty came one factor for exploring the surface gained prominence. In short, food supplies were never meant to last for such an extended period of time. Contact had to be made and trade established if the station's survival was to be ongoing.

Caution was not thrown to the wind. Several plans were made, discussed, examined, cast aside and re-examined ad nauseam. Gabby, Mary and Brooke were an integral part of the underground operation. The girl's education quickly became a key aspect in the ongoing function of the station. The three girls however if not enjoyed then endured a singular bond. Many of the station's technicians had family above ground when the attacks began and the war started. As Gabby discovered in her talks with Dr Eames, each 'employee' was chosen, trained and assigned to this post, a post that required a certain mental toughness and a particular dedication to duty. The girls and their teacher, before his death, were an anomaly, a fluke. Thrown into a bizarre situation and locked away underground while a war raged upon the planet's surface. Gabby had not cared especially for anyone left behind but she empathised greatly with her classmates and teacher. It was Mary who endured silently, the almost paralysing pain of loss without the knowledge of what had really happened to her family. The question of 'are they?' 'aren't they?' A damning song of frustration playing constantly in her mind. Brooke however suffered intensely. In school, both Gabby and Mary would be the first to consider the tall, blond girl, a complete bitch. A bully, a terror to anyone that didn't fit into her plane of existence. That view, even after the war began and Mr Harris's death, did not alter, even though the girl suffered as they all did. Gabby and Mary avoided her as best they could, wishing not to be a witness to Brooke's over dramatic lamentations winding up to hysterical levels requiring sedation. As thirteen-year-old girls, Gabby and Mary, could not endure Brooke's histrionics as a reminder to their own form of suffering, but as time went on they understood in greater depth that Brooke wasn't performing for anyone and that she was suffering in her own unique way. With encouragements from McCaffrey and Professor Eames, Gabby and Mary resolved to help their once classroom enemy. All were wary at first, with Brooke demonising both the girls, now teenagers, for neglecting her and not caring. Both Gabby and Mary to their credit admitted that Brooke was correct and realised that standing together and sharing their grief, their weaknesses made the three of them stronger. Brooke for her own part improved and although she still suffered episodes of black moods and depression she had two friends close at hand at all times.

As the wealth of earth above them provided a protective cocoon from the outside world the three girls were essentially adopted by the remaining staff and military personnel giving them the support, both emotional and psychological, as they matured into young women, though many of those staff would admit to purposely ignoring the girls at times as all three journeyed through adolescence to adulthood and all the teenage troubles that invoked.

Those with families left above ground invested themselves in the three, perhaps motivated by guilt at first over the apparent abandonment of their own kin, in time however it surfaced as a deep abiding affection. As Gabby, Mary and Brooke entered adulthood, a natural passing of responsibilities began to settle upon the three's shoulders. McCaffrey represented one of the youngest 'original' members of the group and with more pressure to visit the outside world for resources it was becoming quite clear who would be at the forefront of that investigation, namely, the three young charges in their care.

**

"That's close enough!" McCaffrey barked his order, automatically bringing his weapon to his shoulder and releasing the safety. The messenger looking down the barrel of the lieutenant's assault gun and raised his hands before him in a gesture of peace and compliance, but Gabby noted the hint of contempt in the messenger's eyes. Gabby placed a hand on her friend's shoulder and McCaffrey lowered his weapon, but only by a few inches, he kept the safety off and removed his finger from around the trigger.

Only twenty minutes had passed since the two friends had speculated on whether an attack was forthcoming or an offer of some kind. With only a little relief Gabby had watched a tall, dark haired man under a white banner march without fear towards the station's security fence.

The messenger's eyes flicked back and forth between the young woman and older man a few times before settling upon Gabby.

"My Lord Andas offers greetings and extensions of peace on this ground. It is his desire to speak with your leaders to plan for the future of all." The messenger bowed and then straightened awaiting a response. Gabby looked at McCaffrey who merely grunted his opinion at her. Gabby took a deep breath and walked towards the messenger her eyes searching his, hoping to find a connection she recognised as human. She failed.

"I will hear Lord Andas's words and plans for the future." Gabby replied with formality, knowing that it was one of the things these dragon riders seemed to enjoy. The messenger's eyes brightened and a small smile danced across his face.

"Very well. If you and any others you wish to escort you will follow me?" The messenger posed it as a question but Gabby knew without a doubt this man intended it as an order. Gabby shook her head and a small fire was lit in the man's eyes.

"I'm sure Lord Andas can appreciate my situation. How would 'my people' look upon me if I simply allowed you to lead me out of here. Regardless of *your* intentions my authority would be diminished." Gabby cocked an eyebrow at the man and tilted her chin up, effecting an arrogant stance of her own. The messenger nodded and something bordering on respect cast a shadow on his features.

"Perhaps a neutral venue would be of better service." The messenger suggested to which Gabby nodded her agreement. "We must survey the area and determine the time and place. I'm sure you can appreciate we do not wish an interruption by those that call themselves Grey Rose." Gabby gave the man a small bow and watched as he turned on his heel to return to his master.

"Neutral ground?" McCaffrey whispered. "Around here?" Gabby shrugged.

"Well Switzerland is a little far away."

*   *   *

"More than likely that son of a bitch will kill anyone we send out there to talk." McCaffrey commented entering the room with several rolls of paper under his arm. Everyone bar Gabby nodded in agreement.

"Or take them hostage and demand we open up for him." McCaffrey finished, laying several rolls of technical diagrams on the large table the group was gathered about. Gabby turned to Mary and cocked an eyebrow. Mary shrugged and let out a sigh.

"Whatever we do this problem isn't going away." Mary leaned forward and placed her hands on the table. She stared at them a few moments before continuing. "We've known this day has been coming for a long time, ever since Gabby's run in with this lot." Mary's eyes drifted around the table until they met Dr Bilson's eyes. The doctor swallowed and, Mary thought, the man's own fear was outshining the total of all in the room. "We've tried to make plans accordingly but we have to be clear about this, not all of us can leave if we wish to survive." Mary turned back to her friend. Gabby reached for one of the sheets McCaffrey had laid on the table and tapped her finger on it.

"We'll go with the escape tunnel. I'll get us out of here." Though the room was quiet before, an absence of sound seemed to shroud the room entirely, coupled with a slight darkening of the light. Mary clapped her hands startling everyone.

"Okay. Let's get prepared and not caught with our pants down." McCaffrey snorted and shook his head and all except Mary left the room. As the door closed, Mary shoved a finger close to Gabby's nose.

"Are you out of your goddamn mind? What the hell are you playing at?" Gabby took a step back, not in shock at her friend's vehemence but to grab Mary's outstretched hand.

"We have no other moves to make, Mary. We're surrounded here. It's taken them far longer than we thought to find me…us." Mary shook her head in protest but Gabby stepped forward now and placed her hands on Mary's shoulders. "We've known that time was a gift and perhaps what we know can be helpful to the Grey." Mary spluttered in contempt.

"The bloody Grey! Great bloody help they've been, useless bastards!" Gabby shook Mary's shoulder's gently.

"That's crap and you know it. We're the ones holding back information, not The Grey. Maybe we should have shared our talents with them sooner but that's a bridge we all burned a long time ago." Mary rolled her eyes and Gabby responded by shaking her friend's shoulders harder. "Hey! If not for them I wouldn't have made it back here."

"So we get this information to The Grey? And then what? What could they possibly do with it?" Mary blustered, not allowing Gabby to speak. "All these years and bloody Bilson keeping his mouth shut on why this place is here until we were 'allowed' to know, and now we've got a sodding army camped on our doorstep wanting to know why as well!"

Gabby opened her mouth to speak but merely shook her head. She suddenly felt extremely tired. Her eyes didn't seem to want to stay open and her legs trembled fiercely. Mary's expression changed in an instant. She reached out and guided her friend to a chair. Even sat down Gabby's legs continued to shake and as she rubbed her hands on her thighs she knew they would shake too if held up.

"I'm sorry, sweetie." Mary knelt in front of Gabby and laid her hands on her friend's. "I… you're my family, you know? I wouldn't have survived this place without you." Tears welled up in Mary's eyes. "And to think I might lose you." Mary dashed the tears away and sniffed fiercely. "But that's me being selfish. This is your plan; you've got the hardest place in it." Gabby placed a hand on Mary's cheek.

"They're here because of me." Gabby raised a hand to stop any protests from Mary. "I know it's not my fault but it's just the way it is. If we can stall them long enough or make them believe what they sense is me, well, who knows? But at least that gives us a chance."

* * *

The majority of dragons had by all accounts left the area surrounding the power station. Whatever actions they had taken to secure it for their leader had apparently reassured him enough to order three quarters of his army away, not that they couldn't return at a moments notice. Gabby watched from just inside the station's perimeter as the riders left behind fashioned a large tent a short way from the main gate. After a few minutes watching the construction Gabby didn't know whether to scoff or admire. The 'tent' was in fact more of a pavilion, measuring at least ten metres square with a peaked central column that gleamed in the weak sunlight of the day. Slits in two sides of the pavilion walls were opened and tied back with dark red rope and Gabby was able to see through the pavilion and down the road. Approximately two hundred metres distant she saw a green flash of dragon hide and Gabby shuddered automatically in response. She pulled her heavy coat tighter around her neck and placed her hands under her armpits. The cold breeze flowing in from the sea however still seemed to find gaps and holes to infiltrate her warm clothing sending occasional violent shivers through her body. Gabby's breath plumed rapidly in front of her face in the cold and she tried to calm herself and lower the beat of her thrumming heart. Gabby was well aware on her few encounters with these dragon riders that not only were they incredibly formal and polite as underneath burned a volatile being, but they expected their opponents to be just as respectful as them. Professor Eames on learning of this disparity in the dragonriders behaviour told her to imagine a country where everyone had a gun and could carry it around, that would call for everyone to be polite to one another. Gabby, Mary and Brooke had thought about this point for a long time before concluding it was utter garbage, Gabby especially thought so when she imagined her parents shooting up their veins before shooting up a shop for money. With this knowledge in place Gabby knew it was vital for her to maintain an appearance of strength regardless of how hopeless the situation was, it was another thing these riders respected. Gabby shook her head at the folly and strange behaviours of people.

While Gabby's thoughts had drifted the messenger she'd encountered earlier strolled from the pavilion to the main gate. Gabby refocused on the man, but ignoring him this time, effecting the poise of what they considered a leader.

"My Lord Andas requests your gracious presence." The messenger bowed and indicated the large tent behind him.

What an idiot.

Gabby almost laughed aloud her nerves were so taught and her fear close to the surface. In fact, she desperately wanted to relieve the pressure building in her heart and head, to simply show these people how ridiculous they were. But she didn't, the stakes were too high. Gabby bit the inside of her cheek, not enough to cause bleeding but enough to bring her back to the moment.

"Not now." She whispered to herself wishing, not for the first time, Mary was unable to speak to her in this fashion.

A horn sounded focusing Gabby's attention and staring beyond the tent she saw the one person in her life she felt hatred for, the one person she admitted to herself and to no one else, in the dark of night she would put down and risk her soul to possibly make the world a cleaner place, Lord Andas or as she knew for a short time, Jack.

The procession came to a halt and thrust their spears, point down into the ground. Lord Andas remained in the semicircle created by his guards a moment before following suit with his own spear. Gabby cocked an eyebrow at the man she had briefly known as Jack. He was dressed in a way a far cry from the simple hooded robe he had been wearing during their first meeting. The majority of his ensemble was a form of steel, resembling a knight's suit of armour but with many added weapons, barbs and hooks crafted into the shoulders, elbows and knees. On his head was a steel helm that left his face visible but on the crown of the helmet was a large curved blade giving the impression that someone had tried to cleave the owner in two. A cape of green and black hung from his left shoulder to his knees, though currently it was billowing like a sheet in the wind from the growing harsh breeze off the sea. He entered the pavilion alone and stepped to the centre with his guards taking position at the entrance.

Gabby took a long slow breath as he studied her in almost minute detail. As she was wrapped in heavy clothes she knew he wasn't interested in her physical attributes, at least not in a heterosexual fashion, but he did want something from her, something she would not give. Gabby waited until he was done and then she lifted her chin to stare upon him in what she hoped was an imperious resolve. He inclined his head and beckoned her forward with his hands outstretched slightly to his sides. Gabby nodded in return and strode into the pavilion to face Lord Andas.

* * *

"It's so good to see you again, Cassandra." Gabby noted he still used the name she had lied to him about those three years past. "For a while there I thought I'd never find you." Lord Andas, or Jack smiled and Gabby thought he was actually genuinely pleased but she made a point to remind herself why he was pleased.

"Thank you. Now may I ask why your army is camped on my doorstep?" Jack gave a small laugh that contained no humour.

"Technically these are my lands and of course my brethren's, I seek no permission nor require it. One reason I am here; to educate, to inform and to bring everyone together."

Well that's three reasons already.

The day we feared

Gabby thought sourly.

Jack clasped his hands behind his back and ambled casually around the pavilion, as much as his armour allowed. "In the past I have been guilty of taking the offensive too quickly. Of not hearing out those who don't understand me and mine. I never thought to try and instruct them first but merely punish them." He stopped and gave Gabby a quick look. Satisfied she was still listening he continued. "So much has been lost these last fifteen years on dragon and human side. The war is over but still many continue to fight because they don't understand." Gabby frowned at the young leader.

"What? Understand what?" She asked. Jack shook his head as if amazed that even she didn't comprehend his statement.

"That you lost. Humanity lost." Jack's eyes went distant as he looked into his own past. "At first it was decreed that any defiance from individuals, villages, towns and even cities would result in complete annihilation." Jack gave a contemptuous laugh. "As if they could stand against us? We'd already disposed of the military and any weapons left behind were useless against us." Gabby felt a chill not caused by the increasing breeze from the sea and she too looked beyond the walls of the pavilion and imagined the destruction brought by this man and his dragon army. "So many died simply for refusing to yield. Regardless of how many, age or sex they all met with the same fate." Gabby's chill was slowly being replaced by the heat of anger. Those small flames of anger were being fanned by her imagination as she heard the desperate cries and wails of millions. Mothers screamed and babies cried. It was the imagined sound of a baby crying for its mother that stoked Gabby's outrage.

"Fine." Gabby's comment was barely audible as she ground the word out through clenched teeth. "So what is the other reason you're here?" Jack turned his full gaze upon her and Gabby saw the righteous fire blazing from the man's eyes, brought on by his very own words.

"Oh I think you know." He took a step closer to Gabby, his eyes gleaming with that strange red tint she remembered from their first encounter, causing her to back away a step. "The power surrounding you that night in the village remains just as potent, if not stronger here. That is why I was interested in you." Gabby stayed silent and Jack took it as a sign to carry on. "Dragons have their own kind of magic, well, we view it as magic, to them it is merely an ability to move from place to place without covering the distance between the two points." Jack stepped past Gabby to look at the station. "But you? My dragon identified a powerful energy within you, something akin to his own. After you fled that day I've sought you, followed your trail until it went cold." Jack turned to Gabby, a grim expression now on his face. "Oh I punished those who offered you rest and food. Those who did not answer my questions were dealt with more permanently." Jack's voice had dropped to a whisper as he observed the growing horror on Gabby's face. Jack shrugged. "I continued until the trail of that energy disappeared. But imagine my incredulity when I discovered another." Jack walked quickly to the side of the pavilion he had entered by and signalled to his escort outside. Gabby heard a multitude of clanking sounds as four guards in Jack's escort came into the pavilion. Once there they parted and revealed the bound form of another of Gabby's companions over the years, Brooke.

"Let her go!" Gabby demanded with no hesitation, allowing her anger to show freely in her voice. Brooke's eyes were red and distant and her face and clothes covered in dried mud. "What have you done to her?" Gabby yelled, grinding the question through her teeth. Jack put his hands in front of him in in an effort to calm Gabby down.

"No harm has come to your friend, I promise you. We located her in a village not too far from here. Actually one of the villagers betrayed her location to us which I found odd as I believe it's a village you trade with." Jack's eyes now seemed to glow intensely red. "I despise humans like that. But anyway," he said waving his hand as if the incident were nothing more than a troublesome insect, "we intercepted your friend and laid out a fitting punishment for those involved. Your friend was kind enough to witness what happens to those who offer solace." Jack smiled at the memory until he saw the look of horror on Gabby's face. "Oh don't worry it wasn't that bad. Remember the village when we first met? Well we simply removed the hands of the men and boys." Gabby's hands trembled but she didn't know if it was more from fear or anger. She stepped swiftly to Brooke, only to be stopped by a rider's arm blocking her way. Gabby was quicker and with one hand grabbed the man's wrist while she placed her other hand flat on the man's elbow. With one forceful twist of his wrist and a push on his elbow the man cried out in immediate pain and fell to his knees. The remaining members of the escort closed in to help their fallen rider but a sharply barked order from their Lord brought them to a stop.

"How dare you bar this woman from her comrade?" Gabby looked up and saw Jack's face burning red to match his eyes. Jack stormed forward and Gabby quickly released the rider, pushing him away. The rider stumbled upwards and fell into Jack's hands, who spun him around until they were face to face. "I gave strict orders that no harm would befall a guest of mine in this pavilion!"

The rider tried to answer but Jack leaned back slightly and backhanded him with his wicked looking gauntlet. Gabby gasped and turned away as blood and flesh were splattered across the ground. The rider screamed immediately, grasping his lacerated face. "Take him away. He is not fit for duty with me any longer." Jack gave the rider a final push and before he could hit the ground the riders caught him and dragged him out of the pavilion. A strained roar came to them and Jack tilted his head, listening intently. Gabby watched and saw Jack's lips moving as he conversed with a dragon some distance away. Jack finally shook his head and sighed.

"My apologies. To disobey an order during wartime may be excused depending upon the outcome but during a truce is unforgivable. Tonight many riders and dragons will mourn the loss of two brothers." Gabby was only half listening as while Jack was hell-bent on a grand apology she'd moved to Brooke and tried to get a response from her. The young woman's face was free from any injury, her eyes were red and swollen but Gabby assumed what Brooke had witnessed involved a great deal of tears. Gabby smiled softly and gently laid a hand on her friend's cheek.

Are you okay?

This guy is totally crazy! The things he did to those villagers!

Brooke began to tremble as fresh tears welled in her tortured eyes.

"You're safe now." Gabby whispered and she drew Brooke into an embrace. A few seconds went by and then Gabby felt Brooke's arms moving upwards to return the gesture.

"Splendid!" Jack enthused. "I'm so glad we could reunite the two of you."

You're safe now. I need you back in the station and tell everyone we'll proceed with the three of us and the tunnel.

Gabby leaned her head back and saw the interest and concern in Brooke's watery eyes.

I'll be okay.

Gabby reassured Brooke silently. *Just be in position and ready for me.*

* * *

Brooke had returned to the relative safety of the station supported by McCaffrey and Jack's escort had retired from the pavilion, shutting the fabric doors as they left. With the fresh breeze from outside cut off the enclosed area seemed to become stifling almost immediately but Gabby attributed the feeling to the situation rather than the conditions. Jack clasped his hands behind his back once again and strolled the inner perimeter of the pavilion, his eyes however never left Gabby.

"Now your friend is returned I will pay you the respect of asking for what I want." Gabby didn't reply and simply waited. "Since that first day I encountered you I've searched whenever was possible. Sometimes the initial traces would be strong but decay quickly. Other occasions I would have sworn on my life you were close by; the trace was too old or weak to follow." Jack halted and took a deep breath before continuing. "Finding your friend was nothing more than luck really and of course you both exhibit the same energy, so I hoped it would lead me to you. Your fellow humans decided to profit from her request for help by informing me of her presence at their village." A look of disgust washed over Jack's face akin to finding clothing covered in animal faeces. "They've been dealt with. They were useful but I abhor that kind of behaviour. Stepping on another's back to escape the foul air, and while you profit from the clean air you're driving them deeper into the dirt." Jack waved a hand brushing aside the issue. "So you know why I'm here, *Gabby*." Gabby gave him a half smile, completely devoid of humour. "Brooke was good enough to tell me your real name. It is of no consequence though. I want to know about the energy you have at your disposal. How powerful is it? How do you use it? And most importantly, how can *I* use it?" Gabby nodded as she considered Jack's words, at least she wished to give that impression, and she hoped her acting skills were good enough.

"It took me a long time to find out what the power was." Gabby began to explain, sitting on the grass enclosed within the pavilion. She crossed her legs and looked distantly into a dark corner of the large tent. She noted the flash of interest in Jack's eyes. He came to her and sat as best he could in his armour in front of her.

The day we feared

"Excellent. Well, now maybe we can proceed?" Gabby heard the change in Jack's voice. She turned and saw the red glow she remembered so well shine in his eyes. Gabby experienced a bout of vertigo and a cold tendril of this man's mind probing her thoughts.

He's trying to access my memories. He'll see we know of The Grey!
Gabby called out to her friends.

Gabby if you're sure of this plan then let him in, it won't change anything, only buy us some time. Let him have them.
Mary advised softly.

Gabby clutched the grass and gripped it hard enough to turn her knuckles white as the first cold tendril was rapidly joined by others and Jack's mind invaded hers.

The Core — Gabby's memories

"Your mother was a frigging crack-whore, bitch!"

"At least she had a reason to whore herself out instead of giving it for free to everyone!"

"How dare you! At least my mother was there for me!"

"Oh I agree. Every single goddamn day! Moaning and complaining to the teachers about all the nasty children daring to speak to her precious little pet!"

McCaffrey stopped dead in his tracks as he reached the door to the girl's living quarters. According to one of his junior officers the shrieking had started ten minutes previous and was escalating as the seconds passed by. With a look that clearly demonstrated the weight of teenage years had descended upon him McCaffrey entered the room.

Brooke, her face swollen and red with utter hatred ran straight into McCaffrey and before he could react she'd sidestepped him and ran out of the room. McCaffrey blocked the exit from the living quarters that housed the three girls and settled his eyes on Gabby. He crossed his arms and for probably the tenth time that month resolved to have the girls assigned separate quarters after Brooke and Gabby had nearly come to blows on the ten previous occasions. Gabby was standing in front of the former lieutenant, eyeing him with extreme irritation as he was denying her exit from the room and chasing Brooke down.

"Who's side are you on anyway?" Gabby spat each word out viciously. McCaffrey frowned at Gabby.

"Oh don't be such a bloody baby," McCaffrey remonstrated with the younger girl "What the hell were you screaming at each other for this time?" Gabby rolled her eyes and shrugged with all the eloquence a teenage shrug can produce.

The Core — Gabby's memories

"She stole my pillow alright! I came in and it was on her bed!" McCaffrey looked from one girl's bed to another, without moving his head. "She. Took. It. Without. Asking!" Each word was fired from Gabby's mouth, as she was exasperated that he would miss such an obvious point, regardless of the fact she hadn't told him. McCaffrey nodded as if considering the matter seriously.

"And what was she doing with it?" He asked cautiously, expecting some awful horror story to emerge that he didn't really wish to hear about. As Gabby drew herself tall and straightened her shoulders to launch another scathing attack against her roommate she cried out in pain and anguish, pressing her hands hard against her ears.

"Jesus! Make it stop!" She shrieked, dropping to her knees and rocking forwards, banging her forehead on the floor. McCaffrey rushed over and crouched quickly next to the suffering girl.

"What is it? Make what stop?" But Gabby couldn't hear him. He grasped her shoulders and lifted her to face him. Tears streamed down her face and he could see her hands shaking with the force and effort she was placing on the sides of her head. It was her eyes that opened McCaffrey's mouth in shock. Blood was pooling in the corners of both eyes and McCaffrey watched in something close to fascination as just like a glass filled too much there came a point when the water bulged however briefly over the rim of the glass before pouring over the lip. An all too calm part of his brain supplied the fact it was surface tension. Gabby's eyes were demonstrating the effect. The mixture of blood and tears reached bursting point and then cascaded down her face. Gabby saw McCaffrey's reaction and she swiftly wiped her eyes and stared at her hand. Blood dripped from her fingers to the carpet, soaking into the thin fabric and expanding rapidly. McCaffrey watched this happen dumbfounded and then snatched at Gabby's wrist before the girl had a chance to clap her hand back against her head.

"What is it, Gabby? Tell me!" He leaned in so his nose was almost touching hers.

"The noise!" Gabby wailed. "it won't stop!" McCaffrey leaned backwards, confused and at a loss. The girls had been in his care for a few years now and he'd taken the role of a substitute father to heart. Watching the world turn into a massive shit-storm via television, satellite and every social media app had of course knocked everyone down but especially the three girls. The resilience they'd shown in the aftermath however inspired McCaffrey and several members of the crew of the station to take the girl's education and wellbeing seriously. It hadn't always been easy, especially for Brooke, but as far as McCaffrey was concerned these three girls were his stepdaughters. Watching Gabby whimper and cry out in pain at what seemed to be nothing, McCaffrey feared this argument with Brooke had caused something akin to a breakdown. He moved closer to Gabby and wrapped an arm over her shoulders, hugging her in tight to him.

"It's okay, Gabby." He tried to muster as much confidence into his tone as possible though he knew Gabby couldn't hear him. "I'm here, I'm here." Gabby collapsed to the floor again and it was McCaffrey's turn to cry out. "No!" He whispered fiercely and he grabbed the girl underneath her shoulders and placed her over his own. He turned to the door just as one of the medical doctors was passing in the corridor. Having seen McCaffrey out of the corner of her eye they grabbed the doorframe to stop themselves.

"Gabby too?" she asked breathlessly. Gabby whimpered on McCaffrey's shoulder and he started forward.

"What the hell is going on?" He demanded.

"Brooke and Mary were just brought in." The doctor stepped forward, her training re asserting itself and allowing a calmness to enter her tone. She lifted Gabby's head slightly but could not get a response from the girl. "Come on." She instructed. "Let's get her to medical."

* * *

The white light is pure, uncontaminated by the world upon which it rests. It has always been here... no, not always. It was brought here many, many years ago, close to the beginning, before the green and blue took a hold.

Its form is immense. It has grown unrestricted all this time in the depths, amidst the rock and stone, but also surrounded by water at times as the world changes her own form.

It seems impervious but is vulnerable.
It is powerful but is merely a tool.
It is dangerous.
It is wondrous.
It is here.
We are here.

The noise?
The noise has ceased. It called to us and now we hear.
Hear what?
Everything.
Three of us are witness to this miracle. We see and accept but we do not understand.
There is another here but it does not see, it does not accept. It wishes merely to conquer, to enforce its own will upon this beautiful form.
It does not see us but it will, we know this. It makes us afraid for this one will tear the world asunder and destroy the fabric of all to know its own power.
We see and accept but we do not wish to understand.
One will come and the darkness will fall.
One will join and the light will destroy.
Salvation will come from destruction.
We are afraid! No! No!

* * *

Gabby heard but did not process the cough and sound of shuffling feet close to her. Another noise constantly nagged at her awareness, attempting to bring her up from the depths of restful sleep. Voices sounded in the black surrounding her but they made no sense. Gabby tried to ignore them, she wanted to fall back into the dark and rest.

"Mutating?"

"That's a theory at best."

The word hooked and pulled at Gabby's mind and she rose with the wave of wakefulness unable to pull herself back down to the realms of sleep. The word was repeated though not out loud.

Mutating...

Gabby swallowed and winced at the roughness in her throat. She cleared her throat and coughed and opened her eyes.

"She's awake!"

Gabby saw a person standing next to her and a bed just behind them, not that she was able to identify them as yet. Noises drifted in and out, mangled together to create a confusing garble. A thin tube was pushed against Gabby's dry lips and she automatically opened them. Cold water entered her mouth and throat creating a strange sense of burning but also a sense of relief and satisfaction at the sensation.

More words are aimed at her but Gabby groaned in protest and slipped back to sleep.

* * *

"Gabby?" A soft voice disturbed the night but not the constant beeping of the medical equipment in the room which swamped the gentle question. "Gabby!" The voice changed to a harsh, impatient whisper, followed by a half disgusted sigh. "Bloody hell." The sound of two feet hitting the cold floor were masked by protesting bed springs.

"Gabby?"

"What!" Gabby rolled onto her back and stared up at a ceiling she didn't recognise. She frowned and shivered uncontrollably as panic raced around her skin, chilling it and causing goosebumps.

"It's me, Brooke. Are you okay?" Brooke padded over to Gabby's bed and Gabby relaxed as she recognised, not Brooke's face but her friend's long hair, swinging loosely in the dim light of the room. "They've taken off your restraints so you should be okay to move now." Brooke sat at Gabby's side, dipping the bed slightly and rested her hand on Gabby's arm.

"What?" Gabby shook her head in utter confusion. "What the hell is going on? Restraints?" Gabby raised up on her elbows and pedalled backwards to a sitting position. A quick look around the darkened room didn't reveal too much detail except for Brooke's empty bed and another in the far corner of the room. "Where's Mary?" Gabby leaned forward, lowering her voice and then pointing. "Is she over there?" Gabby saw Brooke's hair flick round as the girl stared into the dark corner.

"She was earlier today but not now. She's been gone at least four hours." Gabby gave a shake of her head again as she continued to examine the room. Next to her own bed was a stand holding an empty IV bag, she checked her arm and saw the red mark and slight swelling where a needle had punctured her skin. Gabby rubbed her finger on the mark.

"What do you know, Brooke? That last thing I remember is arguing with you." The outline of Brooke nodded in agreement.

"Same here. I woke up yesterday with my arms in restraints. Doctor gave me a once over and released me but McCaffrey told me to stay and rest here while you and Mary were still here." Gabby winced as the scab from the needle came off under her fingernail. In all the years she'd known McCaffrey and other residents of the station she had difficulty believing their reason for such strange behaviour was sinister. "Have they been doing weird shit to us all these years?" Brooke speaking the thought Gabby didn't wish to entertain. Gabby stared off into the darkness, glad that her friend couldn't see her expression of doubt.

"No." Gabby stated, trying her best to keep the firmness in her voice. "There's something else going on... there must be."

"Then let's find Mary and see what's what." As Brooke finished her sentence Gabby's attention was drawn to the door. The door was wooden but contained a large glass window in the upper half. A faint light was visible in the room beyond the door which at first Gabby assumed was a desk lamp or a computer screen.

"Gabby?" Brooke gave Gabby's shoulder a shake. She didn't know why but the light fascinated her. There seemed at first glance nothing special about it, it was a soft blue glow emanating from just below the window level of the door. Gabby frowned and while still staring at the glow, reached out to turn Brooke's head towards the light.

"What? Why are you... oh." Gabby nodded though Brooke wasn't looking at her.

"Are you just as drawn to that as I am?" Gabby asked, her voice rising in pitch to match her confusion and embarrassment.

"Yes and thank god you are, I thought I'd have to change my medication again." Brooke half laughed at her own joke.

"Good. Good." As Gabby was thinking what else to say the light moved above the edge of the window and into view.

The soft pulsating blue light continued to rise until it met Gabby's eye level as she had jumped up to stand next to Brooke when the light first moved. Both girls were drawing in rapid breaths and now held hands as they both stared at this strange phenomenon.

"What the hell, Gabby?" Gabby squeezed her friend's hands knowing the girl would be seriously frightened for the effect on her mental health. In truth her friend's distress brought Gabby's confidence to bear as she would not allow Brooke to suffer so.

"It's okay. I see it too, alright?" Gabby pulled Brooke in close to her and placed a hand on Brooke's cheek, she felt the coldness there brought on by fear. "Come on."

"What!" Brooke shook her head violently sending her hair swinging into Gabby's face. "You're bloody kidding!"

"Just take a moment, Brooke. I don't sense anything to be afraid of, do you?" Brooke took a step backwards and stared at the blue light for a short time. She then inhaled for what Gabby thought was a minute before releasing the breath explosively.

"No. I don't know why but I know it's not dangerous." Brooke admitted. "Doesn't mean I'm not frightened."

"I know. But we need to find Mary and what on earth is going on and the only way out." Gabby pointed straight ahead to the door, "is that way."

Brooke stayed silent but gripped Gabby's hand and gave it a squeeze. As the girls moved across the room the light moved further away, illuminating another door. As they reached and opened the first door the blue light dissolved into the woodwork of the outer door and the room became dark.

"I bet I kick something in here, I'm not wearing shoes." Brooke whispered and Gabby smiled at her friend's brave attempt to keep herself moving forward. The girls crossed the small room without incident and Gabby laid a hand on the door handle, as she did so multiple, horrid images flashed into her mind of what they might find on the other side. Corpses, grotesque creatures, zombies, a demon invasion from Mars, a band of penguins running loose with chainsaws. Gabby paused as her imagination tried to convince her to turn back and go to bed.

"You okay?" Brooke's voice was just enough to break the spell and Gabby rolled her eyes at her own form of personal torture she had always endured, an overactive imagination. Gabby didn't reply and pushed down on the handle and opened the door. The station's corridor was empty with the exception of the blue light; it was also the only illumination present. The main fluorescent strips and the emergency lights were dark.

"God it's quiet. Why is it quiet?" Brooke curled a hand around Gabby's upper arm and held on tight. Both girls stood in silence and with the exception of their own breathing no sound could be heard. The soft glow began to move again and this time Gabby and Brooke followed without question. As they walked, Gabby tried to glean an idea of where they were and where they could possibly be heading. The first time she and Mary had walked these halls and corridors

The Core — Gabby's memories

they'd noted the many painted lines indicating which colour to follow to find a specific facility, now however in the blue glow the colours merely looked light blue, blue and dark blue. These supposedly familiar corridors that had been home to the two girls for so long now looked alien, altered subtly to make them feel uncomfortable without knowing why. It was Brooke who actually figured out where they were heading when she picked out a sign in the gloom.

"There!" She said pointing excitedly. "Oh, why are we going there?" Gabby shook her head as she looked from the blue light to the sign and back again, apparently they were heading to the secondary nuclear core housed here in the underground bunker.

The remainder of the journey along the main corridors leading to the core was uneventful but Gabby could not relieve herself of the idea that they were followed every step of the way, and it took every ounce of self-control not to continually check over her shoulder.

Large metal doors that the girls had never ventured through were standing open and for the first time a light was visible beyond the pale blue of their guide.

"Shouldn't we be wearing those silly suits to go in there?" Brooke's voice quivered with nerves and Gabby shared her fear. The core was off limits to the three of them. Only once had Gabby asked to see the core as part of her ongoing studies of nuclear physics but it was met with a resounding 'no.' That answer had led to Gabby attempting entry in the early dawn hours but even after a few years underground, a watch was still rigorously kept on the overbearing doors at all times. Except for now. Gabby stared down the hallway. She wanted to continue and would carry on alone if that didn't mean leaving Brooke behind in the dark, empty, cold corridors. The blue light simply hovered just beyond the door, no longer moving and Gabby was starting to suspect something about one of her friends, at least their location.

"Mary's down there." Gabby stated flatly with a thrust of her chin. Brooke scoffed and opened her mouth to reply only to close it without answering. Gabby grinned widely, in the main as her nerves were still taut, and prodded Brooke. The blond girl jumped slightly and looked at Gabby with wide eyes.

"Yes, yes I think...know she is." Brooke flapped her hands into the air. "How do I know that?" Gabby took one of Brooke's hand into her own and led her forward again.

"Let's find out."

*   *   *

Mary adored Shakespeare. The use of language, the play of the words was like music. When she first read Hamlet a lot of the prose, the meaning of sentences and some of the plot were beyond her ability to comprehend and appreciate. But something drew her back time and again to the story and every time she read and studied it she understood a little more while she allowed the remainder of the story to wash around her like waves on the sand. Comprehension led her to a fundamental understanding that the words she read were about humanity itself and regardless of the storyline it always came down to people's actions and feelings however they were dressed up in Shakespeare's beautiful words.

Mary's passion for his work had never wavered, not even after the declaration of war above ground and then humanity's final surrender. Mary lost a good portion of herself during that time between the pages of Othello, Antony and Cleopatra, Richard III and so on. During that time, she also experimented in writing prose and stories, she discovered she could start a storyline but hadn't the patience or yet the knack to see it through and her small desk was full of half written poems and books.

These thoughts floated as pollen on a warm day, buffeted gently by the breeze as the heat caused it to rise through the clear air. It brought with it however a sense of frustration. Mary was experiencing the world around her through new eyes and senses and part of her was annoyed as she would never be able to describe what was happening. It seemed that the gift Shakespeare was imparted with was not within her.

Mary raised up on her tiptoes and pushed gently at the metal flooring below. The cold she felt quickly disappeared and her feet acting almost separately of her tried to find purchase in the air she now floated in. Mary heard small gasps of wonder from around her and she smiled lazily, enjoying how her actions impressed others. She looked down and happened to lock eyes with McCaffrey. The man who'd become a surrogate father to her, Gabby and Brooke was talking but she couldn't hear his words. Instead all she could hear was a constant high pitched whine which was quite a distraction but as it wasn't painful Mary tried her best to ignore it. McCaffrey continued to talk, gesturing for Mary to return to the metal walkway she had been standing on moments before. She sighed and nodded, not wishing to upset him. Mary faced forward and the blue

The Core — Gabby's memories

glow that had captivated her since her arrival in the core flickered in what she thought was recognition. While descending Mary marvelled at the sight once again. When she'd woken in the infirmary Mary was extremely groggy and unfocused. The doctors had tried speaking to her, she remembered that, but she had no idea of what they were saying. After a short time, her eyes had grown heavy and sore so they'd left her alone. A restful sleep followed although on waking she was immediately terrified to find herself standing on the metal catwalk she was currently levitating above.

The fear passed quickly as she was drawn in by the sight and sensation of the object in front of her. The artefact was at least two stories high. The catwalk Mary was standing upon brought her eye line close to the apex of it. It glowed blue, but it didn't seem to rest on one shade alone. The longer Mary watched she noticed the shade lightening painfully slowly to almost white before returning to the original blue colour, it would then darken only slightly and the process would repeat again. The change in shade reminded Mary of a merry go round, albeit an awfully slow one, with the shades of blue chasing around the artefact in a never ending slow dance to silent music. Peering cautiously over the railing, Mary saw the foot of whatever she'd encountered affixed to a large circular steel clamp with massive screws at least the thickness of her arm drilling into the object, no doubt holding it in place. At intervals moving higher, more metal rods were connected to the blue artefact but these seemed for another purpose as the rods fed into machinery rather than any type of scaffolding.

At this point Mary's fear was drained away and without knowing why she'd reached out to the strange object she'd discovered. Touching it was impossible, Mary's hand fell short by a good six feet but she realised with shock but no alarm that she *could* feel the surface. Mary moved her hand gently through the air and the smoothness the object seemed to portray was transferred to the skin of her hand. She laughed in wonder and pulled her hand back, wanting to see around the artefact, as the catwalk was built in a circular fashion. A circuit of the walkway revealed the smoothness was contrasted by sharp lines that Mary thought looked razor sharp. These lines weren't jagged but rose from the surface, creating smaller versions of the object extending down its length. Mary had paused with a frown as something nagged at her, it was the sense of familiarity or knowing an answer but being unable to free it from the information held captive in the brain. Mary had reached out again, this time more cautiously. Now she felt the power of the thing and the heaviness in the air.

She closed her eyes and instead of seeing darkness she saw the object with a new sense. It looked more than anything like a network of veins, each one pulsing with energy. That energy was transferred into the metal rods and into machinery built around the circumference of the room and disappeared only for more to flow outwards. "You're alive." Mary blew out a breath with a rasping laugh and opened her eyes. The blue light pulsed and now Mary saw the display as one gigantic heartbeat, feeding its living energy into the network of pipes around her transforming them in turn into something approaching pulsating arteries. To the main object itself, the answer had come to her as she watched the power flowing around the artefact, it was simply the size that kept her from recognising it. It was a crystal.

* * *

Gabby and Brooke moved through two more sets of large metal doors, each unguarded and both with signs promising or threatening the weight of the law would be brought down on all uninvited guests. The girls ignored them, there was no law anymore. The corridors remained quiet and the blue glow was still acting as a guide for them. Both Gabby and Brooke had made numerous guesses from the sublime, top secret military drone, to the ridiculous, a fairy. Neither knew exactly what it was nevertheless they both were aware it was not any of the guesses they'd ventured. The corridor began to slope downwards and turn to the left. The blue glow disappeared and the girls hurried on finding that the turn was in fact a drawn out spiral, explaining why the glow had been lost from sight. A short trot brought them back to their companion and they continued downwards. Gabby noticed that whatever their destination was there were no more signs, no offices or checkpoints, just this one long corridor descending further into the earth.

They walked on at a steady pace for a further five minutes with nothing of interest occurring or presenting itself to clue the girls into what was happening inside the core. As they descended Brooke was becoming increasingly tense, her hand, intertwined in Gabby's was causing Gabby quite a bit of discomfort. Gabby continued on without a complaint. The two girls argued a lot and swore a good thumping during their altercations but when each had calmed they carried on as normal until the next trigger. As annoying as Gabby found Brooke they had formed a wary friendship and the two girls shared a certain kinship in their visits to the doctor regarding their mental wellbeing. Gabby knew, as did everyone, of Brooke's difficulty adjusting to life below ground, but the girl was making an effort now and Gabby wasn't about to complain about her hand hurting as Brooke attempted to hold herself together.

Gabby wasn't sure when the sounds started, only that she was suddenly aware of them. Voices from below, distorted by the distance and shape of the corridor droned for a short while and were then punctuated by sharp barks that Gabby hoped were people shouting. Not that she found that reassuring. The blue glow floated on, ignoring the ominous noises and the girls followed until reaching one final metal door. This one, as the others, was open, but it resembled a huge circular vault door from a bank. Large metal rods could be seen housed within the door and in the wall the sockets they inserted into to protect the core from the rest of the bunker. The blue glow stopped at the vault door's threshold and slowly dimmed until the girls realised it had completely disappeared. Hand in hand, with a final squeeze that made Gabby wince they crossed into the core.

* * *

Mary simply could not hear any of the words spoken by McCaffrey and she was starting to harbour the suspicion that he was messing around and moving his mouth without saying anything. The whine that pervaded Mary's hearing increased slightly, making her wince and then stopped abruptly. The effect was astonishing and Mary cried out and fell to her knees, clapping her hands over her ears.

"Mary!" McCaffrey's voice was muffled, far away, drowned out by the machinery surrounding them both. Mary opened her mouth wide to try and ease the pain in her ears, she then held her nose and blew air into them to try and equalise the pressure she felt. McCaffrey placed his hands on her shoulders and brought her face up, his eyebrows high on his face in response to the expression on hers.

"Mary!" With a satisfying pop her ears cleared and Mary slumped slightly in relief. She grinned and gave McCaffrey a thumbs up. "You can hear me yes? Good." McCaffrey released Mary's shoulders and sat back on the catwalk, murmuring curse words to himself as he fumbled a handkerchief from a pocket to wipe the sweat from his face. Mary sat next to him and leaned on the metal railings.

"I think we need to have a chat." McCaffrey turned his head slightly at Mary's request, her voice was different, it had gained a maturity. He nodded to speak and gazed down through the small openings in the metal of the catwalk floor to the audience far below comprising nearly every person in the bunker. He opened his mouth to reply.

"HEY!" Both Mary and McCaffrey came to their feet swiftly and leaned over the railing. The gathering on the ground floor had parted to allow two people, in medical gowns, in. "CAN SOMEONE TAKE FIVE MINUTES AND TELL US WHAT THE PISS IS GOING ON?" Mary grinned at Gabby's shouted question.

"AND WHAT THE HELL IS THAT?" Brooke added pointing at the massive crystal dominating the room.

* * *

"I don't know if you remember but the first day we met you figured out there was something strange about this place?" McCaffrey was sat at one of the large dining tables in the refectory, pouring drinks for himself and the three girls. After Mary and McCaffrey had come down from their high perch normality resumed, as much as possible after Mary's levitating act. Power was restored and light and life once again ran and energised the bunker. McCaffrey had promised answers so one quick change of clothes later had them meeting in the refectory as each girl was ravenous. McCaffrey said he would talk while they ate so he wouldn't be interrupted.

"If you don't I do. You said the plans didn't make sense. Well you weren't supposed to see them on the screen but at the time there was no damage done and then the attack started and the issue was never raised and never felt important enough to bring to your attention." McCaffrey paused while the girls had their plates refilled with scrambled eggs and toast. As they tucked in he continued. "Back then of course I, we, still thought that our time down here would be measured in days or maybe a week or two and all the staff were still beholden to the Official Secrets Act. By the time we truly understood how long we could be here it was a moot point as what difference would it make if you knew or not." McCaffrey leaned on the table and rubbed his already red, tired eyes. He sighed and looked sadly at each of the girls. "You know I've taken it upon myself to be there for you, make sure you're okay, as best as I could anyway." The girls stopped eating and gave each other an embarrassed glance, silently acknowledging that an adult was making them feel uncomfortable with a display of affection. McCaffrey caught the look and he chuckled softly, his smile then dropped and his expression became a mixture of guilt and love. "I would never let anything harm you, please believe me. I had no idea that our 'secret' could affect each of you in such a way." Mary reached out across the narrow table and placed her hand on McCaffrey's, Gabby and Brooke followed their friend's gesture.

"We believe you." Mary chided McCaffrey gently. McCaffrey nodded and looked down at the table so the girls wouldn't see the tears in his eyes.

"Excuse me, sir? The doctor is waiting for you in his office." McCaffrey pulled his hand away and cleared his throat. The engineer nodded in greeting to the girls.

"Thanks, appreciate it." McCaffrey replied and the engineer left without another word. "There are countless documents and files about what you've seen but next to nothing on what you've experienced." McCaffrey winced but it was at the pain of his next words rather than something physical. "I've asked Dr Bilson to debrief you." The girls moaned in unison. "I know, I know." McCaffrey held up his hands as if warding off the girl's disgust. "He's a bit different."

"He's a dick." Brooke stated simply eliciting snorts of laughter from Gabby and Mary. McCaffrey nodded.

"True, but we need his input." Gabby tutted and blew out a breath in frustration.

"Great." She whispered sourly.

The Doctor — Gabby's memories

Gabby, with Mary and Brooke, entered Dr Bilson's office behind McCaffrey. The former officer directed the girls to a small sofa against one wall as the Doctor studied each of them. Their first encounter with Bilson occurred a few days after the dragon's initial attacks. Being of the same opinion as the military, that the situation would be resolved sooner rather than later, he graced the girls with a cursory glance that dismissed them from his current reality. When it became clear that the war was taking a disastrous turn for the human race and the unexpected company would be staying for the long term he left the girls under no doubt that he didn't want them there, they were a distraction, a random vector he had not considered in the construction and running of the bunker. It was obvious to the girls and those around them that the doctor considered the war above ground as a means to an end in testing the facility and human life merely another distraction or variable he couldn't account for.

Now, years later, with the doctor a witness to events in the core, he looked upon them with interest, maybe even a certain affection, but it was the affection a scientist shows his lab rat that he uses for testing. He knows the creature may yield wonderful results and he may care for it but he will be the one who will experiment and test until the creature is dead.

Gabby squeezed herself between Mary and Brooke, wriggling her shoulders for a little extra room. McCaffrey took a chair before Bilson's desk and placed a hand on it, drumming his fingers lightly as he considered what to say. Gabby took the quiet for the opportunity to cast her eye over Bilson. She hadn't seen him much recently but she remembered those initial encounters with a good deal of smouldering anger. Back then he was actually a handsome man, just over six feet in height and slim. His hair was light brown and wavy, his eyes green and piercing. It was his demeanour and coolness however that to Gabby seemed to subtly shift those qualities that created an attractive face to one that harboured a cruel twist. His mouth would smile but there was no investment of humour or humanity in it. His eyes, though piercing, invited a cold stab to the heart rather than a sense of warmth.

The years underground had taken their toll on the doctor and Gabby was quite shocked at his appearance now. If there was one person stuck down here below ground for years who could come out unscathed she would have bet a great deal of money it would be the doctor. The wavy hair was grey and lacklustre, it had not received attention from a pair of scissors for a while and it hung loose and in greasy strands to his shoulders. The eyes had lost their power to intimidate and were quite watery and weak. It was the doctor's weight that shocked Gabby the most, never a man to carry any spare weight, the doctor currently could not weigh more than eight stone by Gabby's estimate. She bit her lip and felt a flush of embarrassment. As much as she disliked the man in front of her she didn't wish him to be seriously ill.

"Considering the events of the last seventy-two hours I think it's time for explanations for them." McCaffrey said, breaking the silence and causing Gabby to jump slightly inviting looks of mild protest from her friends either side. Dr Bilson stared at McCaffrey for a few seconds and then turned his watery gaze on the girls. Gabby at that point wasn't sure which was worse, the doctor's former piercing gaze or the wet, almost excited look he now gave them.

"Full disclosure would put us in breach of the Official Secrets Act." Bilson replied, his voice surprisingly strong and deep. McCaffrey scoffed at this.

"When we take back the surface of the planet and find a government official who gives a rat's arse then we'll worry about it." The doctor smiled and once again it contained no humour.

"Very well. I do have a few conditions of my own." Bilson leaned back in his chair slowly and crossed his hands across his stomach.

"What conditions? We're not here for a bargaining session." Gabby complained before McCaffrey could reply.

"Oh I understand that, young lady. But I must be clear here, this is an opportunity for me to advance understanding of what happened to the three of you in relation to this 'experiment.'" Bilson waved his hand in the air indicating the bunker itself. Gabby gave Mary and Brooke a quick look as she could feel them tensing up.

"Alright." She conceded. "We may need to hear what you have to say but there are limits do you understand?" The doctor's face grew impassive and Gabby tried hard to repress a strong shudder.

"Very well." He stated abruptly. "Are you sitting comfortably?"

* * *

"At the turn of the millennia, two brothers, both miners, were excavating within Naica mine in Mexico. They were one thousand feet down and rather than the conventional imagery of mining as pick axes and the like they were actually drilling." The doctor paused as he opened his desk drawer and retrieved his pipe. He thumped the bowl into his opposite hand a few times before continuing. "The cavern they drilled into was unlike anything either brother had ever seen and as it turned out, nothing the world had ever seen. Now you have to understand that Naica was within private hands, the owners were cautious to the point of obsessiveness over this discovery. They contacted various geological societies, in the U.S, the UK and Europe but were so vague in their communications that their requests for an onsite visit were ignored at first." All this while the doctor had continued to prepare the tobacco for his pipe, all done without him once taking his eyes away from the three girls. "Eventually a university undergraduate was sent, more than a cruel practical joke really rather than an attempt for a serious analysis. The joke of course was revealed to be on the professor responsible. The student discovered crystals the like that had never been found before or since. What you saw within the core is just a cutting of a much larger sample, measuring sixty feet in length and fifteen in diameter at its widest point. Once the university undergraduate impressed upon the mine's owners the importance of such a find they acted quite responsibly, for a private company anyway, and sealed the main entrance to the mine to discourage any looting. I think they realised there's no such thing as a secret down there, especially as the student got extremely drunk in a local tavern and started bellowing at the local traders who were attempting to sell him some small pieces of crystal. The cat was out of the bag and it only took people a short time to realise something odd was afoot at the mine." The whoosh of a struck match made Gabby twitch and she watched in fascination as the doctor sucked and sucked on the stem of his pipe until the tobacco in the bowl started to glow. "More specialists arrived over the next month, many from universities and geological societies and this is the beginning of my association with the find. I'll tell you now that my area of expertise is not nuclear physics or energy production from that source, and you'll learn why soon. In the beginning we were simply interested in the whys and the wherefores of how these crystals were formed. The clue was the temperature and the fact that for possibly half a billion years that particular cave was flooded, it created the perfect environment for such massive growth." Bilson stopped to allow a trickle of smoke escape the corner of his mouth while at the same time he clicked his teeth repeatedly on the stem. For reasons unknown this turned Gabby's stomach and she moved her gaze to McCaffrey, who although knew the purpose of the bunker, had never heard the story from the doctor first-hand and he was enraptured by the recounting. "So all in all, a wonderful discovery yes? Absolutely, to enter that cave is to marvel at nature and her accomplishments, but it was also a grim reminder that humanities effect on the planet could erode or even destroy such natural works of art. You see as soon as the water was pumped away the crystals had no supportive structure and I have no doubt have continued to breakdown." For the very first time Gabby witnessed distress cross the doctor's face, it was fleeting however and vanished as the doctor coughed to cover his emotions. He cleared his throat and tapped the stem of the pipe on the palm of his hand. "Anyway, it was during a sampling that one of the professors on site noticed some anomalies with his electrical equipment. Naturally this was assigned to the ninety percent humidity and incredible heat of the cave affecting the circuitry and dismissed the aberration while new equipment was drafted in to complete the work. It was only after a sample was retrieved, and I'm talking a small sample here the size of a cricket ball if not smaller, that these anomalies seemed to occur again and again to any electrical equipment with the crystal close by. Tests were performed and it was discovered that the crystal was burning the electrical circuits or motors out through the incredible amount of energy it was producing. What's more for a person or any organic organism to be in such proximity would be considered hazardous but here's the rub; it was deemed totally safe to life and therefore it's applications to the energy industry were staggering!" Bilson's eyes shone with fervour from his own words but Gabby could see his eyes gradually dim as he looked about his small office and reality crept back into his mind.

"I bet the oil companies and certain countries weren't happy about that?" Mary asked, not really expecting a positive answer. Bilson nodded and he smiled his awful, false grin.

"We kept it classified but some secrets are too scary, too big for those even in government to handle and naturally those people talked. Working through the legal systems of Mexico those bastard corporations managed to wrest a company from private hands and into their own."

"And no one did anything?" Brooke thumped her hand on the arm of the sofa in frustration.

"What could we do? They'd bribed the legal system and also had so many contacts and members of any government you would care to mention in their pockets it was as if the mine simply disappeared, or better yet from their point of view, it had never existed." The doctor's face once again betrayed the emotion the man still endured after all these years of a great discovery abolished, deleted, taken from the annals of human history. Gabby had to admit to a certain amount of sympathy for Bilson at the moment but then he looked at Brooke's own expression of sorrow.

"Don't profess to know what this loss meant to me, young lady!" And Gabby's sympathy vanished in an instant.

"Actually," Brooke responded quietly, "I was thinking about the loss to the world." Bilson scoffed and worked the pipe back into his mouth.

"So the crystal here?" McCaffrey asked, guiding the briefing back on track.

"Before the mine was shut down a team was contracted to gain a much larger sample and return with it, obviously they were successful." McCaffrey frowned.

"But how? If governments were whitewashing the whole thing?"

"Ah yes but there is always a way. It was a joint task force from a few of those countries sick of being at the behest of their oil rich counterparts, then after the task was done this site was selected for the testing. Unfortunately, that meant maintaining a fully functional nuclear reactor onsite and allowing 'civilians' access." He finished with a dismissive glance at the girls.

"Right." Gabby drew out slowly. "So the crystal is super powerful and you've harnessed that energy down here, I understand that, clean energy blah blah blah, but if that's the case then what the hell does it have to do with the three of us?"

"Its magic." Mary whispered, earning her a derisive glare from Bilson and widened eyes from her two friends and McCaffrey. She met each gaze defiantly. "I experienced something wonderful, powerful but passive." She shifted her position on the sofa to speak to Gabby and Brooke. "No one's asked me yet how I ended up there so I guess it's my turn." She cocked an eyebrow at Bilson and offered him her own look of contempt. "When I woke the doctors checked me out and I acted as if everything was okay." Mary's eyes softened in wonder. "But I could feel something pulling, no not pulling, beckoning to me from the core. You were both still out so I waited until night and made my way down there. Whenever I encountered one of those metal doors or guards, the doors opened and the guards fell asleep right where they were standing!" Mary gripped Gabby's arm in excitement. "The rest is a bit fuzzy, I remember feeling so content, so right! It was as if I finally understood why and I don't even know the question. I wanted you both there," and Mary shared a wide smile with her friends, "at this time I was on the catwalk and I saw a blue light solidify deep within the crystal itself. It floated to the outer edge of the crystal and then just popped out! After that it fled the room as I was thinking about you in the infirmary." Gabby nodded and smiled.

"When we followed it we both had a sense it was you down there." Brooke added.

"What about the floating?" McCaffrey interrupted. "Was that a conscious thing?" Mary held out a hand and waggled it back and forth.

"I don't know. The energy reminded me of floating in the sea with waves gently lapping around me. It seemed natural then to rise up and allow that feeling to take me over." McCaffrey sighed and rubbed his tired eyes.

"I think we have to take it offline."

"Out of the question!" Bilson responded flinging his pipe onto the table, spilling hot ash over his papers. "As long we are here, as long as I bloody well breathe the crystal will not be shut down! There is no danger!"

"You don't know that!" McCaffrey responded harshly. "It knocked the three of them out cold for three days and we have no idea of the long term effects on them and us!"

Both men had locked eyes and both were flushed with anger.

"May I say something?" Gabby interjected calmly, her question delivered in a way that Bilson and McCaffrey knew it wasn't a request. "Clearly we're dealing with something extraordinary, something beyond our understanding at present, but even if you disconnected the crystal it would still," Gabby flung her hands in the air as she searched for the right word, "radiate and continue to do whatever the hell its doing?" Both men blinked rapidly and a wry smile dawned on McCaffrey's face. He turned to Bilson while pointing at the girls.

"I told you they were excellent students." Bilson reached for his pipe and grunted at the waste of tobacco.

"Then we continue and find out. If we can use this newly found power correctly, who knows, maybe one day we can venture onto the surface." Gabby laid a hand on each of her friend's legs and they placed a hand each on hers. "Let's begin." She finished.

Testing — Gabby's memories

"I can sense the energy, even behind these doors. It's strong and feels like a pulsing heat in my chest, spreading out through my blood."

"Are you sure it's not heartburn?" Bilson asked in his usual insufferable tone.

Gabby huffed in annoyance and gave the walkie-talkie she held in her hand a disgusted look. Testing with Bilson had started with great promise as the girls were pleasantly surprised to be welcomed into Doctor Bilson's laboratory with something akin to warmth by the doctor himself. Gabby had to remind herself the man was glad to be in a position to experiment on them rather than any genuine feeling towards the girls.

Testing started simply enough, blood pressure, ECG's, urine samples, height and weight but very quickly more intrusive tests began as each girl found themselves lying inside a massive MRI machine. Mary questioned why on earth is was located down here and the doctor had replied the facility was set up as a fully functioning miniature city and due to the number of people that were meant to be onsite in the event of an emergency it was to have a fully functioning hospital with all the diagnostic equipment plus actual operating theatres. To that end, brain scans were scheduled via CAT scan and EEG. Gabby was quite looking forward to having a dye injected into her and watch it travel around her brain. The same test was to be performed to check blood vessels though Brooke didn't like the idea of having a radioactive substance running loose in her body. The situation was almost a deal breaker for her when she discovered her urine would be radioactive for a short time. Gabby and Mary mollified her though joked quietly about not having to turn on the light to pee at night as they would be glowing.

Tests that began as fascinating quickly became a chore, interest at pouring over images of slices of a body dissolved after Gabby and Brooke began naming body parts to what it reminded them both of in the refectory, much to Mary's disgust. Still the tests continued and were repeated, a variation added each time, allowing for the diagnostic equipment. The girls would be standing, lying, sitting, moved closer to the core when possible or further away. Metals and other materials would then be used as a makeshift shield to see if the energy output from the crystal to the three girls could be blocked or disrupted. In every case the answer was no. Doctor Bilson however was not convinced of the total validity of the tests and results and he required them to be repeated, as the only register they had for the girls being in contact with the crystal so far was the girls themselves, none of the equipment had yet to show any conclusive physiological change in any of them.

With this in mind the doctor suggested the girls must have a passive link to the crystal which, for whatever reason, was not appearing on any of his equipment. His conclusion was tempered by the fact that every piece of electrical equipment in the bunker was specially built and shielded from the huge energy output emanating from the crystal itself. It was decided then to recreate what had occurred at the core with Mary but in the laboratory. Every medical sensor possible was placed on or around Mary as she attempted to focus and channel the energy located within the core of the facility but to no avail and after two hours of monitoring Mary called a halt to the test herself as she was clearly upset at failing. The three friends talked well into the early hours of the next morning, in part consoling Mary but also attempting to discover a solution. It was Brooke who suggested recreating the experiment inside the core but on presenting the idea to Bilson the next day they were told the core was off limits to them, McCaffrey himself issuing the order to protect his three charges, at least until they knew what was happening. With some refinement it was this idea which had led to Gabby scowling at a walkie-talkie. Mary had suggested that Gabby and Brooke were on her mind as she first explored the crystal, she had wanted them with her so perhaps it was a merger, a symbiosis between the crystal and the three of them rather than an individual. Bilson scoffed at the thought, calling it a wild guess and was brought up short by Gabby when she reminded him that Mary had levitated next to the crystal so he shouldn't ignore her. Gabby's own refinement to her friend's idea placed Gabby near the core acting as 'first receiver' of the crystal's energy. Bilson had objected naturally stating Mary should be in place in the depths of the bunker but Gabby wasn't prepared for Mary to become as upset as she had during the test in the laboratory.

Gabby knocked the walkie-talkie hard on the metal door and scratched her nails across the small voice receiver.

"Gabby! What the hell is going on down there?" Bilson yelled from the laboratory. Gabby smirked at his response to her aural torture, feeling only a little guilty.

"Sorry, dropped it. Anyway I'm in place. Brooke where are you?" Static burst into the corridor, echoing slightly. Gabby stared down the long stretch leading to the main facility and a shiver caressed her spine at the apparent emptiness. She imagined the entire bunker empty save for herself and the dark shadows beyond.

"Hello!" Brooke's voice yelled into the silence. Gabby jumped and gasped sending her heart fluttering and a sweat to erupt.

"Jesus, Brooke. Not so loud." Gabby complained, her voice pitching higher than normal.

"Sorry but I'm in place. Just at the bottom of the escape stairs."

"Has Mary moved on?" Bilson interrupted.

"She and McCaffrey are heading into the main station now."

* * *

The operations room buzzed quietly along and had done so without human intervention for these last few years. With everything automated above ground the engineers in the bunker could have easily left the station to run independently, with remote access feeding them a slew of data on the nuclear reactor. Built five years previous to the onset of the war, Elm-sea was technically the safest power station ever constructed. The location of the bunker deep underground made for vigorous safety checks above and beyond the norm. Nuclear technicians who had survived underground were determined to carry out checks one week in four however to ensure operations were carrying on as normal after the war was declared officially over. To that end the room Mary entered for the first time since she'd fled the surface wasn't dark or cold. No dust coated the surfaces and the ceiling and walls remained clear from many an industrious spider's work. Mary bit her bottom lip as she gazed about the room.

Apart from the lack of people it was exactly the same as she remembered, not that it had reason to be different.

"You okay?" McCaffrey asked laying a hand on Mary's shoulder. She gave him a brief smile and nod, hoping to reassure him. Her eyes stopped at the entrance, or to her view, exit from the room and into the power station proper. When the alarm had sounded due to the dragon attacks the heavy, grey metal door closed automatically in an instant, sealing Mary and her friends away from their classmates and families. Mary closed her eyes and felt the sharp pinprick of tears form. She thought of the many nights spent sobbing herself to sleep only to wake a few hours later, groggy and confused but almost blissfully ignorant from lack of sleep as to why she felt so awful. The memories would return swiftly and wipe the remnants of sleep away and a day of loss would begin again. For Mary the lack of knowledge concerning her family's fate drove her to distraction for a good deal of the time. Did they survive the initial attacks? Were they caught up in the conflict that followed? The village all three girls had lived in was a fair distance from the city but an airbase was less than five miles away and Mary would often nightmare that her parents and siblings had sought refuge at the base only for it to be obliterated by the dragon's hellfire while she sat screaming in desperation while witnessing it live on television.

As the girls became acquainted with their new home underground Mary started to notice the far away looks on many of the faces during breakfast, lunch, at work or even reading a book. The person seemed to be focused on whatever they were doing but their eyes betrayed that they existed in their own personal hell. Mary realised that these people, these employees, military or not happened to be caught in the same situation. They also had families and friends on the surface at the mercy of the dragons and the truth in their eyes and expressions Mary recognised was the same as hers. They were lost inside their own version of events. From their loved ones escaping and staying safe, to husbands, wives and children suffering endlessly before the ultimate release of death. Time passed and the medical staff became the number one resource for the survivors trapped underground as they sought relief via psychological or pharmaceutical avenues. Mary for her own part felt no reluctance in sharing her fears and grief with Gabby and McCaffrey as they in turn did with her, it was Brooke who required a more substantial intervention by using anti-depressants. Mary was worried for the girl at the time, thinking the drugs would turn the girl into a husk, a shell of the person she used to be. Time, if not a healer, at least allowed Mary to observe the improvement in Brooke and she received a great deal of credit from McCaffrey for how she would take care of the troubled young lady.

"Mary? Come in? You there?" Brooke's voice asked along with a crackle of static. Mary cleared her throat and wiped her eyes as she focused on the task at hand.

"Yes I'm here." She replied simply, glad that Brooke couldn't see her expression.

"Gabby wants to know if you can go to the vending machine in reception and get her a cola?" Mary chuckled with a bit more force than necessary banishing her remaining memories of that day.

"Tell her we're not leaving operations, Brooke." McCaffrey answered this time on his own handset. The sound of a long suffering sigh came though Mary's handset and she could imagine Brooke gesturing in the over dramatic fashion of hers when no one understood her sense of humour.

"Okay. Let's do this." Mary said firmly, pulling out a chair from one of the consoles and sitting as comfortably as possible. The chair wheels squeaked and squealed in protest after years of neglect but the padding was still in good order so Mary started a routine of deep breathing exercises to relax and clear her mind, actions that Gabby and Brooke would also be performing. The goal being to 'sense' Brooke and for her in turn to tune into Gabby.

Mary tensed and relaxed a muscle with every breath taken in and released. She began with shoulders, bringing them up as forcefully as possible to her ears as she breathed in and then slowly relaxing them down as she exhaled. Mary continued on like this, moving down her body by muscle group. Clenching and releasing until her body seemed to be melting into the chair she was sat upon.

Mary allowed her calf muscles to relax and she closed her eyes, picturing the staircase she and her friends had fled down into the bunker. She drifted past the doorway and saw the metal grids comprising the floors and decks of each flight. Bright yellow lights burned on the walls, two per flight lending a harshness to every texture and shadow. Mary descended serenely, the movement of her mind's eye reminded her of the gentle bobbing of a balloon caught in a small breath of air and in the operations room she smiled. Mary continued, focusing now on a swifter descent to Brooke and the stairs became a yellow blur until she saw her friend sitting near the entrance to the bunker, not on a chair but on the floor, legs crossed with her back against the concrete wall. Mary stopped for a moment to take in her friend's face. When Brooke was sixteen she appeared ten years older, the bouts of depression drawing themselves onto her face, seemingly pulling her features downwards as a match for her emotions. Two years on and at eighteen Brooke now resembled her age, a testament to her friend's and the doctor's commitment to her wellbeing. Mary felt a warmth flush her chest in the operations room and she saw an orange glow expand from where her mind was positioned in front of Brooke. It covered Brooke imbuing her with the same glow. It moved smoothly until it covered her entire body and then it melted into her clothes and skin. Brooke gasped and arched her back. Her mouth split into a wide grin and she looked around the bottom of the stairwell.

"I assume you're down here, Mary?" Brooke asked in a deep tone, one Mary hadn't heard before. Mary nodded and tutted to herself. She moved forward and gently grazed her mind against Brooke's forehead.

I'm here!

Brooke laughed again and this time it was Mary's turn to gasp in wonder. She experienced a wealth of emotions pouring from the girl sat cross legged before her.

You...you never told me you felt this way!
Mary said, half accusingly.

I wasn't sure either.
Brooke replied, laughing out loud at the wonder of the non-verbal conversation and the secrets it had revealed. *No. That's not true.*
Brooke paused and she screwed up her nose in thought. *I knew how I felt about you. I was just scared you wouldn't feel the same. You used to think I was such a bitch.*
Brooke's mind dimmed slightly as she finished, Mary interpreted it as the equivalent of a shy whisper or embarrassment.

You were.
Mary said quite matter of factly, sending a pulse of affection with the seemingly harsh thought. *But we've all come such a long way and now we know.*
Mary stated firmly and Brooke nodded, a smile once again on her face. *We'd better continue. Gabby's waiting.*
Do you think she'll understand?

So, you think I can't hear the two of you from down here?
Gabby's mental tone was filled with amusement.

You bloody eavesdropper!
Brooke accused her friend.

It can't be eavesdropping. This is all in our heads.
Gabby reminded Brooke.

Alright. Alright.
Mary interrupted. *Do you think anyone else can do this with the crystal?*

At the station or anywhere?

We can't answer anywhere. But why us? Why us three?

Mary could still sense Brooke and Gabby as a soft weight in her head. Like her, the question of their apparent joining led to silence.

Perhaps it needs us? I mean you can definitely sense a presence from the damn thing. Maybe it's lonely.
Brooke said breaking the silence. Mary shrugged.

Maybe we'll never know. But it does make you wonder if others at the station have this ability and are keeping it quiet.

What? Like Bilson?

Silence descended once more only this time like a black shroud over the girl's contact as each went quiet with the possibility of another *hearing* their conversation.

HEY, BILSON! YOU'RE AN ARSEHOLE!

Both Mary and Gabby erupted into howls of laughter at Brooke's silent yell. Brooke's high pitched shriek of laughter echoed in the stairwell and all three though separate in location were joined in the warm tears that ran down their faces.
Phew!

Gabby finally said, gaining some control on her mirth. *I think you two need to have a chat, preferably some place private.*

Mary once again felt the warmth from earlier but this time recognised it as affection for her friend standing down near the core.

Agreed!
Mary and Brooke chimed in together.

You know.
Gabby remarked. *If this was a musical we'd break into song right now.*

Shut up, Gabby!

The village — Gabby's memories

Gabby dropped behind the stonewall and into thick mud onto her hands and knees. Her breathing was almost out of control and accompanied by whimpers of fright. Her mind raced with one profound yet simple question at what she'd witnessed and the voice following her.
Sweet Jesus! What the hell? Oh, sweet Jesus, what?
Over and over, speeding through her thoughts, matching the rapidity of the air drawn into her lungs. A breath became a sob and tears spilled onto the muddy ground as Gabby pictured the scene. It was close to midnight and ten men and women, adorned in armour Gabby recognised out of history as that worn by knights but updated for the twenty first century, bedecked with wicked looking spikes and hooks. Each standing with their respective dragons and holding court on a small village of people, survivors of the war. The village itself dated back to the construction of the main farm in the area during the early nineteenth century. As the farm grew, cottages and houses for farmhands were built within walking distance of their place of work. Dirt tracks that allowed the transport of produce to market by horse and cart were replaced by stone and then tarmac as the years went by. To Gabby it was a surprise to discover it. Her trips away from the station to this moment had revealed nothing of the situation of the world above. The maps housed at the station showed the surrounding roads but gave no indication of habitation and Gabby had only noticed it because of the glow of orange fire. A small green, created a century before, was home to a few wooden benches and a war memorial, in remembrance for those young men lost so long ago. It was here that torches had been lit and placed in a large circle, then the men and boys of the village were separated from the women and girls and made to line up in front of a

green dragon. Gabby saw the hopelessness, the utter desperation in their faces and in the way they held themselves. She thought she should feel shame for them, that they would not stand up even with their families close by and to be cowered so. Gabby swiftly realised, as she watched the dragons from her hiding place, how physically overwhelming these creatures appeared up close and that these people had suffered years of it.

"We know members of the resistance fled here and they were offered food and rest." Gabby identified the man speaking but the angle of light from the fire didn't allow her to see any features. "That is not in question and we're not here to interrogate you but merely educate." The figure speaking raised both his arms as if pleading with the frightened crowd. "All we wish is to be as one. That road is difficult, I acknowledge that but I know if we work together a better world can be achieved." The arms dropped and the speaker's head looked down at the ground. "The resistance uses a symbol, quite a famous one used by a gentleman named Churchill and I know many of you are aware of it, especially those of you from the old world. It is my intention as a first step towards peace, to educate you away from using it." As his words finished the first man in the line was grabbed up by two of the larger riders and dragged before the green dragon, his arm forced towards the dragon's mouth. The man screamed, followed by the cries of fear and protest from the rest of the village. Nine dragons reared back on their haunches and sent a torrent of orange fire into the sky, silencing the noise. In the bright light Gabby saw the instant the dragon snapped at the man's hand, taking it cleanly. He screamed once and then mercifully passed out. The limp body was handed over to two of the group standing guard on the village's inhabitants. They laid him gently upon the ground and tended his vicious wound. Many were crying but the majority of the men forming the line in front of the green dragon were silent, but it was not a silence of defiance but of disbelief. To witness such a horrific act had temporarily confounded them all.

Gabby backed away a step from the tree she was using as cover and she felt a sharp pain in her hand. She flinched and gave her hand a confused look as she removed the clenched fist from her mouth, she had no memory of placing it there. In the flickering orange light, she could see her teeth marks curving about the forefinger of her right hand. Another scream penetrated the night and Gabby jerked in shock. Shaking her head, she turned and fled, all thoughts of maintaining cover scattering as she pushed through bushes and low hanging tree branches. More screams in the distance pushed her further and further away from the nightmare she had witnessed. She ran while sobbing incoherently and stumbled with no conscious thought of direction, Gabby simply had to get away.

Plunging through a hedgerow Gabby immediately bashed her hip on stone sending her falling to the ground. White pain lanced into her back but Gabby simply scrambled up again, her feet and hands pushing, grasping at the wet grass for purchase, adrenalin vanishing the pain away. Dimly aware she was now in a graveyard Gabby automatically slowed and scanned the darkness keenly for more obstructions. By good fortune Gabby located a gravel path running through the graveyard and followed it until it led her to the opposite side and a low stone wall. Gabby paused and wiped the sweat from her brow and neck before leaning both hands on the wall and resting.

"Who are you? Speak!" A man's voice rang out in the night.

Gabby squealed in shock and vaulted over the wall, dropping to the ground, her breathing out of control.

"Well, well. What have we here?"

A torch brightened the area instantly and pointed straight at Gabby on all fours in the mud.

A hand grabbed Gabby's shoulder and lifted her up roughly. She yelled in protest and attempted to wriggle free but the grip was too strong.

"Out on a night like this." The owner of the vicelike grip mumbled. "Dragons in the sky and you're running around like dinner." A roar echoed through the night, scaring resting birds from the branches of nearby trees. "Shit!" The voice dropped to a harsh whisper and the torch was extinguished immediately. Gabby was forced back into the mud and held there. She struggled again and felt hot breath against her ear. "If you wish to survive the next five minutes with your limbs intact I suggest you keep still!" The last word was punctuated by the hand holding her down pressing down harder. Gabby closed her eyes and focused on her breathing. As she brought her fear under control she heard a terrific noise from the sky and Gabby visualised a great old wooden clipper, it's huge sails unfurled and whipping and snapping in response to the wind it had sought and found. The hand pressed down on her shoulder harder and whoever the man was holding her down placed his head close to hers. The sails whipped again, closer this time and the truth dawned on Gabby causing her heart to palpitate, she was hearing a dragon in flight for the first time, beating its way across the sky. The realisation froze any reasonable thought she might have had and for what seemed like hours, Gabby was forced to lie in the wet mud trying to hide by sheer act of will. After a few minutes or hours Gabby shivered and felt the cold mud sapping away at her heat, leeching it for its own deeds, and Gabby thought incoherently *what the hell does mud want with my warmth? What will the dragon do to me? I'm scared, oh please help me, so scared. What did McCaffrey want yesterday, Mary said it was important. Who pushed me into the mud.... what mud? I must change the orders for, for...Brooke's birthday?*

Gabby jerked awake, the soft yellow light around her creating a haze that she could not see through with blurry, sleepy eyes. She scooted her legs up to her chest and pushed backwards, jamming herself up against a stonewall.

"Ah, you're awake. Good." A soft voice from the haze reached her. She rubbed her eyes furiously, dashing away the last remnants of sleep. A figure approached her and as she rubbed the last of her dreams away a young man sat himself down on the edge of the cot she had been sleeping on. "I hope you're well rested. It seems you've had quite a night." Gabby blinked and swallowed nervously. The young man sitting close by was clothed in a simple white robe, tied with a black rope. A large hood hung loose down his back showing his curly, blond hair cut to the shoulders. Gabby had been in the presence of many older men during her residence at the station with the only people of comparable age being Mary and Brooke, this was the first male she had met even close to her own age. He smiled and Gabby considered it genuine as it crinkled his eyes and though she thought his face quite plain she had to admit his eyes were large and beautiful. In the light of the cellar she swore they had a faint red cast to them. Feeling heat rising uncomfortably to her cheeks Gabby cleared her throat and looked about the room she had woken up in.

"I take it the dragon passed us by?" She asked quietly, judging by the cool air, stone walls and earthy smell that she was in a cellar or basement of an old house. Her eyes found his and he nodded.

"Oh yes. You're quite safe now." The young man's eyes went distant for a moment and then returned their focus on Gabby. "I've brought you some food and drink. Please help yourself and rest." Gabby frowned as she didn't feel the need to rest but the young man rose and crossed the cellar quickly, leaving her with an open mouth as he exited and closed the door behind him.

* * *

The village — Gabby's memories

Gabby considered herself a polite young lady. The emotional struggles of her past were well and truly behind her. Her abusive, drug addled parents were more than likely dead and despite her declarations of hate for them, she found herself grieving more than she'd ever thought was possible. The staff and military officers remaining at the station had become her family, as well as Mary, Brooke and Dr Eames to a certain extent and she felt a great sense of pride that she'd been chosen to lead the first in a series of reconnoitres into the world above.

That said, she was bored and extremely frustrated. The door the young man had exited through a short while ago was locked and Gabby had resorted to banging on the wooden door with her fists and then, when there was no response, she started to holler, kicks replacing the pounding of her fists. Over her own noise she heard the turn of a key and went quiet immediately, stepping back from the door. The door opened cautiously and the head of the man Gabby had met earlier came into view, his eyes round and eyebrows raised. Gabby placed her hands on her hips and tilted her head, expectancy written in her expression. The young man twitched a nervous smile and entered the room fully, closing the door softly behind him.

"I'm sorry." He said, sensing correctly that Gabby was not going to speak until he'd offered an apology. "I wasn't sure if this area was safe so thought it proper to lock the door. We're still quite close to the village you ran from." Feeling a bit ill-used, Gabby's eyes searched the man's face for any sign of mockery but on seeing only sincerity she acquiesced and offered a wan smile.

"Fair enough." She admitted with a shrug. "Surely they must've moved on by now? I need to get back to my people."

The young man lifted an arm indicating two stools near the cot Gabby had woken on and they both moved away from the door and sat down.

"I'm just being cautious." The young man ran a hand through his hair to the nape of his neck which he massaged eliciting a small groan. "Long night on watch." He commented with a wince. Gabby nodded absentmindedly as she thought about the horrors she'd witnessed the night before. There was something about that night and hearing the cries and shrieks from the terrified villagers that was playing on her mind and not just the awful violence. A hand gripped her knee and Gabby jumped slightly. "Come back. You were miles away!"

Gabby blew out a deep breath as the young man withdrew his hand. She frowned and gave him a penetrative stare.

"Did you ask me something?"

"Two things. Where do you need to get back to and what's your name?" The young man smiled warmly at her.

Gabby blushed slightly at his attention to her and her own inattention.

"Not too far away and my name is Cassandra."

Oh my god! I lied! Why did I lie?

Even as Gabby asked herself she knew the answer. McCaffrey was extremely specific on what to say if during any of these excursions she should happen to meet people and she felt uncertain about her surroundings and that was to lie.

"That's a lovely name." Gabby nodded and the blush that had commenced its journey to her face earlier came on full force as a result of her misinformation. She quickly ducked her head and affected a 'girly' demeanour, hoping the young man would consider her quite taken by his compliment.

I hate myself right now.

The young man leaned forward until he could meet Gabby's eyes.

"It's lovely to meet you. I'm Jack."

* * *

Gabby trod carefully on the small, mossy stone steps leading out of the cellar and into an overgrown garden. Jack had returned to the surface for a look around after their conversation and declared the area safe enough to move about in. As she took in a breath of clean air she stared into the clouds above. A blanket of grey lay overhead and a stiff wind rustled bushes and trees, despite the strong breeze the roof of grey remained as if painted onto the sky.

What on earth am I missing here?

Whatever was bothering Gabby she could not focus or point her mind in the direction it needed to go. Jack turned and gave her a reassuring grin.

Is it him?

Puberty and their teenage years were tremendously difficult for each of the girls. The slew of hormones rushing around young bodies, the onset of periods and dozens of other matters that seemed vastly important to teenage girls was in the main denied to them. The three girls went through the physical changes to their bodies together but the emotional and psychological matters of growing up and changing were ignored by those around them without children of their own and who didn't know what to do with three highly charged individuals. Any women stationed at the reactor with the military had already left, leaving the three with no contemporaries to speak with. The only female left on site was a medic and according to Mary at least two hundred years old. Neither Gabby, Mary or Brooke relished the opportunity to speak of their adolescence with a group of male scientists. The result, as Gabby was appreciating now, was to be entering her twenties and experiencing complete confusion with a member of the opposite sex of similar age. Gabby cleared her throat and looked away from Jack.

"How far is the village? Maybe we should go back... see if we can help?" Jack nodded at Gabby's suggestion and turned away. Gabby shrugged and looked back to see that Jack had brought her to a half destroyed farmhouse. The walls closest to Gabby had survived the ravages of war and time until they reached the first floor then it looked as if a huge rock or boulder had smashed its way through the house, taking away the wall and a great portion of the roof with it. Gabby stepped backwards and she saw the charred remains of furniture hanging on what was left of the first floor. To the left of what remained of a wooden door she saw a blackened figure, small and shrivelled and Gabby felt her heart pound hard, instantly bringing a sheen of sweat to her face. Her eyes widened and mouth dropped open.

"It's okay." Jack whispered behind her. "It's a doll, a toy of a baby." Gabby released a huge pent up breath accompanied by a sigh of utter relief. Jack took her arm and guided her away from the farmhouse.

"I should get you home." Jack squeezed her arm for emphasis. "You've seen how dangerous it is out here and I'm guessing you might be seeing it for the first time." Gabby stopped walking and looked into Jack's eyes, noticing once again how they seemed to be flecked unusually with red.

"It's that obvious huh?" Jack simply nodded at her unneeded question. Gabby smiled at her own innocence and she wondered if she could trust this young man. He had helped her after all and saved her from the dragon searching for her. She looked around and saw, not too far away to her left, a small church and graveyard.

"Oh, is that where you found me?"

"Yes. You gave me one hell of a fright, Cassandra." Jack replied.

"How long did that dragon hang around?" Gabby continued, moving away from Jack slowly towards the church.

"Twenty minutes I guess. You were sound asleep by then." Gabby shook her head as she carried on walking, amazed that her body's response to a life and death situation apparently meant, fall asleep.

"Well if I haven't said it already." Gabby raised her voice as she sensed Jack wasn't following her. "Thank you." Jack didn't reply and Gabby pushed her way through the long, wet grass, veering away from the church slightly and heading for the graveyard.

Now why am I curious about where I fell asleep?

Gabby wondered. Ever since coming up from the cellar her sense that something was amiss had increased but she simply could not fathom what. She took a quick look behind and saw Jack was still standing by the farmhouse, facing her way but not moving. The utter stillness in his form and expression gave Gabby a chill so she turned away and walked on.

What did I miss from last night? Apart from the gut wrenching horror and fear.

Gabby grimaced and she was forced to endure a wave of nausea as she relived the violence she'd witnessed once again. *Must try and get back to the village, maybe I can help and they can tell me what the hell is going on.*

Gabby stopped in her tracks close to the stone wall enclosing the graveyard. One word played repeatedly in her mind.

Village…village…

Why is that important?

Gabby's eyes unfocused as she stepped slowly forward.

Village. I ran from the village to here. That's where Jack found me…

Gabby's foot kicked a heavy object that made a metallic knock in the long grass and she growled in exasperation at the interruption. She looked down and froze. Partially concealed by the long grass was a body. She looked down further at what she had kicked and saw a slim, black tube. Gabby crouched down, sickened at her proximity to what seemed to be a dead body, and picked up the black tube. Glass fell from one end into the grass and Gabby turned it on its end to see a broken bulb.

So this is Jack's torch? Why is it broken?

Gabby placed the torch down and stared unblinkingly at the still form on the ground. Whoever it was had landed face down. Gabby shuffled forwards, holding her breath and twisting her face in repulsion. She reached out and

The village — Gabby's memories

grabbed the shoulders of the body. The body groaned and Gabby yelped in fear and shock. She scooted backwards as a bloody and muddy face was turned her way.

"Christ! Did...did that dragon land on us?"

Gabby started to shiver. The voice coming from the man on the ground was the one who'd startled her the night before.

No. No. The village...he knew I'd run from the village.

Gabby would have never thought it possible but she physically felt her heart drop in her chest as her confusion cleared over what Jack had said to her.

There's no way he could have known...

Still squatting in the grass and listening to the man who'd actually tried to hide her last night Gabby turned slowly and looked back towards the farmhouse. Jack wasn't in sight anymore and whatever his reasons he must've known what Gabby would find over here.

He's playing with me. That sick bastard.

"Give me a hand up, lass. They might still be about and we're defenceless out here." A terrifying roar from the farmhouse sent Gabby and her would be rescuer to their feet together. "Inside!" The man ordered grabbing Gabby's arm, pulling her along. The church and its promise of sanctuary from whatever had created the awful noise was a short distance away. Gabby allowed herself to be taken, the speed and wet grass causing her to stumble. Her anger fuelled her embarrassment and as she became flushed it served to repeat the cycle again, her indignation and outrage causing her jaw to clamp so hard it began to ache quickly. The man guiding her, the one who had truly tried to rescue and hide her the previous night glanced the way of the farmhouse. He drew a sharp breath inwards and tried to force Gabby to the ground. Fear, anger and the adrenaline rushing through her system caused an effect she knew about but had never experienced or given credence to, until now. Time seemed to slow as Gabby followed the man's gaze and though her head moved normally it seemed to take an age for her to execute such a simple task. Sound distorted and as she looked towards the farmhouse she heard the man's long drawn out cry of warning. A huge green beast was flying in the grey, sullen sky. It's wings pushing hard against the air to gain purchase. As the creature finished one stroke Gabby recognised the sound from the night before, it was the mainsail of the ship she'd imagined cruising across the night sky. The man continued to bellow but Gabby paid him no heed. Her eyes had found the dragon's rider mounted close to the shoulders of the great beast. It was Jack.

Gabby did not move. Jack riding on the back of his great, green dragon flew ever closer but still Gabby did not move. The man had given up on saving her as apparently she wanted to commit suicide by placing herself in front of a dragon. He ran for the church doors and out of sight. Gabby couldn't fathom why she felt so calm. Since the first few days of the war she had never faced such a direct danger as this. The green dragon was close enough now for Gabby to see its sickly yellow eyes. They were tracking back and forth from her and, she presumed, the man who'd tried to get her inside the church. As amazing as seeing a dragon this close and flying, the beauty of it was marred by its intent and the look of utter hatred upon its face. Gabby assumed the dragon had seen combat as she saw an extensive wound to the jawline, which had healed, in a fashion, malformed and horrific. Against the backdrop of grey, the green of the dragon gleamed as though the brilliance of its internal fire penetrated through the thick hide. Gabby shuddered and with sick realisation knew she wasn't calm at all, the extent of her terror at such a sight had riveted her to the spot. A cold part of her mind scoffed in disdain that she would stand pathetically in harm's way as terror didn't allow her to fight or flight and instead merely act like a small rodent playing dead when faced with a predator. The green dragon pushed against the air once more and Gabby felt an eternity pass as she watched the dragon slowly tilt its wings downwards, followed by its vast body. Jack came into view and even at such a distance Gabby sensed his eyes locked onto her and nothing else. With the passage of time seemingly the same for the natural elements of the world to erode a mountain Gabby took a step backwards, away from the church and its relative safety. The dragon began its descent and as it flexed its claws Gabby whimpered.

* * *

Whoever the man was standing in the church doors screaming, begging for Gabby to get inside, Gabby wished he would be quiet. As the green dragon swooped in lower to Gabby's position she heard voices from beyond the man shouting and she wanted him to shut up so she could hear them.

WE'RE NEARLY THERE!

The village — Gabby's memories

What the hell is he doing and what has he found?

I GUESS WE'LL FIND OUT SOON.

For the first time since seeing the green dragon Gabby managed to look away, albeit briefly, to try and find who else was nearby. Except for the distant farmhouse, the church and graveyard Gabby could not see anything or anyone else. The voices were forgotten as the dragon screeched as it skimmed the roof of the church, it's eyes and claws locked onto its prey. Gabby's legs buckled forcing her to the grass as her fear reached a level she could not consciously deal with. Gabby's eyelids felt incredibly heavy and if handed a pillow she would've happily fallen asleep right there in an attempt to escape in any way possible. A single blink lasted an hour and Gabby swore she saw the movement of the Earth, spinning its way around the sun in the darkness behind her eyelids. A crackling sound erupted into Gabby's awareness and it reminded her of many a science fiction TV show where an explosion would always cause an electrical fault to erupt, creating havoc and lots of sparks. The man from the church bellowed incoherently and Gabby, with great effort, opened her eyes. The green dragon had stalled its descent and banked sharply to Gabby's right taking it on a long arc back to the farmhouse. Gabby tracked its movement and saw above the farmhouse a seething black hole set against the dull sky. Bright electrical blue energies danced and writhed around the circumference of the dark area, either reaching for the ground or unleashing their spent up charge in the air around them causing small pockets of thunder to echo across the landscape. The green dragon shrieked in defiance at this sight and set its flight straight towards it. Some of the fear left Gabby as she witnessed this and she pushed herself to her feet. Her legs still trembled but new strength was surging through her muscles, responding to the apparent diversion in the sky. As she continued to watch the green dragon close on this hole in the sky a hand clamped onto Gabby's shoulder and she was yanked again towards the church.

"Wait!" She protested. For whatever reason and despite the paralysing terror she had just experienced Gabby had a strange feeling that something dreadfully important was about to happen. Whatever it was it was now going to happen without her. The man was nearly twice her size and had no problem in half carrying, half dragging Gabby to safety.

HERE WE GO!

The voice returned and still Gabby could not place the source. She must've have shouted out as the man turned to survey the land in front of the church.

"Trust me, there's no one else here. Only the two of us are stupid enough not to have left." As he finished speaking they both entered the church. The man released his tight grip on Gabby's shoulder and stepped quickly to a large object half covered by an equally large tarpaulin. With one swift action, he pulled the tarp away revealing a black motorbike that Gabby guessed at being at least sixty years old.

Where is… never mind…down! Get over him!

I'll try.

That's it! Close your eyes!

An incredible sound erupted from outside. It was like the electrical energy Gabby heard from the black hole but this was different. It seemed to build and build to an almost excruciating whine before discharging with one great whoosh of noise.

Did you get them?

"Come on, girl! Get on!"

During the noise and the voices Gabby heard, the man had kick-started the motorbike to life and that now growled with its own fire. He gestured wildly at her to take the seat behind him. Gabby turned to the doors and considered disobeying and running outside to see what sounded like a titanic battle in the air. A roar of utter menace shook the roof of the decaying church sending a cascade of dust to the floor. Similar to the motorbike, it was the kick-start Gabby needed, she backed away and raced to the motorbike. The man nodded his approval and handed her a black helmet. Gabby pushed the helmet down onto her head and grabbed the man round the waist just as he released the clutch and the bike hurtled forward and through the church doors.

* * *

The motorbike seemed to snarl and growl as it was ridden along the bumpy and jolting paths of the area surrounding the church. Gabby had wrapped her

The village — Gabby's memories

arms around the man's waist as they set off as the acceleration nearly resulted in her being left behind in the church with a sore rear end. Over the noise of the motorbike and the restricted view of the helmet Gabby could see nothing of the events near the farmhouse. Clearly something had emerged from the black hole she'd seen form in the sky and whatever it was, was an enemy to Jack and his green dragon. Gabby was tempted to loosen her grip and take a look, mainly as her back felt awfully exposed, but every knock and jolt she felt through the bike's suspension persuaded Gabby otherwise. The bumpy ride across the countryside continued and just as Gabby started to calm the man in front of her turned slightly and shouted.

"We've got company!"

Gabby didn't turn but followed his pointing finger to the bike's wing mirror. In the distance she saw three dragons beating their wings furiously in an attempt to catch the bike and its riders.

BASTARD HAS FLED AND CALLED THE CAVALRY.

I know. Let's track these three. They're chasing whoever was in that church.

GLAD TO.

As the voices disappeared from Gabby's mind she took note of the dragons chasing them. None were the green of the dragon Jack was riding. There was also something else even further afield in the grey sky, barely visible in the small, jumping mirror. Gabby only caught sight of it the one time but above the three dragons she swore she saw a fourth red one.

"Hold on!" Came another muffled shout from in front and the bike bumped and jumped even harder as they left the dirt track for a fallow field covered in rough ploughs and troughs of mud. Gabby increased her grip thinking the man was an absolute lunatic. She peered over his shoulder and could see he was heading for the tree line of the woods nearby.

* * *

As close as the trees appeared to be, as fast as the motorbike seemed to be going Gabby could not help but cringe and cower with her back fully exposed to the pursuing dragons. In every second that passed Gabby imagined a huge talon impaling her back and lifting her clear of her would be rescuer. She tried to locate the dragons again using the bike's wing mirror but the field they were in caused the bike and mirror to jump around to the extent that all Gabby was able to do was hold grimly on, until the man riding the bike screamed with such volume she heard him over the roar of the engine. Gabby loosened her grip and looked over his shoulder. They were at best twenty metres from the boundary of trees so Gabby fought her fear and brought her arms to her front, allowing her to still hold onto the man's clothes. She turned and immediately saw why the man was screaming. One of the three or four dragons chasing them was less than the distance to the trees directly behind them. A vast, scaly grey head and emerald green eyes were focused on Gabby's back and she screamed incoherently in accompaniment with the man.

"He's going to ram us! Jesus! Hold on!"

Gabby could not take her eyes off the approaching dragon. It was not even beating its wings. Petrified, Gabby could still not see how the dragon had reached them and she could not fathom why on earth it would now ram them into the trees!

Shit! That grey one is going to ram them!

Gabby cursed at the stupid voice invading her head making such an obvious comment.

I BLOODY KNOW!
She shouted back. *Now shut up!*

What the...?

The rest of the sentence from her inner companion was washed out as the bike entered the canopy of trees amidst the crackle and snap of low branches. Further escape became impossible as the dragon caught the rear of the motorbike with its nose and then continued to plough into the trees, crashing into large branches, sending leaves and wood flying and knocking down the smaller trees close to the treeline. Gabby was pitched forward over the man in front of her as the bike tipped forward onto the front wheel and she flew over the bike itself.

Sound disappeared except for a high pitched whine. Almost prosaically she noted that her flight through the air was slow and at the same time a blur.

The village — Gabby's memories

She somersaulted and saw the blur of green and brown on the ground melding together into fuzzy patches. Her roll carried on and she saw two black smudges crashing and rolling across the smudge of the ground. They came to a stop much quicker than she only to be replaced by the grey blur of the dragon smashing its way to her. The dragon vanished from sight and the blurry green colour of trees returned with small areas of grey where Gabby could see the sky. The high pitched whine went on and as another somersault commenced Gabby closed her eyes feeling a strange vibration in her throat and an ache in her jaw. It was then she realised that the whine was in fact her screaming.

By no small amount of luck Gabby's arc through the woods crashed her into small branches causing cuts and scrapes on her hands. Some cut through her clothing and raked her ribs and thighs but none seriously. As she landed her body had turned enough sideways allowing her to land on her left shoulder. The impact was horrific, jolting her neck and smashing her head into the ground, denting the helmet she wore severely. A crack sounded and her shoulder shifted with an intense white fire of pain punching into her body. Gabby continued to roll and with every touch of her left shoulder she screamed in absolute agony. Hitting a rotten tree stump stopped her roll and Gabby sucked in deep breath after deep breath, each one accompanied by a sob. She cradled her left arm and cried until a roar from a good distance away dried up her tears instantly.

"If you can hear me, run! Get the hell out of here!"

It was the man's voice, the one who had saved her. Gabby heard the pain and fear in his tone and she shook her head as she desperately looked for a weapon of some kind to help him.

"Find The Grey! Tell them Andas was here! Now go!"

A roar cut off the last syllable the man spoke and then she heard him scream again, only once, only briefly, then silence.

"Move. Move. Move." Gabby let go of her left arm sending a streak of fire into her shoulder and pushed herself up slowly. With her right hand she levered the battered helmet from her head, wincing as new pains from her neck caught her breath. In the grey dreariness below the umbrella of trees she saw movement from the way she had come. She took one more second and then turned and limped painfully into the woods.

Gabby wasn't sure how far she had walked through the woods as night fell or for that matter how long she had been walking. The last couple of hours, or perhaps minutes, Gabby had spent humming a low tune in rhythm with her steps. It also served to keep her mind from replaying the day's events again and again. It worked with limited success. The monotony of walking was only broken when she was forced to find an easier path or she found a root or stubborn branch with a foot or arm and it sent lances of pain into her shoulder and neck causing her to bite her lip hard enough to draw blood and tears. Gabby saw the grey dragon's eyes locating hers and she imagined the gruesome creature smiling, revealing yellow stained daggers of teeth, dripping with blood and torn flesh. Gabby's left foot caught a root and she cursed through clenched teeth as her shoulder throbbed with pain. She lifted her top away from her skin and saw the joint was red and swollen, she laughed harshly without any humour as she realised the vision of the dragon had at least been driven away by the pain. Gabby looked about in mild shock at how dark it had become while she'd daydreamed or in her case, nightmared. The noises of the wood seemed to increase with volume now she was paying attention and despite the fact she didn't know where she was, where the dragons were or what animals might be in the woods casting their eyes on her at this very instant, Gabby found that she was too exhausted to worry. She leaned back against the nearest tree and slid onto her bottom feeling the cold soil seep in next to her skin. Gabby grimaced at the cold and drew up her legs to support her injured arm. Looking into the darkness she began to make out the black lines of trees, branches and bushes, every now and then an animal would scurry in the distance, never coming close enough for Gabby to identify. As her eyelids grew heavy she smiled at the body's determination to snatch some rest regardless of the day's terror filled pursuits. An owl glided soundlessly to the tree Gabby had chosen for the night and perched to find it's night-time meal. It hooted into the darkness and though many creatures heard the sound of the winged predator Gabby was not one of them and she slept soundly.

"Gabby! Christ I can't believe it! I found you!" Gabby opened her eyes and was dimly aware of two people crouched down by her. She was cold and her entire body ached, all Gabby wanted to do was sleep.

"A member of The Grey came to us and guided us here. They said you were in trouble." Gabby heard a small sob and she tried to focus on what was happening. She blinked several times and eventually saw her two friends, Mary and Brooke, fussing over getting warm clothes for Gabby from their packs and then arguing in hushed whispers over the location of the food. Gabby couldn't help herself and laughed weakly at the bickering partners.

"I love you, guys."

*　*　*

Gabby, Mary and Brooke didn't return home to the station immediately. After tending to Gabby's wounds, involving a sling, pain medication and a significant amount of stinging antiseptic, the girls ate travel rations while Gabby told of her adventures of the past few days. When her tale was finished a heavy atmosphere permeated the trees and air, surrounding the three, seeming to shroud them from the pleasant weather on view a short distance away where the tree line ended.

None of the girls wished to speak. Each was aware of the terrible war that was waged when they became trapped at the station, but this was one of their first ventures into the outside world since the beginning. In truth each of the girls harboured secret hopes that when they travelled away from the station they would find everything as they'd left it to the point they would go home and find their loved ones waiting impatiently for them. To have wild dreams and outrageous hopes dashed was a hammer blow.

The sound of muffled footsteps brought them back to the world.

"Who's there?" Gabby despite her injury rose swiftly to her feet only to have Mary step in front of her friend.

"Sorry, my fault. I said a guide from the Grey came to the station? Well he led us here. I asked him to wait while we sorted you out." Mary turned and called into the trees. "Come on in." Mary gave Gabby a comforting squeeze on her undamaged shoulder. A young man came into view striding confidently through the narrow animal paths of the woods. His clothing was all one colour, brown, which Gabby thought wasn't the most logical form of dress for a member of the Grey. The jacket, trousers and even the boots were brushed to a matte finish so there was no hint of glare from the sun's rays piercing the canopy of leaves. His hair was cut short and seemed black when he stepped from the light into the shadows and a dark shade of blue when the light caught it. Gabby frowned as he stepped closer, not that she recognised him, but she sensed something familiar in the man's overall bearing. As Gabby formed a question to ask her friends what they knew about this apparent Good Samaritan a grey rabbit darted in front of the man causing him to curse and roll his eyes. The rabbit hopped cautiously towards Gabby and then sat back on its hind legs, casting what she thought was a critical eye over her. The man entered the space the girls were resting in but Gabby could not take her eyes from the rabbit. She slowly raised her uninjured arm and pointed at the strange creature.

"You can see this right? I mean you gave me proper painkillers?"

Brooke smiled and placed a hand over her mouth to hide her amusement, much to Gabby's irritation. Mary laughed nervously and then cleared her throat.

"Um, yes. You thought dragons were a bit too much fantasy. Why don't I introduce you that might be easier?" Mary held a hand out. "This is Fern." Gabby gave the man a welcoming nod.

"Pleased to meet you. I've heard I have you to thank for my friends finding me?" The man grinned slyly and Gabby sensed irritation flush her face. "What?" She asked Mary, trying to flap her arms in exasperation, wincing as her shoulder made her moan in pain. She closed her eyes and clasped her arm adding support to lessen the pain.

"We should get you home and have that shoulder looked at by a healer." The man named Fern suggested, Gabby nodded and sat slowly. She laid her head back against a tree. A strange thought crossed her mind. She hadn't heard the man move but the voice was from in front of her, in fact close to her feet. Another thought cocked her eyebrow upwards, the word *healer* was an odd terminology to use rather than doctor or medic.

"Mary?" Gabby kept her voice low and soft. "Is the man still standing to my far left?"

"Yes, Gabby." Was the simple answer and it allowed Gabby to draw a conclusion that proved to her she was suffering a concussion or worse.

"Was it the rabbit talking to me?" Gabby heard gentle snorts of laughter from her two friends.

"Yes, Gabby." It wasn't Mary who answered this time and Gabby opened one eye to stare. The rabbit was still standing directly in front of her, only now it was leaning on a stick or staff. It nodded in greeting. "Hello." Fern said. Gabby placed her hand over her face and shook her head.

"No, oh come on. I mean seriously…."

* * *

The village — Gabby's memories

An hour had passed in surreal fashion for Gabby. Her friends seemed quite comfortable that a talking rabbit, and not just any talking rabbit, but a rabbit imbued with magic, was in their midst speaking of what plans to make next. The young man from the Grey kept quiet for the majority of the time, not even introducing himself, allowing the rabbit to speak and only interjected when Fern asked questions of him regarding travelling that Gabby did not understand.

Twilight approached within that hour and the man went about the business of setting up camp for the night. The bundles Mary and Brooke had with them contained bedrolls and more hard wearing food as no fires were to be allowed lest they be spotted from the air.

"We're still in what can best be described as enemy territory," the rabbit explained, "though that could account for nearly all the land of this world." He finished, a dark look appearing in his face, surprising Gabby that such a creature could be so expressive. Gabby was still convinced she'd suffered some form of head trauma. For the time being however, until they made their way back to the station, she ate her food, drank her water ration with a heavy dose of painkillers, relieved herself and settled down for the night on a bed of leaves put together by the man from the Grey. It wasn't cold beneath the trees but neither was it warm. Mary and Brooke placed their own bedrolls either side of Gabby's and lay close to keep their injured friend warm.

"So glad we found you, Gabby." Mary whispered and they both sniggered at Brooke's acknowledging snore.

"That girl was always able to sleep anywhere, though to be fair she used to take a lot of drugs." Gabby commented in a mock serious voice.

"I know you think I'm asleep but I can still hear you." Brooke slurred in a sleepy tone. Gabby and Mary chuckled in the darkness.

* * *

Compared to her two friends, Gabby was the most pragmatic, most practical of the three. Her use of common sense, logic and intelligence was considered a boon by the staff of the station, teenage mood swings notwithstanding, but as she approached the buildings she had called home for the past ten years Gabby experienced a warm rush in her chest coupled with the darkness she felt encroaching on her mental wellbeing brightening slightly.

The journey home proved boring, thankfully, though painful. Gabby's shoulder had improved and the swelling reduced but she feared some permanent damage had been caused. Their guide from the Grey remained mostly silent on the return, when he did speak to tell them to wait it was done so in hushed tones. Their other visitor, Fern, had left the morning after finding Gabby in the woods. She could not reconcile the strange animal into her view of the world even though Mary and Brooke quite sensibly explained it was a world that contained dragons. Gabby conceded she would try and bring some of her sense and logic to the situation but secretly promised herself to ask Doctor Eames to check for any head wounds.

McCaffrey was the officer manning the gate when they arrived and any pretence at maintaining a proper watch at all times disappeared the moment he saw the three friends. He fumbled clumsily and noisily with the chains of the gate, cursing all the while, and when they finally rattled to the ground he wrenched the gate open and sprinted to meet his three charges. His eyes went back and forth all three, checking them out physically for any injuries. When his gaze met Gabby's shoulder she saw the widening of his eyes and the blood run from his face. She smiled bravely for him as he neared and held out her good arm for a gentle embrace.

"I'm okay I promise." McCaffrey wrapped his arms around her head and pulled her onto his chest. He kissed the top of her head.

"Christ, Gabby." And she felt his lips moving in her hair. "I'm sorry. If I had any idea I never would've let you out here, especially alone." Gabby placed a hand on his chest and pushed her old friend back a short distance.

"What's done is done. We have some idea of what's happening in the world now and," Gabby turned to indicate the man from the Grey, "we've hopefully found allies." McCaffrey gave Gabby one more quick squeeze and released her to check on Mary and Brooke.

"We're fine." They both chimed in together, stepping a pace back. "I don't want a hug." Brooke complained. McCaffrey gave them a shake of his head and caught the two of them in a strong embrace, eliciting muffled squeals and complaints. Gabby looked at the man waiting patiently a few metres away.

"How did you know where to find me?" Gabby had wanted to ask the question for the last few days but decided to wait until she felt her feet on familiar soil in case the answer left her feeling as if she could see the spin of the world

The village — Gabby's memories

again. The man smiled and pointed at the building. Gabby frowned but McCaffrey had seen the gesture after releasing Mary and Brooke.

"A representative from the Grey is waiting for us. I've tried to question them but they were having none of it. The only thing the stubborn bugger would say is her name and they would wait for you three, and him, to return." McCaffrey glanced at the silent man, grimacing in embarrassment. "No offence." The man smiled slightly and nodded.

"What's her name then?" Brooke asked, setting off for the gates and home. The rest followed, including the guide.

"Cerys."

* * *

"Absolutely not!" Bilson thundered, his gaunt face twisting with fury. "I will not have the integrity of this site compromised by strangers!"

"'Integrity of the site?'" Brooke scoffed. She gestured disdainfully at the doctor. "Notice how he's not concerned about the *safety* of the site and the people in it! Just his frigging experiments!"

"How dare you, you little…"

"ENOUGH!" McCaffrey ordered to the infuriated doctor and young woman. Both desisted and cast sullen expressions at the other. McCaffrey took a deep breath and pointed at Gabby standing at the sealed main entrance to the bunker.

The guide from The Grey and their visitor identified as Cerys were awaiting Gabby, Mary, Brooke and McCaffrey's return to the surface in the main power station observation room. McCaffrey had decided not to invite their guests into the heart of their 'home' until he understood what trouble Gabby was witness to. Only then after discussing potential risks would he parlay with this new group.

"It's a fact they're responsible for us locating Gabby." McCaffrey continued in a calmer tone. "However we don't know their involvement with the group of dragon's Gabby found. For all we know they are the same group of people." McCaffrey crossed his arms and leaned against the concrete wall, his expression clearly showing the dark worry he felt.

"That's true." Gabby conceded. "But why be so coy about it? Believe me they don't need any form of deception or ruse." Gabby closed her eyes and pictures flashed of the 'punishment' meted out by the green dragon. "These creatures and their riders deal in force, and even if I'm wrong I honestly don't think there's a damn thing we can do about it."

The corridor fell silent as Gabby finished. No one met another's gaze for a short time.

"Then we plan as best we can for both options." Mary finally broke the damning silence. "I hate to agree with the doctor but we can't let on at the power contained down here regardless of whether they consider themselves on our side or not. Does that satisfy you, Doctor?" Bilson grunted and threw a withering look at them all, he then marched off down the corridor towards the main bunker.

"Just be sure you say nothing about what's here!" He called over his shoulder. The four of them watched in silence until the doctor had disappeared from view.

"Dickhead." Brooke whispered breaking some of the tension.

"Secondly." Mary continued with a smile for her partner. "We draw up evacuation plans. I'm sure the military didn't invest in this place without some form of retreat in mind?" All three young women turned to McCaffrey as one. He grinned and shrugged nonchalantly.

"Maybe." Was all he offered.

"*Maybe.*" Gabby said rolling her eyes at her old friend. "There's something we can do, the three of us together. We know how much energy that crystal creates. Perhaps we can learn to channel it somehow?" Mary and Brooke nodded in agreement.

"It would have to be at close range." Brooke reminded them. "In all our tests we've never been able to extend much beyond the perimeter."

"At least it's something for us all to work on." McCaffrey said with a more confident look upon his face. Gabby looked towards the closed door leading to the many stairs beyond.

"I guess we better find out why they were so interested in saving me."

* * *

"Thank you all again for allowing me to stay here while we awaited your companion's return." The woman Gabby identified as Cerys said kindly. "I hope it shows good intentions on our part." Gabby smiled noncommittally and took a seat on one of the old swivel chairs in the operations room, indicating Cerys and the guide should do the same. McCaffrey pulled a chair in close to Gabby and waited for her to speak first.

"You certainly have my sincere gratitude, Cerys." Gabby looked towards the guide. "And to you of course. I hate to think where I could've wandered the state I was in." Cerys smiled and Gabby found herself quite taken aback by the complete genuineness of it.

"Now you'll be wanting to know who we are and how we found you?" Cerys asked, pre-empting Gabby and McCaffrey.

"It is something of an issue." Gabby acknowledged. "You have to admit the circumstances are strange to say the least."

"Absolutely." Cerys agreed. "But then none of you have lived in the world for how many years now? I think you'd have to admit the world has changed beyond recognition for you." Cerys leaned forward placing her hands on her knees. "It has become a terribly dark place. The world suffered enough before the war but now?" Cerys sighed and rubbed her hands on her legs. "Suffering is rife and only a few are spared pain and hardship. In terms of numbers, billions of humans now live under the yoke of oppression enforced by the few." Cerys noticed Gabby's surprise. "Oh yes. Dragon numbers compared to ours are ridiculously small yet they still maintain dominance over the human race."

"But how?" McCaffrey spoke for the first time, shaking his head in disbelief.

"A mixture of things, like the worst bloody cocktail you can imagine. Ferocity, the dragons are merciless in battle and off the field. The militaries of every developed country are gone, or at least gone into hiding so well even we can't find them. And adaptability, we humans do adapt so quickly to any given situation even if that means we're the ones crawling in the shit for a meal. The genius of the dragons and their riders is to make us feel grateful for that goddamn meal."

Gabby and McCaffrey stared at the floor together but both lost in their own thoughts.

"That's why we're here." Cerys added softly. Gabby ran a hand through her hair and looked back up at the young woman whose eyes were now gleaming with resolve. "The Grey are devoted to ending the dragons reign and in part that is why we are here." Gabby cast a glance at McCaffrey who seemed as confused as she.

"You see, Gabby. When you were fleeing those dragons, by chance, it was with a member of the Grey. A friend of mine who is 'talented' when it comes to matters about dragons keeps in touch with our agents and set off to help him."

Gabby put her hand up causing Cerys to pause.

"There wasn't anyone else there. He didn't have time to send a message." Gabby stated stubbornly.

"By radio, no, I agree. But, Gabby I think you know what kind of message I'm talking about here. You've experienced it yourself." Gabby frowned and shrugged. "No matter," Cerys continued. "It'll come to you. To cut a long story short, when my friend came on the scene they detected a very strange energy from you, Gabby. One that was familiar to them but somehow different. Unfortunately, they couldn't stay themselves and search for you and our agent, so I, my good friend here and Fern were asked to intervene and locate you. I'm glad we all had a happy ending, Gabby but I'd be a fool now if I didn't point out that this entire area *reeks* of that energy."

Cerys sat back, her tale complete. Gabby at that moment was glad of the dim lighting in the operations room so no one could see how pale and drawn she knew she'd become. Not only did it make her feel sick that such ferocious creatures were now in power above ground, the effect was worsened by the woman sat in front of her proclaiming quite calmly she knew of the power here if not the actual source.

McCaffrey cleared his throat drawing Cerys's attention away from Gabby.

"Okay you've made your point about being able to sense an *energy* here. As far as we're concerned this is a nuclear power station we set up in." McCaffrey shrugged and sat back with a sigh, affected a relaxed pose. "I'm not in a position to verify the validity of your claims but you know it's just low level radiation you're detecting?"

Cerys blinked rapidly for a few seconds and tilted her head at McCaffrey. After a few seconds more her expression altered to one of frustration coupled with sadness.

"I see." Cerys turned her head to look at the guide. "I'm not one for mincing my words." She whispered turning back to Gabby and McCaffrey. "So I will say this and go. If the dragons took an interest in you as we did it will only be a matter of time until they come calling and please believe me when I say you won't like that." Cerys stood and straightened her jacket. "You wish to protect what you have, I understand that. You don't want it placed into the wrong hands and you doubt if we're the right ones. Perhaps you're right to be cautious." Cerys held a hand out to Gabby. Gabby rose and took the woman's hand in her own. "Regardless of what you might be thinking if you need our help, our protection, just call." Gabby frowned as Cerys gave her hand a hard squeeze before releasing it and picking up her travelling kit.

"Who?" Gabby's throat closed up as if the question she had to ask didn't dare to be heard out loud. Cerys placed her kitbag on the floor slowly and stared intently into Gabby's eyes. She walked forward and this time took Gabby's shaking hand and enfolded it in both of her own.

"It's okay." Cerys whispered. "I can see your terror, your shame at being duped even if it was for such a short period of time."

"Who was he? That man, the one on the bike, he called him 'Andas'"

"In some ways your one of the luckiest people alive, Gabby. You met the leader of the riders and his dragon and survived." Cerys squeezed Gabby's hand with some force. "That's why we think you all and you in particular, Gabby are in danger." Gabby's eyes widened and she felt the sting as unshed tears pricked her eyes.

"Thank...thank you again." Gabby stammered, unable to confide the station's ultimate secret to this strange and seemingly empathic woman. Cerys nodded and released Gabby's hand. The guide gave Gabby a sad smile. Gabby realised she didn't even know the young man's name who'd helped her back to the station. I'm sorry I didn't ask sooner but what's your name?"

"My name is, Blue."

Evolution — Present Day

"You can hear them." Jack/Andas whispered, his breath catching. A fleeting expression of wonder danced across the dragon-rider's face. Gabby frowned at his strange response as she surfaced from the visions of her own memories. Jack pursed his lips before curling them into a cruel smile. "The trouble that one, well two, has caused me. You have no idea!" He laughed in delight and clapped his hands together and noticed Gabby's confusion. "You don't know? Oh, my Gabby you are quite the special one indeed." Jack rose with a clanking of metal and stretched. "And to see you've encountered so many of my old friends." He continued with a shake of his head. "Well that's for later. Let's deal with you and yours. The power my dragons sense from you is extraordinary. They tell me it is akin to whatever energy they use to travel." Jack said, his eyes sparkling with wonder, perhaps even awe as he looked down into Gabby's own eyes. "Thank you for sharing with me. That I can experience your friend's memories and emotions speaks volumes of the power you have at your disposal."

Gabby blinked as she continued resurfacing into the waking world. Jack's invasion of her own memories had caused her to relive her past experiences with great clarity. She remained silent, digging her fingernails into the palm of her hands to keep it that way as she tried to re-orientate herself. McCaffrey had warned her the main problem most people face in conversation is keeping quiet when instinct will be to speak. She cocked her head to the side in false interest, inviting him to continue.

"Of course my dragon sensed it within you in the woods that night. It was faint at the time but it was there. It was unfortunate our time together was limited as I so wanted to show you my world." Gabby's heart punched her chest wall with one vicious beat sending a hot flush to her face. Her lips trembled as she tried to force the words of anger back down her throat. Jack caught the redness affecting Gabby's face and he raised his eyebrows in query. Gabby pressed her lips together firmly and rose quickly to hide her face away. "Yes I know." Jack whispered. "You're old enough to remember the old world. You harbour the anger from the war and what you've seen out there." Jack moved towards the hanging cloth acting as a door and lifted it letting in the aroma of the sea. "Change was necessary. Revolution was my gift to my dragons and humanity." He said, staring out at the power station. "And now I sense yet another change in the offing. A potential to end humanity's enduring arrogance that they can retake this planet." He turned and his lips curled into a smile. "You see I don't remember the old world. Through others I know what the human race had become. Controlled by an elite or governed by corporations. You all lived in a world that allowed children to starve, fought countless wars over resources to be perpetrated in the name of freedom. For people to live on the streets of the wealthiest countries." Gabby faced him and for the very first time she saw the malice, the malevolence and utter hatred he felt for his own race. "The Grey will be next. From your contact with them I see they mean very little to you."

Gabby's heart would not slow. Her determination to extend the dialogue was wavering far sooner than she wished. As Jack's words ended they came out her unbidden, unwanted but necessary.

"Yes I remember the old world. My life was shit. My parents were shit. I didn't give a damn about anyone." Gabby's vision swam, pulling Jack in and out of her focus, as unshed tears filled her eyes. What she saw of his reaction repulsed her further. His expression was one of understanding, and he reached out to share his empathy with this similarly tortured soul. Gabby dashed the tears from her eyes with her wrist. "You think we're the same?" She asked in a deathly whisper causing him to recoil in shock at his misreading of Gabby's emotions. "I was lucky. My carers were good people. My foster parents were good people. I met an extraordinary friend." Gabby emboldened by her indignation strode forward to join Jack at the pavilion opening. She faced him and pointed at the station. "In there I met more. And you...you took it all away. That day. That memory still causes me sleepless nights but those are better than the nightmares that come when I do sleep." Jack backed away from Gabby a step, his face pale and drawn. "And yes the world was a shit hole as well. Innocent men, women and children suffered daily for the excesses and greed of others. People were fuelled by fear and hatred of each other by the very politicians who were expected to make a stand and do what's right." Gabby sneered at the man before her. "That still doesn't give you the right to act as you have."

"I thought you were different, when we met I sensed something in you that reminded me of something I lost."

"Perhaps I reminded you of your humanity." Gabby spat, shaking her head and turning away from him in disgust, all her pretence at staying civil according to her plan, gone.

"There is not one day that passes that my only wish is I couldn't end the scourge of the human race from this planet a day sooner. There is something inside you, something inside that station that I need to finish this." Jack reached out and gripped Gabby's upper arm causing her to cry out in pain. He pulled her in closer until his nose was almost pressing against hers. "You will take me to it or I will kill every last soul in that building." Jack tightened his grip and Gabby gasped in pain. "Decide!" He ordered giving her a small shake. Gabby grimaced in pain and nodded. Jack loosened his grip, allowing her to stand straight. She calmed her breathing, slowing her heart rate, allowing the anger that had possessed her to disperse as it was no longer useful here. "Well?" Jack barked, his brows drawing together in frustration. Gabby slowly raised her free arm and placed a finger to her lips.

"Shush. I'm deciding." Even though she didn't think it possible Jack's brows drew even nearer to one another. A humming sound suddenly pierced the air and Jack instantly released Gabby and left the pavilion his eyes searching the sky for the location of the noise. Gabby closed her eyes and smiled, this was the most dangerous part of her plan as she was completely defenceless but if it allowed the station to survive even ten minutes longer she thought it worthy of the risk. Calmly she allowed her senses and mind to open themselves to her two friends, Mary and Brooke inside the station. She found Mary within the operations room, sitting quietly and chewing on a fingernail. Gabby paused and Mary smiled as they joined. On the two travelled, through the door and down the many stairs to the facility they had called home for so many years now. As swiftly as light they traversed the entire bunker, their destination the core. They entered and saw Brooke waiting impatiently beside the object responsible for their joint power, the crystal. Gabby and Mary, together, grazed Brooke's mind and she merged with them. Gabby was immersed in the love her two friends felt for one another and the love they both had for her as their friend. Back inside the pavilion, tears ran down Gabby's cheeks, but not in fear or anger now, but for love.

"What are you doing?" Jack demanded, his entire personae altered and his true self showing. Gabby opened her eyes and despite the calmness she felt within she experienced a surge of fear. His face was almost white, cast with a green tinge. His eyes were now completely red and they swirled and danced, seemingly dipped in blood. Gabby thought it a trick of the light but his jaw appeared to jut out further.

"I'm defending my home." She replied and pointed above her. Jack peered up as a white, almost translucent shell rose from the ground near the main gate and the perimeter fence of the station. The buzzing sound intensified and the shell continued higher into the air, curving swiftly over the station until it had formed a dome of soft white light. Gabby breathed out in relief, fully aware however she was now standing on the wrong side of the barrier.

That'll take the lead out of his bits.

Mary commented dryly.

Snaps and cracks disturbed the buzzing in the air and Gabby stepped backward quickly as Jack screamed in defiance at the sky. He hunched over violently as the cracks continued to puncture the air around him and he dropped to all fours.

Gabby! What the hell is going on!

Mary's and Brooke's voices were merged adding weight to the call. Gabby shook her head as Jack continued to scream in agony. She dashed for the opposite side of the tent and hauled back the entrance. The dragon army, both beast and rider were standing, waiting rather than attempting to aid their leader.

Oh shit! I don't know. What…I…sweet Jesus, he's changing!

Gabby cried out in her mind and out loud. Jack reacted to the noise and his head came up. Gabby could plainly see that no trick of the light could explain what she saw. Jack's cruelly handsome face was gone. The jaw was stretched a good six inches from the nose which itself had flattened out. The forehead had shrunk or tilted backwards and a bony ridge had swiftly formed above Jack's eyes. The eyes were still red but had sunk deep into the skull. Gabby couldn't be sure but he seemed to be grinning at her.

"This is why I'm here. This is why I wanted you and your power, it is pure." He growled and long strands of saliva fell to the ground. "I cannot use my dragon's energy fully, but yours," Jack chuckled but the sound was a gurgle, "oh your power will help me, help all of us transform into beauty." A huge crack sounded from Jack's spine and his scream caused Gabby to slap her hands over her ears. It continued on and on until his voice gave out. The silent scream went on and as he pounded the ground Gabby saw his fingers extend and his hands flatten into pads.

He's trying to merge dragon and human!
Gabby called out, a wave of nausea passing through her.
So that's it. That's what he wants.
A new voice commented in a measured tone. But Gabby realised it wasn't a new voice. She'd heard it the first time during her race to get-away from Jack. Jack collapsed to the ground, his strength spent. Gabby gave the army waiting not one hundred meters away a quick look, they still maintained their vigil in silence.

What do we do now?
Gabby sent to Mary and Brooke. *It's not as if we planned for this!*
Though neither responded Gabby could sense their confusion and inability to form a cogent response. Jack twitched and Gabby jumped back a step. She groaned with indecisiveness. With the barrier in place, the station was safe for the time being. She had hoped this might lead to more time for the evacuation as she continued a dialogue with the person on the ground before her, now she was completely at a loss as to how to proceed. One thing was clear however, Jack could never be allowed to enter the station whatever the cost.

Jack groaned and a transformed hand groped along his back. Gabby shook her head as she noticed ridges pushing against his riding clothes. A talon flicked out and sawed through part of the material, then with a huge shrug of his shoulders Jack came to his knees causing the clothing to tear and a haggard, deformed pair of wings to emerge from his spine. Gabby acted instinctively, while she watched in horror at the gruesome spectacle before her she stumbled sideways, out of the pavilion and towards the station.

Gabby! You have to calm down otherwise the shield will fall!
Mary's desperate tone tore Gabby's gaze away from Jack. She eyed the shield only just erected and immediately saw several parts 'thinning,' in response to her panic.

I can't! I can't!
She sobbed as more snapping of bones from Jack's direction made her flinch and hunch her shoulders. The shield wavered for a few seconds more as if

somewhere a switch was repeatedly switched on and off in rapid succession, and then evaporated completely. A roar of triumph brought Gabby to her knees. Jack stood, or tried to stand. One leg was bent backwards from the knee, driving the foot toes first into the ground. The other was normal in all except size. The muscles in the thigh and calf were distended, bulging hideously against the leather of his riding trousers. As with his spine, Jack released a single talon and carved a line down the front of the leather, allowing the gross muscles to bulge outwards and blood to gush down his leg where his talon had shredded skin. All the sights and experiences the world had offered Gabby could in no way prepare for the visceral sight of a man transforming, or at least attempting to transform, into what resembled a dragon. Jack's magenta eyes wept blood from the pain induced by his body, but his mouth held a hideous grin.

"This is what I sought for all!" The voice was mangled by the elongated jaw and the blood rushing from broken vessels within Jack's face causing a deep throated gurgle. "You have the power I need within that building and I shall have it! Give it to me or I will drag every last one of your companions out here and nail them to the floor for my rider's and dragon's pleasure!"

So much for honour amongst dragon riders.

The voice not belonging to Mary or Brooke remarked laconically, totally unfazed at the sight that stole Gabby's strength from her legs.

You've done your best, Gabby. But now it's our turn and regardless of what happens this day it will end one way or the other.

Gabby nodded numbly and felt some of the dread dissipate by the calm words of the stranger, spoken in her mind. Jack stumbled forwards, catching himself on his unaffected arms. He bellowed unintelligibly over his shoulder and a squad of soldiers responded by setting off in his and Gabby's direction. His eyes never left Gabby as he slowly, carefully pushed himself up.

"Your defence is gone. I thought we had a connection you and I, and I'd hoped for a peaceful resolution. No matter." Jack spat and black blood splattered the ground. "You and your friends have nothing." He stumbled forwards once again, quickly figuring a method of locomotion with his new limbs. "You and your friends are nothing. Just like the rest of your pathetic race! You have no one. There is no help, no aid coming and there is no god except me to offer you salvation!" Jack was less than six feet away and Gabby's breathing was so rapid her chest was light and she was unable to look away from the creature before her.

"So what is your answer? Cower and live or stand and die?"

Gabby's lips trembled and Jack watched with morbid anticipation, waiting for her response. He lifted himself upright and flexed his massive hands, now altered to large pads, and flicked talons outwards in readiness. Gabby bit her lips together and felt the sting of tears as her dread, for herself and her friends occupied her thoughts. The tang of blood entered her mouth. Gabby already knew what her answer was to be and the taste of her own blood painted the words she spoke.

"Neither." Gabby said, her voice harsh from fear. As the word left her lips she found herself standing straighter. The weight of the moment was gone and despite the horror in front of her Gabby realised she was more afraid of failing to honour her friends and the millions of people left on this world and the billions whose desiccated bodies littered it still.

Jack tilted his head in brief confusion, as if the word had no meaning or it hadn't been spoken at all. Even without his human eyes Gabby saw the moment comprehension formed in Jack's red orbs. His face twisted, not in anger but agony. That his moment must wait. That this one human whom he'd discovered a brief connection with was exactly like the majority of every single one of her race, defiant.

The squad of soldiers were at the pavilion awaiting orders and now Gabby could see the expressions they wore. Horrid fascination mixed with true fear. The fear so pure that every single one of them was now contemplating desertion or adulation.

Gabby took a step back but Jack reacted instantly and lunged forward on his new legs. His talons were aimed at Gabby's chest and Gabby knew in an instant she couldn't dodge their wicked sharpness in time. She wanted to close her eyes but couldn't. Her gaze fixated on the points of the talons and she wondered if they were sharp enough to penetrate her without hurting.

Jack's distorted face came into view as his body was at full stretch behind his arms. He was whispering or shouting at Gabby, she couldn't be sure, though the words were simple enough to understand.

"Then die!"

NO!

NO!

Gabby's friends screamed in unison from inside the facility into her mind at such volume it should've made her cringe from the assault on her senses.

To Gabby they were two voices lost in the wind but one voice came through powerfully.

GET THE HELL AWAY FROM HER!

Gabby was rocked backwards slightly from the impressive power of the voice and she sensed rather than saw the enormous figure rear up from behind Jack. Two great paws grabbed Jack's shoulders and halted his deathly lunge towards Gabby instantly. Claws snapped around his arms pinning them down and Jack screamed in defiance at losing his quarry. He was lifted and Gabby caught a flash of red skin from whatever was attacking Jack. With one fluid movement Jack was hoisted thought the air and launched towards the pavilion. The soldiers watched dumbfounded as their leader crashed into the apex of the large tent bringing it crashing to the ground and enveloping him.

Gabby shook her head as she tried to process events as swiftly as possible. She slowly looked away from the collapsed tent and the soldiers attempts to cut it open to release Jack. A growl and puff of black smoke made her jump and she found herself staring at a red, scaly face. The jaws were huge and held daggers for teeth. Her eyes drifted upwards and found the creature's eyes swirling with many colours. The creature lowered its head and Gabby saw a human sitting astride the spine of this enormous red dragon. They were dressed in what Gabby identified as rider's clothing, soft leather jacket and trousers but these were dark brown and not the standard black associated with dragon riders. The face was covered by goggles and a piece of headgear that enclosed the remainder of the face and hair except for the nose and mouth. The rider leaned forward and offered Gabby a gloved hand.

"You must be, Gabby. I believe you know Cerys and Blue?" A woman's voice asked. A voice that sounded strangely familiar.

An infuriated scream reached Gabby from the collapsed pavilion and the rider waved her hand impatiently at Gabby. "Come on, I haven't got all day. We're the Grey Rose. We're here to help as promised." Gabby laughed, half crazed that she was still alive and being offered help from the very people she'd denied assistance to and from. She grasped the offered hand and was pulled up by the rider and assisted by the dragon's leg pushing her up. Before taking her place behind the rider, Gabby paused and crouched down.

"I'm sorry but who on earth are you?"

The rider smiled and removed her goggles, revealing large, dark brown eyes that seemed familiar. She reached down and gave the dragon's spine an affectionate rub as if the army closer than five hundred meters away didn't exist.

"This beautiful guy is Cole." To that the dragon nodded a greeting which Gabby returned, completely flummoxed at the whole situation. A host of roars, growls and bellows sounded from the sky surrounding the station. The dragon named Cole turned in a circle to give Gabby and his rider a full view of the great mass of dragons circling high above them. Gabby cowered against Cole's back as the full enormity of the situation turned her thoughts dark. A hand was placed under her arm and she was lifted to face the rider. With a free hand the rider pulled off her head covering, releasing long, brown curls to her shoulders. Gabby saw scars about the face and head, previously hidden.

"Don't worry." She said with a terrible grin full of hatred. "They're with me." Gabby looked up again and saw the dragon's circling in closer to the station. Some landed while others took up positions above the highest buildings. "It's them you have to worry about." As the rider said this, a slew of horns interrupted the trumpeting of the dragon's near Gabby causing a new hoard of dragons to rise from Jack's army. More dragons appeared in the sky but away from the station this time. They glided in to land with the main army. The rider pulled Gabby onto the dragon's back to a sitting spot behind her.

"Okay, my love. Up we go." The dragon tilted backwards and Gabby sensed the enormous power the creature contained within its back legs. The energy was released and Gabby's stomach turned over as they left the ground forcing her to grab the woman's back. Gabby frowned, the world momentarily forgotten as she realised she'd grabbed the leather scabbard of a massive sword. The dragon's wings thrust strongly against the air, bringing Gabby back to her situation and they swiftly attained height above the station.

Gabby are you okay?

Mary screamed and Gabby became aware that her two friends had been shouting at her continually since the red dragon had appeared. Not able to trust even her inner voice Gabby merely squeaked in reply.

Dragons soared, dipped and turned all around her. Their colours were many, but all were massive, dwarfing any creature Gabby had ever encountered up close.

"Oh I'm sorry, Cole tells me I'm being rude." The rider said over her shoulder, half turning so Gabby could see her profile. "I'm Ellie. Pleased to meet you."

Gabby's eyes widened at such a casual introduction but then she caught Ellie's cold expression in profile as the rider leaned over Cole's shoulder and studied the army ranged against them.

The red dragon bellowed and every dragon close to the station circled in close or lifted from the surface to rise and meet them. Gabby saw dragons of so many colours she laughed in nervous fright at the sight. Two beautiful blue dragons coasted in on either side of the dragon named as Cole and trumpeted a greeting. Gabby saw one dragon to her left was rider-less but she recognised the rider to her right.

"Blue!" The woman sat in front of Gabby called out. "Have the wings form up on Lapis and Lazuli." The rider named Blue let his eyes briefly meet Gabby's before he disappeared beneath the red dragon.

"What the hell is going on?" Gabby screamed.

"Cerys told you to call for help and you did."

"What?"

"Just sit back and listen okay… but not with these!" Ellie pointed a finger at her ear. Cole tipped forwards and Gabby's stomach lurched. Every dragon was now set behind the red dragon and split into two groups with each of the blue dragons at the fore.

Riders of the Grey Rose. We will not cower in the face of death. We will not stand aside and allow tyranny to prosper unchecked anymore. The lives of the people here depend upon us even though our lives may be forfeit, but that is true of all when the time comes and nothing, no power on earth can stop that!

For every one of us they take, we will take five. For every inch of ground they take, we will take five more of them.

Remember what they've taken. Remember what they've destroyed and make a vow on this day to bring about their ruin!

Gabby heard cries and yells of defiance and jubilation from behind her. All the while her own mouth was wide open in astonishment as she recognised Ellie's 'voice' in her mind.

"You were the fourth dragon in the sky when I escaped on the motorcycle?"

"I've been watching you for a while, Gabby." Ellie called over her shoulder. Before Gabby could answer a massive wall of noise sounded from the army camped opposite. Hundreds of dragons took to the air, each screeching their own battle cry.

"Cole." Ellie ordered. "Let's get this over with."

Epilogue — The Prisoner

The woman's first waking breath was a scream. But no noise resulted from her act of fear. The unheard scream altered to a whimper of panic and her eyes frantically shifted left and right for any indication of what was happening. The room was still in darkness and though vague shapes were visible to her the woman could make no sense of them. A cold sweat enveloped her body as terror, the like she hadn't experienced for many years, took a tighter hold. Responding to the instincts of her youth she tried to turn, compress her body into a small knot but failed as she discovered her limbs were paralysed. Tears of outright panic streamed into her ears and she thrashed her head about, clenching her teeth, making small tight sounds of horror as her body failed to obey her commands. Imagination took over and during her ceaseless thrashing she saw movement in the darkness. The woman became completely still in an instant, her eyes fixated where she thought something had moved. Feeling exposed and totally vulnerable her breathing responded by quickening. She tried to clamp her mouth shut to stop the short, sharp breaths from being heard but they simply forced their way out through her nose. Tears of panic transformed into tears of near hysteria as she detected more movement, a swift sliding of something tall. With her last ounce of reason, the woman cried out into the darkness of her mind.

HELP ME!

ELLIE! ELEANOR! WHAT'S WRONG? WHAT'S HAPPENING?

Lights flickered and then snapped into harsh life. Eleanor squinted and turned her face away from the glare. A loud thump brought her attention into focus and her body back under her control. Another thump and with adjusting

Epilogue — The Prisoner

eyes Eleanor saw a guard standing with a frown at her cell door. He glanced to his side quickly and an intercom crackled to life.

"Are you okay?" The man's tinny voice echoed slightly in the room. She nodded, the reality of her situation dispelling the terrors of the night as swiftly as they had taken hold of her. The guard nodded and Eleanor managed a small smile of appreciation. Despite her position here she and her various guards made the best of a bad situation and knew each other fairly well.

ELLIE! WHAT'S GOING ON?

Eleanor's smile widened as Cole's voice warmed her mind.

I'm sorry, my love. The dreams have started up again.

She explained

I THOUGHT AS MUCH.

Cole replied quietly. *I could feel your distress and was able to 'see' some of it.*

Eleanor rose from her small bed and stretched the kinks and small cramps from her waking body. The dreams had first started approximately a year ago. Their intensity and frequency had lasted six months before finally fading to be replaced with more mundane dreams. During that time Eleanor had documented each dream as their detail and realism seemed to dismiss any notion that these were just night terrors visiting her. Eleanor's hypothesis was correct when the Institute themselves investigated when one of their local spotters' detected energy that apparently had no source that would appear each time Eleanor slept. She was questioned as they obviously believed it was some kind of ploy or escape attempt, but as time went on and Eleanor's notes and diary were analysed they accepted she was as much in the dark as them. The content of her notes however were dismissed and the documents confiscated.

This must mean something.

Eleanor continued striking her fist into her other hand. *But it's all coming out of order.*

Cole was silent but Eleanor could sense him listening patiently as she worked through the problem.

Eleanor nodded and looked about her cell. White, durable plastic for the most part, furnished with a bed, chair and desk. The desk held her current personal task. Stacks of paper, all filled with her neat penmanship detailing her life. She moved the few paces required to get to the desk and carefully shifted her work to the side before pulling out a clean sheet of paper.

I need to get the Institute's attention.

Eleanor told Cole, tapping her fingers on the desk. *Otherwise I think something much worse than them is coming.*

End of Book One of The Lucent Series.
In book two Eleanor must try to understand her dreams of Ellie and Gabby and what they mean to the survival of humanity.

Afterword

Hello to the end of the first book in the Lucent Series.

I thought I'd take a small opportunity here to write about how this novel came about. As always if an author prattling on about their own work is as dull as the proverbial dishwater to you please close the book or app and thanks for reading! (If you could leave a review it would be much appreciated)

Onwards brave souls.

With the conclusion to the Baiulus Series my initial inclination was to immediately continue the story of Ellie, Rox and Cole et al. I started to write the follow on story of how these characters would combat the Institute and an entire world of talented, and developed quite a lot of the first act when I read an article and subsequently watched a documentary regarding a 'cold spot' in the universe and why it exists. For a writer the most outstanding theory was this area of space as I've described in the book is the imprint of a universe next to ours.

I stopped work and started making notes and reading more about parallel universes, multiverses, paradoxes and so on. The idea of a choice leading to many outcomes is not a different one in literature and film but I decided I wanted to apply this to my story. Significantly I wanted to use it in relation to my characters, take one moment that was crucial in their history and change the outcome and see where that took them. Suffice to say I made everything that went right before go completely wrong this time around and developed the story from then on (this will be revealed in more detail in book two, sorry about that). It also meant casting aside the first act I'd written for the moment as I predict I won't actually require any of that material until the last book in the series.

Work on this new series went very well but I encountered a 'nice' problem. At 100,000 words (and growing) the book was too big, had too many concepts and way too much journeying from the present to the past and back again. I thought I might've overdone it for this book alone! I made a choice to completely eliminate my main character from the story until the very end as Ellie's history is too rich and deserving of a lot more attention than I could give her here. This brought Gabby, Mary, Brooke and Blue to the fore and I hope their story is worthy enough to stand alone.

This book also marks a departure in how I approached the writing. For The Seren Trilogy and Baiulus Series each book was written in order and I never 'jumped' around different parts of the book, finishing the middle before the beginning for example. This book however was written so each chapter could be effectively moved at my will to any place in the narrative and hopefully maintain the same cohesion. As fun as the experiment was it gave me headaches I was constantly changing my mind on who and what should go where, who was more important, what information should be given to the reader at any given time. Suffice to say, I made my bed and lay in it. I just hope it's an enjoyable read.

Well back to it. I'm currently working on book two and all the headaches and moments of joy that writing brings.

Thank you.

Darren Lewis
November 2016

About the Author

As I'm sure every author on the planet would say, 'I love reading.' In fact, it's not just love, it's a passion. Some of my earliest memories are of reading school books to my parents and then speaking about those stories to my teacher.

I consider myself extremely lucky to have a family that share this passion and by the time I was ten years old, I believe my parents had a book collection that could be counted in the high hundreds. Their collection ranged from horror to science fiction, romance to thriller and at a young age I was allowed to read some of the more 'adult' books by Dean Koontz, Stephen King, Isaac Asimov and so on. If I could take one thing away from that experience, it was that I never considered myself too young to read these authors.

My first real love affair with an author happened at thirteen years old when I read a book of my brother's entitled 'The Pawn of Prophecy' by David Eddings. I was enraptured, captivated I suppose, and wanted to read every single book of the series in one go. Here was the problem, however. I had bought my own copies except for book three of a series of five and I'd just finished book two. My older brother had a copy and it's an unwritten rule of the house that whoever buys a book reads it first... no exceptions.

So what did I do?

I waited until my brother went out for the day and stole away to his bedroom and 'borrowed' his copy. I read that book in six hours and returned it before he came home. I did feel a bit guilty and waited for the fallout to occur but it never came. To assuage my guilt I'll point him in the direction of this bio and see if he ever knew.

I never really tried writing at that age apart from school assignments as it was something I never considered myself able to do. I might've been able to think of a premise but could never follow through on the story.

I left school at nineteen and entered the print industry where, in various guises, I would stay until the age of 38. During this time I'd found the love of my life and luckily for me, married her. We had a beautiful daughter and a son on the way. Again, I had never seriously written anything while employed in print and with having my own family my time was used up, but in a fantastic way. I will never look back and think I should've been writing during this period as my family and job were my priorities.

Fate stepped in at this point. Redundancies were made at the print company and I chose to accept. At the same time, out of the blue, my daughter, Ellie asked for a story. A story for her. It seemed to be the key to unlocking the ideas trapped inside and my first story 'Ellie and the Rabbits' was born.

It took another year but I added two more stories to complete what is now called 'The Seren Trilogy.'

It was now that my path crossed that of Creativia as my brother (yes, the same one as above!) had also been writing and accepted to be published. I thought I would give it a go as well, not mentioning that I was related to the other Lewis, Creativia was publishing. This was probably the second key moment for me as in my mind it affirmed what I wanted to do now my former career was over and I was fortunate enough that Creativia accepted my stories for publication. I continued with Ellie's adventures and added five more books which are now The Baiulus Series.

It hasn't all run smoothly. Over the last couple of years I discovered, or the doctors did, major problems with the nerves in my feet which means I can't walk as much as I love to do. I had to alter my male driven ego away from being the main bread winner of the family but my wife has never been anything but supportive in allowing me to pursue this path of being a writer. It took me a while to get familiar with though I also love spending so much time with my children.

The most important lessons I learned from all this?

If you can, do what makes you happy, not what makes you rich!

Also, it took me a few years to realise I can write whatever I want, whatever I please, and that is freedom.

Lightning Source UK Ltd.
Milton Keynes UK
UKHW041827110321
380204UK00008B/487/J